WORLDS APART

L.G. CAMPBELL

Copyright © L.G. Campbell 2021

All rights reserved

The characters and events portrayed in this book are fictitious. Any similarity to real persons, living or dead, is coincidental and not intended by the author.

No part of this book may br reproduced, or stored in a retrieval system, or transmitted in any form or by any means, electronic, mechanical, photocopying, recording, or otherwise, without express written permission of the author.

Cover Design: Rob Campbell

Edited by: Liji Editing
Formatted by : Liji Editing

PROLOGUE

My parents always told me I could be whatever I wanted, that my art was beyond brilliant and one day they would be seeing my work in the Tate.

Maybe I shouldn't have put everything I had into my art? Maybe I should have concentrated at school more, and got those vital English and Maths GCSE's. My parents aren't like normal parents, they believe in doing whatever makes you happy, to never follow the rules of the world, and to always rebel against the powers that try to confine us. Bottom line, they are hippies. They took me to many festivals, and I've been on many protests.

They're not bad parents, they just weren't the normal type of parents. They taught me to always fight for what I believed in and to follow my dreams. No strict rules, I've never been grounded and I got to chose my outfit every day, even at a young age... hence why there are photos of me wearing my swimsuit with a tutu and wellington boots.

While I am grateful for all my parents did because they were free-loving people who refused to pay into the corruption that was the tax office, money was often tight, and we often went without things. We lived in a small two-bedroom flat on the council estate.

We didn't have much, but I never felt like I was without. My parents showered me with love and would always make up for us not living a materialistic way of life.

They would tell me endless stories, we'd play puppet shows with old socks and a cardboard box, and when I was old enough, my mother taught me how to knit and sew.

"Nothing needs to be thrown away; with the right love, care and attention, anything can be saved," is what she would always say to me.

As I got older, especially during my teenage years, I noticed more and more that I wasn't like the other teens at school. The cool girls with the latest coats or the latest shoes. Instead, I had hand-me-down uniforms that were ten times too big, backpack and shoes from the local charity shop. Pretty much everyone laughed at me or avoided the "weird girl." All except Kyle. He was a little like me, his family didn't have much money, but the difference was his dad was an alcoholic... a violent alcoholic. His mum walked out on him years ago, leaving Kyle behind to grow up in that environment. His broken and tortured soul appealed to me. He was cute, and he didn't look at me like I was the "weird girl." Being there for each other, we soon fell in love.

All was great, we had each other, and we had planned all that we were going to do with our lives together. He was counting down the days to get away from his dad. We were going to travel together, get far away from here, far away from his father. But of course, life doesn't work like that. After a missed period and terrible morning sickness at sixteen, I took a test and found out I was pregnant.

The rest, as they say, was history. We stayed together and got ourselves a council flat. He worked as a labourer, getting paid less than minimum wage and I got a little cleaning job. We got married, and although things weren't as we had planned, and life was tough, we were still happy.

CHAPTER ONE

Eleven years later

Kyle was acting weird, his mood swings becoming unbearable. I knew that things were a little tough for us as I was still on maternity leave, so money was tight.

I was over the moon when we had Betty, now seven-months-old and crawling around nonstop. I needed eyes in the back of my head. Thankfully, Theo was proving to be a fantastic big brother.

"What time is Dad coming home?" Theo asks.

I plaster on a fake smile, that I'm sure he can see through, and shrug. "Who knows, sweetie, I think he may be working late." Kissing the top of his head, I stand to go grab Betty as she currently has her hand under the couch, trying to grab something.

"What is it, baby? Your toy gone under? Mummy get it for you." I smile whilst kissing her chubby little hand.

Running my hand along, trying to feel for a toy, I feel a wrapper and roll my eyes. "Really, Betty, you're like a puppy, sniffing out food." I laugh at her little chubby, dribbling face. I pull the wrapper out. "Theo, honey, please make sure you don't keep leaving rubbish lying around. Betty nearly ate it." I sigh, looking at him.

I look down at the wrapper in my hand and I feel like my world shifts from under my feet. This isn't a food wrapper.

"Mum! It wasn't me," I hear Theo defend himself, snapping me out of my daze.

"Er, yeah... My mistake, honey. Can you take Betty into your room for a minute while I tidy up a bit in here?" I ask.

"Fine, but you know she's just going to pull everything about in there and I'm not tidying up her mess." He grumbles, picking her up and taking her into his room.

I look down at the wrapper... no, not a wrapper, a small bag of drugs. Drugs that our baby girl nearly got hold of. My hands shake and I feel sick at the thought of what could have happened if Betty gotten hold of it.

The front door opens and in stumbles Kyle, knocking into pictures on our wall. He giggles to himself. I stand from the sofa, feeling my blood boil with rage. I'm tired, I've had enough. I have given him enough chances, time and time again. He always promised me he would go to rehab, go and get the help he needed.

"Hey, baby, I didn't see you there." He laughs to himself, swaying on his feet.

He is completely smashed out of his face, his pupils dilated and wide. I hold back the tears that are waiting to burst free. Years of our life together, the time and effort put into our family, the love I've given him wasted.

He opens the fridge and continues to talk to himself whilst he pulls out a beer.

"Kyle," I call him.

He ignores me and carries on continuing to talk to himself. "Kyle!" I yell.

Standing up, he turns and leans against the side and drinks his can of beer. "What?" he asks.

I hold up the bag containing the white powder, and his eyes go even wider, if that's at all possible. "Where did you find that?" he asks, reaching for it. I move my hand away, keeping hold of it.

"I didn't find it, our daughter did!" I seethe.

"Did she take any?" he asks, but not out of concern for her health, more out concern for him.

"No," I answer simply.

"Its over, Kyle. I'm so tired and I can't keep doing this. You can't keep doing this to me and the kids." I sigh.

"What? You don't know what you're saying, you don't mean that... I will get help, I promise," he begs. I know this speech, I know what's coming.

"I... I promise I will change, I will go to those meetings, the ones on the leaflets. I just need time. This isn't something you can just stop. I need to ease off it," he rambles.

I sigh, tired and frustrated. It kills me to end it, we've been together since we were teenagers, we are high school sweethearts. We were both misfits that found each other.

"Shut up! Just shut up, Kyle. You've said all this before. You've gambled our rent money, you've used money we haven't got for drugs and drink, you've made endless promises that you will stop, that you'll go to rehab... That's the thing though, isn't it? You make these promises then go straight back down the pub and get high again or play poker and end up owing money we haven't got, and then you get your head kicked in. Are you even hearing what I am saying to you right now?! It's over. Betty, our beautiful baby girl, picked this up earlier, what if she had eaten it? She would have died! Died! And you think making a few promises is enough? That I'm just going to forgive you for that? Well I'm not. I am beyond done with you. I am so fed up of giving you chance after chance. Get your stuff and leave," I say, my voice cracking.

"But you love me, and I love you," he states.

"It's not enough. With the drugs and the gambling, it will never be enough, you made your choice. This," I say, holding up the bag before turning and emptying it down the sink and running the tap.

"No, no, what the fuck are you doing? That wasn't mine to waste!" he says, almost frantic.

"Even now, you're putting that stuff first. Get your things and get out, I will be in touch about you seeing the kids," I state firmly. I have my mask in place, hiding that I am crumbling on the inside.

His wide drug-induced eyes search mine for any weakness, any sign I will back down. I hold my poker face. He runs his hands through his blonde hair, he bites down on his bottom lip and nods.

"Fine. I will go," he answers and heads to the bedroom and packs himself a bag of clothes. I reach for my purse and take out the twenty-pound-note that I had been saving towards Theo's birthday.

I hand it to him as he comes out. "What's this?" he asks.

"So you can get some food over the next couple of days," I say, offering the money.

He nods and takes it, leaning forward to kiss me. I turn my head at the last second, his lips connecting with my cheek instead.

"I am sorry, Cora. Really, I am," he apologises as he leaves.

I don't reply, I just shut the door behind him and let out a long breath that I had been holding. I let the tears fall as my back hits the door, and I slide down, sitting on the floor crying.

"Mum?" I hear Theo call quietly.

I quickly wipe my face and smile. "Hey, baby, you okay? Does Betty need me?" I ask, standing and making sure I plaster on the fakest and biggest smile I can to reassure him that I am okay.

He frowns. "So Dad's gone?" he asks.

"Yeah, um, yeah. But don't worry, he will still come and visit you all the time, I promise," I say, trying my best to soothe him.

He wraps his arms around my waist and hugs me, burying his little face. My heart feels like its about to shatter for him. "Don't worry, Mum. I will look after you and Betty," he promises.

I kiss the top of his head, swallowing back my tears. "I will be okay, it's my job to look after you and Betty. There's nothing for you to worry about, okay?" I reassure, holding his face. He nods. "Good, now, how about I make your favourite for dinner?" I ask, and a smile spreads across his face. "Good, now go and get your sister for me, please, before she screams the place down."

He runs off and I take a calming breath. Plenty of time for heartbreak later, but first, my kids need me and my son wants toad-in-the-hole for dinner.

We sit on the sofa and I put on Theo's favourite DVD. He eats his dinner glued to the TV while I try and feed Betty. He turns to me and realises I don't have any food.

"Mum, wheres your dinner?" he asks.

"Oh, I'm fine, baby, I'm not that hungry," I lie.

The truth is, when I went to make the dinner, I only had two sausages and a small amount of flour. I managed to make him his own personal toad-in-the-hole, I had a few frozen vegetables left and three potatoes. Betty has the spare potatoes and vegetables. Its not the first time I've forgone a meal so they can eat. Kyle never used to, but then it got to the point that he was never really here. He just took money from us to spend on his habit.

I go to bath the kids and realise the gas has gone, and with no money until tomorrow it will have to wait. Thankfully, we have an electric shower, so I give them a quick wash then dry them as quickly as I can and wrap them up warm, sending Theo to bed in his thick fleece pyjamas and dressing gown.

I lean over and give him a kiss goodnight. "Goodnight, baby," I whisper.

"Night, Mum. One day I'm going to earn enough money to take care of you, so you never have to go without dinner and we always have heaters," he says yawning.

Giving him another quick kiss, I head out of his room as quick as I can and then let the tears fall.

I creep into my bedroom so as not to disturb Betty who is sleeping in her cot. I open my jewellery box and take out my wedding and engagement rings. I haven't put them back on since having Betty as my fingers swelled a fair amount when I was pregnant. I look at them and twist them around on my finger. They're simple and not very expensive, but they will get me at least a few pounds to get us some food and put the gas back on.

I sigh and flop onto the sofa, feeling defeated. I hurt for mine and Kyle's relationship being over. I don't feel devastated or heartbroken at losing him, I feel sad for the years of love and effort I put in, only for him to throw it away for some drugs. I feel more anger than anything, angry that he wasted those years of my life, that he would just throw it all away like it was nothing to him, like me and the kids were nothing to him. He didn't fight, he didn't even try.

Deciding to go to bed, I stand up and place the rings in my purse, ready to take them to the pawn shop tomorrow. I hear shouting coming from outside, glass being smashed and soon I see the familiar blue lights flash and light up my lounge. Not even phased by it now, I peep out of the curtains and see the usual lot mouthing off and fighting back with the police.

"One day I will be out of this bloody shit hole." I sigh to myself.

I climb into bed and as I do most nights, I pray for some luck that will get us away from here to a place that is safe, give them heating and plenty of food in their stomachs.

CHAPTER TWO

Four years later

"Kids, come on, we have to leave for school in five minutes, brush your teeth and let's go!" I yell from the kitchen, quickly downing my coffee.

"I'm all ready, Mummy!" Betty yells, skipping in wearing her pink feather boa and tiara on her head, not forgetting her sparkly sandals.

"Baby, go and take that off, you know you can't wear that in school," I point out.

"But, Mummy, Nana said I am to express myself in any way I can. This is me doing that. I am actpressing myself, showing all my sparkle." She smiles and twirls.

"Uh-huh, well school is for learning, not expressing yourself. But from three-thirty, Monday to Friday and Saturday and Sunday, you can express yourself however you want," I state, taking off her boa and tiara.

She rolls her eyes and puts her hands on her hips. "It's not fair, that's a dickatatorship," she grumbles, trying her hardest to pronounce the word.

I give her a look. She throws her hands up in the air in protest and storms back to her room to put on her school shoes. " Must remember to have a chat with my parents about what they teach Betty. She may be four, but I still think she has it in her to cause a full scale riot at school.

Theo walks in dragging his feet along, looking like he has just rolled out of bed, his school tie all wonky and hanging around his neck.

"Morning, baby, you sleep okay?" I ask.

He gives me a look. "They keep you awake all night again?" I ask.

"Yeah, I swear they just put the speaker up against my wall on purpose," he states, yawning.

Having had enough—"Wait here"—I order angrily.

"Mum, don't, please," Theo complains.

I wave my hand at him and continue to storm out of our flat and go to next door. This has gone on long enough with their loud music and partying at all hours.

I pound on the door and wait with no answer, so I continue to do it until the door swings open with force. "What?!" the guy yells. He is stood there in a pair of sweats, no top on, he is muscled and has a fair few tattoos on him, including the teardrop tattoo by his eye.

His eyes sweep my body, and it makes my skin crawl.

"Will you stop bloody partying all hours of the night?! It's keeping my kid awake. I've had enough of it!" I yell angrily.

He smirks. "Say, pretty lady, why don't you offer me something, an incentive to keep me quiet." He winks, crossing his arms over his chest.

I roll my eyes and don't even try to mask my look of disgust. "Shut up, don't make me bring up my breakfast. Now you're going to keep quiet at night so my children can sleep, or I will call the old bill. You choose... What's it going to be?" I threaten. Gone is his cocky and flirtatious demeanour, instead he looks pissed off.

"You call the pigs, then we're going to have a problem," he threatens quietly.

I keep my head held high and try to keep a hold on my emotions. "Just show some damn respect and keep it down." I huff before storming back to my flat. I slam my door and see both Theo and Betty stood there waiting, ready for school.

"Oh good, you're ready. Come on then, let's get going," I say, ushering them out the door.

We walk together, Theo a few paces ahead so as not to be seen with his mum. Apparently it's embarrassing. We drop Betty off first.

"Have a fantastic day and I love you," I say, kissing the top of her head before she goes skipping into class. "Betty, remember Theo is picking you up after school!" I yell over the fence as she smiles and waves.

I reach my bus stop. "Theo, have a great day and I will see you later. Remember, straight home and I should be back by five," I inform him.

"Yes, I know, Mum. I'm not an idiot."

Some boys start yelling things across the street to Theo.

"Oh, Theo, nice shoes! Theo, where did you get that coat, a charity shop? You managed to wash today? Or is the leisure centre stopping you from using their changing rooms? I will let you have my bag of crisps if you clean my shoes, peasant! Hey, I will give your mum a fiver if she will suck my dick!" one yells, waving his money in the air.

"That's it, I can not have them say those things," I state and go to storm across the road to them but get halted in my tracks when Theo holds me back.

"Mum, don't," he grits through his teeth.

"But, honey, they can't talk to you like that," I argue back.

"Just leave it, Mum, okay? It will just make things so much worse," he pleads. I nod my head and bite my lip, not liking seeing him worried or stressed-out.

My bus pulls up. "Promise me you're going to be okay?" I ask.

"I will be fine, Mum, go to work and I will see you later." He sighs, annoyed.

I quickly kiss him, which he hates, and he scrunches his face up. I wave to him from the bus as he walks off to school. As it pulls off, I sit there and wish I could go back and give those kids a piece of my mind. I sigh and try not to worry about him, kids are cruel. It's just hard seeing someone being cruel to your child, the mamma bear instincts kick in and I want to kick that snotty teen's butt into next week.

Only a short bus ride and I'm at work. I clock in and run into Sylvia, who is rushing in behind me, flustered and dragging her coat and handbag behind her.

"Clock me in!" she yells breathlessly.

I laugh and shake my head and clock her in. She's been warned if she's even a minute late, she will be out of a job.

"Phew, thanks, babe, I don't know what happened... I set my alarm, I got up on time and got dressed, and yet I'm still late. I mean, it's obviously the world telling me, telling us, that I am not supposed to be on time," she says, fanning her face to cool down.

"Yeah, possibly, or maybe you could set your alarm before eight a.m.?" I point out.

"Yeah, I can't cope with getting up before eight, that's slave labour! I need my beauty sleep. I'm twenty-seven, the lines are coming, and I'm not adding dark bags under my eyes to it," she defends.

I snort and roll my eyes. I spot our boss Mr Richards. "Heads up," I whisper in warning to Sylvia.

"Cora, Sylvia, will you get a move on, the vans are waiting out back," he barks.

"So sorry, sir, we do apologise, sir," Sylvia snaps sarcastically.

I elbow her in warning. "Don't poke the bear," I say under my breath.

"Well, he pisses me off, he shouldn't be such a wanker," she adds.

"Sylvia," I hiss, looking over my shoulder making sure he hasn't heard her.

She really doesn't give a shit. It's different for her, she still lives at home with her parents. I may only be four years older than her, but our lives are so very different.

"Oh, I don't care, it's not like this is the only cleaning job in London. Hell, all the posh twats down the road hire cleaners all the time. I'm just biding my time. One day a rich banker will swoop in and sweep me off my feet, and we shall live happily ever after in his million-pound-home in Chelsea." She sighs.

We quickly shove our coats and personal items into our lockers and put on our staff aprons.

"Sylvia, what you are describing is a Cinderella tale. Except you are far from sweet and angelic. Hate to break it to you, honey, fairy tales aren't real. This is the real word and the real world sucks. People like you and me are to stay right here, working our arses off until we finally die. We will never swap our class status, we are beneath them," I rant.

Sylvia pauses and stares at me with a raised eyebrow. "Well, aren't we just the happiest little treasure this morning," she says sarcastically.

"Just saying it as it is." I shrug as we walk out back to the vans waiting for us. We jump in and slam the door shut.

"About bloody time! Some of us want to earn money today," Sharon huffs.

"Oh, go get shagged, Sharon," Sylvia bites back, making me and the other girls snicker with laughter.

"You really have a way with words, don't you?" I state.

"Why thank you." She bends forward, taking a bow.

∼

OUR SHIFT TODAY IS AT A FANCY HOTEL IN THE CENTRE OF London. Hotels hire our specialised cleaning company to come in a do a deep-clean, especially in the winter months when its quieter. The amount of brass to polish is insane. I am bent down, currently polishing part of a door panel, headphones in, not paying a blind bit of attention to my surroundings. The door suddenly swings open, hitting me right in the centre of my head, knocking me off my feet. I land on my back with a thud.

"Ow," I moan, blinking, trying to focus.

"Oh shit, I am so sorry," a deep voice apologises.

He leans over with a concerned look on his face. "Ow," I repeat. He is breath-taking, and aside from the hit to my head, my brain has completely checked out. He has a strong jawline, covered in a light dusting of stubble, but that's not what has my attention... His eyes are the most beautiful I've ever seen. They're a green-hazel colour with a perfect black line surrounding them. It's almost as if they are gold.

"Miss, Miss, are you okay?" he repeats.

"Huh?" I blurt.

"I'm going to sit you up," he informs me and leans close in, helping me sit up, his cologne enveloping me. I want nothing more than to bury my face in his neck and take a deep inhale, and possibly lick his neck.

He crouches next to me as I take out my headphones. "Simon, get me a water, now," he orders.

I go to move to stand. "No, stay seated, have some water first," he orders.

I ignore him and stand up anyway. I brush myself off and look in the large mirror at the nice red lump on my head.

"You should have stayed seated." He sighs.

I frown and turn to face him, handsome or not, I won't be told what to do, and especially from some rich arsehole. "I am okay considering some moron opened the door in my face," I snap.

"Seriously? Who crouches down in front of a door with headphones in?" he argues back.

"I was told the room was empty, I was doing my job and now look... I look like something out of a cartoon," I say, pointing to the lump forming on my head.

"Oh, I see, I see what you're after," he says, reaching in his suit jacket and pulling out his wallet. He holds out a wad of notes in front of my face.

"What are you doing?" I ask.

"Oh, come on, it's what you want, what is it they say? Where there's a blame, there's a claim? So just take the money and we will say no more about it," he says, continuing to wave his money in my face.

I curl my lip in disgust at him. His minion comes running back frantically with a glass of water in his hand, nearly sloshing it everywhere.

"Here's the water." He pants, out of breath.

I reach for the water and smile kindly at the poor guy who is clearly used like a piece of trash. "Thank you, err, um..." I pause, waiting for him to say his name.

"Simon. My name's Simon, I'm Mr Nash's personal assistant." He smiles whilst still panting like he's been running in a marathon.

I smile sweetly back to the poor lad and drink my water until the glass is empty before handing the glass back to him. "Thanks again." I smile. I turn to this Mr Nash and give him daggers. "Mr Nash, I accept your apology for nearly knocking me out, but you can take your money and shove it up your arse. Good day to you," I snap before storming off.

My heart is pounding in my chest as worry kicks in. What if he calls and makes a complaint about me? Then I will be out of a job. I should have just kept my mouth shut. I can't help myself. As soon as he belittled me, just because I'm lower class than he is, my back went up. I hate people judging, and I hate people assuming I'm a certain way because of what I do for a living or because of where I live.

I storm around to try and find Sylvia and find her chatting up the chef from the hotel. I roll my eyes and grab her elbow. "Sorry, I need her for a moment, won't be long, then she's all yours," I yell over my shoulder as I practically drag her away.

"What the hell, Cora?!" she complains.

We get to a quiet bit of hall and I stop and spin around, telling her what just happened.

"Oh shit, you didn't?" She gasps.

"I did," I answer, biting my lip.

"Okay, well... One, why in the hell didn't you take the money? You need the money," she snaps.

"Because I have pride, Sylvia. Because the way he said it was so... So judgmental and grrr, I just wanted to kick him in the balls," I explain.

"Yeah, okay, well that's the difference between you and me. I have zero pride and will do just about anything for more money," she admits.

"Apart from working for it," I quip.

"Hey," she complains. I just raise my brow and she shrugs and nods. "Fair enough, yeah you're right there."

"Come on, let's get back to work, get this shift over with. If I keep my head down and work, soon enough it will be home time." I sigh.

We walk back the way we came. "Yeah, you keep telling yourself that if you think it helps. If you will excuse me, I am going back to talk to that very nice chef." She winks.

"Sure, I'm sure he's giving you all kinds of cooking tips," I retort.

"Oh, honey, endless tips. I'm hoping he will give me some with his rolling pin soon." She winks, entering the kitchen.

I laugh and shake my head, walking back to my cleaning bucket and continuing to polish the brass in the hotel, praying I don't bump into Mr Pompous Arsehole again.

Finally, at the end of my shift, I breathe a sigh of relief when we pack up to leave. As I go to walk out the door, I feel the hairs on the back of my neck standing on end. I turn and my eyes connect with him, Mr Pompous Arsehole. His gaze is intense and I can see a smirk playing on his lips which pisses me off. I lift my chin and then flip him off. His eyes go wide and his jaw tenses. I smile, proud to have ruffled his feathers.

CHAPTER THREE

I wander the supermarket, looking at the food, pricing it up in my head as I go. I'm sure Mr Phillips, my old maths teacher, would be proud of the calculations I can do in my head now. I have thirty pounds to my name, and I need to buy food for the three of us for an entire week.

I head to the clearance section and pick up some reduced chicken that goes out of date today. I smile at my bargain and add it to my trolly. That chicken means I can cook us all a nice roast dinner. I look in my trolly and see I have done okay. I decide to treat the kids to some chocolate doughnuts with my last pound.

Happy, I offload my items onto the checkout.

"That will be thirty-two pounds and fifty-eight pence," the cashier states.

I frown. "Are you sure? I calculated it at twenty-nine eighty-five," I question.

"Yes, I'm sure." She rolls her eyes at me.

"Okay, um, can you put the doughnuts back please, and, um, the..." I pause, looking through my shopping.

"Here, allow me," a voice behind me says.

I turn around and see Simon, pompous arsehole's assistant, stood behind me.

I smile at him. "Oh, hey." He smiles back and hands the cashier some money. It's in that moment, I realise he has paid for my entire shop.

"Oh gosh, here, you don't need to do that, take this and I will owe you the rest. If you give me your address, I will send it to you," I insist.

He pays for his couple of items and helps me load the rest of my shopping into my trolly, ignoring my offer to repay him.

We walk outside and I start unloading the bags and putting the trolly back. He picks up my bags and turns to me. "Where are you parked? I will help you carry these bags to your car," he offers.

I smile and take the bags from him. "Oh, I don't have a car, I will jump on the bus." I shrug.

He looks past me and shakes his head. I turn around to see what he's looking at, but there's no one there. His phone beeps with a message and he takes it out, reads it and replaces it back in his pocket. "Follow me, I will give you a ride home," he offers.

"Oh no, I'm fine. I have a return ticket, you've already done enough," I state.

"It's fine, I have the car for a while, let me drive you." He takes the bags from my hands and walks off across the car park, leaving me speechless.

I quickly run to catch up with him and notice a homeless man sat, huddled with his dog. "Wait!" I yell. Simon turns around and looks at me questioningly. I take a bag off of him and rummage around. I find a packet of biscuits and some ham I had bought for the kids sandwiches. It's fine, they will be okay with just jam for this week.

"What are you doing? he asks.

"Just give me a second." I smile and run back across the carpark to the homeless guy.

"Here," I say, handing him the ham and biscuits. He takes it and smiles. "I'm sorry I don't have more to give you, but I thought your dog would appreciate the ham." I smile and stroke the dog whose tail wags happily at the fuss.

"Thank you. It's appreciated." He smiles.

I run back to the car and see Simon stood there looking stunned.

"What?" I ask.

"Nothing, just get in the car." He smiles.

"You know, it's really nice of you, but you really don't need to be going out of your way to drop me home," I continue.

"It's perfectly fine... And how do you know it is out of my way?" he asks.

I snort back my laughter. "Oh, I know that where I live is definitely out of your way."

"Come on, before Mr Nash calls for me to pick him up," he says, guiding me into the passenger seat.

He gets in and I look around the car which cost more than the entirety of my belongings. I am scared to move or touch anything for fear of scratching anything, or knowing my luck, I will accidentally break something.

"When we get to where I live, I will take the bags up to my place. It's, um, probably best you don't leave the car unattended," I warn.

He smiles and pushes his glasses up his nose. "Okay, gotcha."

I bite my lip, feeling anxious to get out of the car. My mind is going crazy with a million thoughts a minute. Why did he pay for my shopping? Why is he being so kind? Why drive me home and risk getting a bollocking off of his boss? Is he expecting sexual favours in return?

"I won't sleep with you," I blurt out.

He chokes and coughs. "Right, that's good to know... I, um, don't plan on sleeping with you. I am happy with my girlfriend." He smiles.

I blush and bite my lip, feeling embarrassed. "I'm sorry, it's just... Where I am from, no one does something for free or to be nice, it usually means you owe them a favour, or they want to get in your knickers," I admit.

"Christ, it sounds like prison," he mutters.

"Well, most of my neighbours have been in prison, so it would make sense that they bring that part of their experiences home with them." I shrug.

He just shakes his head.

A little while later he turns into my estate, and I can see he's trying to keep his face neutral, but I can see the shock and disbelief.

"How is this even possible? I mean, Chelsea is right there! It's like less than twenty minutes away. How can you have people living like this when there is so much wealth on the doorstep?" he asks in disbelief.

"If you live a decent life, you only see what's in front of you, what affects you. Seeing is believing, unless you have to come here, you would have never known about this estate. As long as the lower class don't encroach on the wealthy, everything is just tickity boo. Well, in their lives it is anyway." I shrug.

Simon looks at me and I catch sympathy in his eyes. I hate that.

"Just here is great." I point.

The young teens on their bikes all look over, eyeing up the car with pound signs in their eyes. I get out. "Oi! You can fuck off. Any of you touch this car and I will drag you down to the station personally. And, Sonny, I know you can't have that happen, you're already on your last strike," I threaten.

Simon gets out and looks at me dumbfounded. "You can really handle yourself, can't you?" He smirks.

"Grew up here, know most of them and their entire families," I state. I bend back inside the car and grab my purse. I look quickly over my shoulder to see Simon unloading the boot. I take out my thirty pounds, and an old receipt and pen. I wrap the receipt around the money and write a little note.

Thank you for your help, it's appreciated. Please take the money for the groceries, and I guess I will have to hunt you down to give you the rest.

Cora x

I place it near the centre console and quickly shut the door, taking the bags of shopping off of him. "Thanks, now go before they have the alloys off." I smile.

"You're welcome, and I won't argue with you. Mr Nash would have my balls if anything happened to this car." He smiles and salutes before getting back in the car.

I lug the bags up the three flights of stairs to my flat, the smell of weed and piss filling the hallways. I rest my bags on the floor and unlock the door quickly, slamming it shut behind me. I walk straight into the kitchen and dump the bags down.

"I'm home!" I yell. I walk into the lounge and see Betty covered in paint, my mum with a paint brush in her hand, painting her with paint.

"What the hell?" I ask.

"Mummy!" Betty smiles excitedly.

My mum turns around to face me. "Hello, my darling! We are creating a masterpiece!" she says smiling, pointing to the rolled-out paper on the floor and what appears to be Betty's body splattered with paint.

"Okay, fine, just clear it up. Where is Theo?" I ask.

Mum pulls a face and nods in the direction of his bedroom. I go straight to him and knock.

"Go away," he yells.

"Sorry, honey, that's not going to happen," I say and walk in.

I find him led on his bed, facing the wall. I perch next to him. "What happened?" I ask.

"I don't want to talk about it," he snaps.

"Okay, fine. I will ring the school then," I state as I stand. He reaches out and grabs my wrist. I turn and look at him.

"Oh my God, baby! What the hell happened?" I say worriedly. He has a busted lip, and what looks like a slight black eye.

He huffs. "The boys you saw this morning, they were saying stuff, mouthing off at break-time about things. Things about you," he says and looks up at me, his eyes filling with tears. "I lost it, Mum. So I dived across the table and hit him. His friends soon pulled me off him and held me while he got his hits in." He winces, his hand going to his ribs.

I immediately lift his jumper and see bruises on his ribs. "That son of a bitch... And this was at school?" I ask in disbelief.

"Yeah, at lunch," he answers.

"I'm going to give that head teacher a piece of my mind!" I fume.

"Mum, don't, just leave it. I have break-time detention for the next month," he says.

"What the hell for?" I yell.

"For fighting." He shrugs. I jump up and pace his room.

"That is ridiculous. Oh, I am so mad right now. I will make a formal complaint to the governor. I have a mind to go round the boy's house and have a chat with his mother," I ramble on. I take a deep breath to try and calm my rage and look to Theo, seeing him smirking at me.

I bend down and cup his face. "I'm not sure why you're smiling but I'm glad to see you smile. Let's get some ice on your lip and eye." I kiss the top of his head.

"Mum, stop kissing me, I'm going to be fifteen soon, it's weird. And also, we don't have ice," he adds.

I pause and smile. "You're right, but tonight I am making us roast chicken dinner with all the trimmings, and while I'm cooking, you can sit with the bag of frozen veg on your face," I state as I open his door. "Oh, and we have doughnuts for pudding." I smile.

He smiles and shakes his head. Mum gives me a wink as we walk back through the lounge. "Theo, look, look at my masterpiece!" Betty squeals excitedly.

I walk straight to the kitchen and grab the bag of veg and hand it to Theo. Mum follows me to the kitchen and helps me prepare the dinner. I tell her what happened, she sighs and shakes her head.

"Poor boy, he is like your father, he's a lover, not a fighter. As long as those vile boys don't ruin his kind heart, he will be okay." She sighs.

"Where is Dad?" I ask.

"He's at a protest for the factory that's being closed down. You know, the one where one-hundred and fifty employees lost their jobs, all because the owner of the company ran it into the ground but made sure his pockets were lined first. His workers though, got nothing. Some had even forgone their wages to help keep the company going in the hope that things would pick up. He should be on his way over soon. Well, providing he hasn't been arrested that is." She shrugs.

"Mum." I laugh and shake my head.

"Darling, don't look at me like that, you know how your father can get overly passionate about these things. Anyway, they always release him within the hour. You know, he's got an invite to their Christmas party in December." She laughs.

"You're joking?" I giggle.

"Nope, I'm not."

There's a knock at the door. "I've got it!" Theo yells. "It's Pops!"

"Well there you go, no arrest tonight." I wink at Mum.

Dad comes bursting into the kitchen. "Victory!" he yells with his fist in the air.

"Hey, Dad." I smile and kiss his cheek.

"Victory for the little people!" he booms, clearly still on a high from the protest.

"Pops, you shouldn't just call them little people, the right word is dwarfism. Miss Wren says we need to always think of our words carefully before we say them as not to cause anyone a-afence," Betty chastises my dad.

I hold in my laughter as do my parents. "Honey, I think what Pops is saying is, he means the workers are also known as the little people, they are not actual little people." I smile. "Now go with Nana and wash up and change in time for dinner."

Mum takes Betty to have a bath and change while Dad talks to Theo about the bullies at school.

How can I love my life and hate it just as much? I have the best family, the most amazing kids, yet I can't seem to give them a better life, no matter how hard I work.

CHAPTER FOUR

We all sit down for dinner, all squeezed around my little four-seater table, with Dad sat on a camping chair. I managed to spread what food I had between all of us. I like to help my parents out when I can, they don't make much money, never really have. Mum sells some of her artwork online or at car boot sales, and Dad sometimes manages to get some cash-in-hand work. Their benefits don't cover a lot and at their age, with zero qualifications, it's not like an employer would snap them up.

"How's your paintings selling, Cora?" Dad asks.

I sigh. "They're not, I haven't had time to paint anything in a while or post them online. They don't pay the bills, so it will have to wait." I shrug.

"See, this is what is wrong with our society. Your mum is an amazing artist, she got an 'A' in her GCSE art. She was predicted amazing things for her future, but what happens? She's not from the right class, her along with so many others are slipping through the net, never finding their chance at a better life," he rants.

I roll my eyes and pull a silly face at the kids, making them smile.

"Felix, shut up and eat your dinner." Mum sighs.

Once we've eaten, it's late, and I need to get Betty to bed. My parents say their goodbyes, but just as I'm about to open the door, there's a knock. I frown and open it.

"Kyle." I sigh.

"Daddy!" Betty squeals excitedly, whereas Theo stands right by my side. Being older, he sees through his Dad's bullshit.

"Hey, princess!" he says, scooping her up in his arms.

I notice—as his sleeves rise up—the bruise and track marks. I immediately want to rip Betty from his arms.

"What do you want, Kyle?" I ask.

"I just came by to see my kids, I'm their father, I'm allowed to see them," he states.

"You are, yes, but at arranged times, not at eight-thirty on a school night when I'm about to put Betty to bed," I say, crossing my arms over my chest.

"Kyle, son, come and visit another time, not now," Dad backs me up.

"You're right, I must have lost track of time, go to bed, sweetie, and I will come visit soon." He kisses Betty on the cheek and puts her down. I give Mum a look and she nods, taking Betty.

"Hey, son." Kyle smiles, putting his hands in his pocket.

"I'm going to go help Nana put Betty to bed," Theo says, walking off.

"Dad, give us a minute," I say.

Once Dad is out of ear shot, I cross my arms over my chest. "How much do you want this time, Kyle?" I ask.

He scratches the back of his neck and tenses his shoulders, his jerky and twitchy movements showing me its been a while since he got his last fix. "Uh, well, I owe some money and I wouldn't ask if I wasn't desperate. I... I got no one else I can turn to. If I don't pay up, I'm a dead man." He smiles nervously.

I look at him. His eyes are sunken, he's lost more weight and his teeth are rotten. Gone is the handsome boy I fell in love with, gone is the father my kids had.

"If I give you some money, will you promise to never come here again? I mean it, I don't want you bringing your shit to my door, to the kids. The only money I have is for the kids Christmas presents," I state.

"Oh, thank you, I promise. You wont hear from me again. I'm gone," he says excitedly.

I curl my lip in disgust that he doesn't even think of his own children at Christmas. I shouldn't give him the money, but then I don't want his death on my conscience.

"Wait there," I state as I walk into the kitchen and grab my pot off the top of the cupboards. I have just one-hundred pounds saved for Christmas. It's not much, but it's all I could save. I have eight weeks until Christmas. If my parents could help look after the kids, I could try and get a few extra shifts in to try and get some extra money.

I take eighty pounds, leaving twenty in the pot, just in case. I need to have something in the tin even if it means I can just get the kids some Christmas chocolate.

I hand over the money to him and he practically snatches it from my hand. "Eighty pounds, is that it?" he asks frantically.

"Yes, Kyle, that's all I have. Funnily enough, when you're a single mother, working in a under paid job and have two children to feed and clothe, and a dead-beat-dad who doesn't contribute in anyway, you're not exactly rolling in it," I say angrily.

"You're right, I'm sorry. This is good. Thanks," he mutters and walks off.

"I mean it, Kyle, don't come back ever again," I yell after him.

I slam the door shut and lean against it, closing my eyes and pinching the bridge of my nose.

"You okay, Mum?" Theo asks.

My eyes fly open and I am quick to put on a smile for him. "Sure. Everything is fine," I try to reassure.

∼

"Please, I need just any extra hours. I will literally work anything. I'm begging you," I plead to my boss.

He looks at me blankly and sighs. "There's nothing I can do, you'll just have to make do with what you have. If another girl leaves, then sure, but I can't give you the hours if they're not there." He shrugs.

"Okay, thanks," I mutter and turn to leave.

"Oh, Cora," he calls. I turn around to face him. "There are other ways to make some money, decent money." He leers, his eyes looking up and down my body.

I curl my lip in disgust. "Thanks, sir, but I prefer to earn honest money, I'm not desperate enough to let a disgusting limp maggot dick anywhere near my body. Have a good day, sir," I sneer as I slam the door behind me. I shudder at the thought of him anywhere near me.

I change and grab my cleaning stuff and catch up with Sylvia. "Any luck?" she asks.

I shake my head. "Nope, but he offered sex for money."

"You are kidding me? God, I think I'm going to throw up my breakfast." Sylvia gags. "The dirty bastard, I hope you told him where he can shove it?"

"I did, don't worry. Although, I hope he doesn't sack me for it," I mutter.

"He even tries it, I will stand by you and we will both make sexual assault claims about him. That slime ball has been caught staring at my arse one too many times. I would be more than happy to help," she promises.

I nudge her. "Good to know you have my back."

We arrive back at the same hotel where I met Mr Pompous Arsehole. I pray I don't run into him again today because I really don't have the patience for him.

Much like the same, I put my headphones in and get to work, doing what people like me do best around the rich and wealthy. You work away and go unnoticed. I'm currently in the ballroom, it's so extravagant with a massive chandelier hanging from the centre of the ceiling. To have a wedding here must cost the earth. I'm polishing the frame of a large mirror when suddenly, out of the corner of my eye, I spot a reflection of a figure standing right behind me. I scream and turn around and with my fist, I hit them, hard.

It's Mr Pompous Arse and he's doubled over, holding his nose. I take out my ear buds and cover my chest with my hand, feeling like I've had a heart attack.

"Why would you do that?" I ask breathlessly.

"Ow, fuck, I think you've broken my damn nose," he groans.

"Well what do you expect when you creep up on a woman?" I retort. "Here, let me see." I gesture for him to take a seat. He looks at me, eyebrows raised. "Oh, don't give me that look, I've seen many broken noses to know what one looks like, stop being such a baby and let me see." I roll my eyes.

"Is that because you've broken all those noses?" he quips.

"Ha ha, just be thankful I didn't kick, or you'd be cupping another part of your body instead," I say, pulling his hands from his face to have a look at his nose.

I lean in closely to look, his eyes are firmly fixed on my face, watching me intently. I frown and bite my bottom lip. Carefully, I cup his face, and using my thumbs, I press lightly around his nose. "Tell me when it hurts." He doesn't answer, he just continues to watch me. I make the mistake of looking into his eyes, his beautiful eyes. I swallow nervously as my mouth suddenly goes very dry. I lick my lips and immediately his eyes focus on my mouth. I shake my head and drop my hands from his face and take a step back.

"You're fine, nothing is broken. You just have a nosebleed. Here, this should help." I reach into my back pocket and quickly take the wrapper off and place it up his nose.

"Did you just put a tampon up my nose?" he asks.

I nod, fighting a smile. "Um, yes. It's effective at absorbing the blood, they use them all the time in football." I bite my lip to stop myself from laughing.

"Those are medical implements used, not sanitary products," he says sternly.

I can't help it, I burst out laughing at him sat there with a tampon shoved up his nose, the string hanging down, speaking all serious and uppity. All my resolve is gone.

"I'm glad you find this situation so amusing," he states, removing the tampon from his nose.

"I'm sorry, but you have to see the funny side," I say, wiping my tears.

He stands there for a moment, watching me, and briefly, I think he may smile, but he doesn't.

"Do you often make a habit of attacking your employers?" he asks, eyebrows raised.

"No, I don't, you were the one that crept up on me. Wait a minute... Employer?" I ask confused.

"Yes, I own this hotel and I employ the firm you work for to clean. I will say that ever since our first meeting, it's been, shall we say, interesting," he says, crossing his arms and raising his eyebrow.

I feel the colour drain from my face. This beautiful pompous arsehole is going to have me fired. Then what? Then how will I feed the kids and pay the bills? And then there's Christmas. I start feeling lightheaded as my breathing becomes more and more panicked.

"Miss... Miss..." he calls before it's lights out for me.

"Simon, get me an ice pack and a fresh orange juice," I hear.

I groan and open my eyes, squinting. "Now, Simon, she's waking up," he orders.

I feel him sweep the hair from my face gently. He looks concerned.

"What happened?" I ask.

"It appears you had a panic attack and fainted," he informs me.

"I need to get back to work, I can't afford to not work," I say, sitting up a little too quickly, making the room spin.

"You're not going anywhere until you're well rested and I'm satisfied you're okay," he states.

Simon comes running back in with a glass of orange juice and an ice pack. Immediately, the pompous arsehole takes it from him and places the ice pack on the back of my neck and hands me the orange juice to drink. I drink it down in one go, I'm so thirsty, and to be honest, I can't remember the last time I had fresh orange juice.

"I feel fine now, thank you, sir. I need to get back to work," I say, avoiding looking at him. I've already dug myself a grave, I do not want to dig myself any deeper.

"Simon, please escort Miss home, she isn't well enough to continue working today," he orders.

"No, no, I'm fine, honestly, no need to worry. Perfectly healthy. Thank you anyway, sir," I say over my shoulder as I grab my things and practically run away before he can force me to go home, or worse, fire me.

I keep my head down and try to push aside the feeling that's brewing... the feeling like I'm about to lose my job, the feeling that life can't get any shittier, but you just know that it will.

CHAPTER FIVE

Roman

I watched her on the CCTV. As soon as she found out I owned the hotel, she looked at me differently. Gone was the fiery spark behind her eyes, instead I saw fear and worry. I hated that, I should have kept my mouth shut and nothing would have changed. I love how she called me out on my bullshit, I loved how she wasn't afraid to stand up for herself.

I followed her on the first day to the supermarket, seeing her struggle to pay for what little food she had. In that instant, I knew she wouldn't accept money from the likes of me. My wealth makes her uncomfortable, but Simon she was relaxed with. Although, I'm sure she wouldn't be if she found out he was an Oxford graduate and his father was the local mayor in Brighton. His upbringing was just as privileged as mine.

She took his help, even though she still argued against it. I made him drive her home. When Simon returned to pick me up from the supermarket, he couldn't hide the emotions on his face. He told me where she lived and what it was like. Of course, I knew places like this existed, but I had yet to visit or even see one for myself. I snort at that fact. I'm exactly what she thinks I am. A sheltered little rich boy.

What got to me the most was probably the folded-up note and the money she left in the car. She had nothing, her shopping was paid for, she could have enjoyed having that extra money. But no, not her, she is—as I am beginning to find out—a strong, caring and incredibly stubborn woman.

"Simon, be ready to leave in ten minutes. I want to see the place she lives for myself," I state.

"Sure thing, Roman. Just warning you now, its not pretty and if we ain't careful, someone will have your alloys off the car," he warns me.

"I know, I couldn't give a shit about the car. Objects can be easily replaced, people cannot." I sigh, watching her clean on the monitors.

"Okay, you're the boss, whatever you say. I've never seen you so riled up before... She's really got under your skin, hasn't she?" He smirks.

I don't say anything, I continue to watch her. She caught my attention from the moment I accidentally knocked her over with the door. Those beautiful blue eyes, those lips, even her scent did things to me. Then she smiled and it felt as if my world had been kicked out from underneath me. I noticed her clothes, they were falling apart. I noticed the dark circles under her eyes. I noticed every single thing about her. Immediately, I wanted to rescue her, to hold her and save her from whatever she was being put through.

I look at the clock, she wont be finishing for another hour, perfect time for me to go and have a look at where she lives. "Simon, let's go."

I stand and grab my jacket off the back of the chair. "Yes, boss." Simon salutes.

As we leave the affluent area of London, it's not long at all until the scenery begins to change and the poverty becomes apparent. Simon was right about one thing, how can somewhere this dire, with this much poverty be on the doorstep of not just London, but on the doorstep of some of the country's wealthiest people? The thought makes me angry and sick to the pit of my stomach. Why isn't there more money put into the poorer areas?

"Simon, make a note for me to ring the local councillors when we get back. I feel there will be an immediate meeting, I have a few questions that they need to answer."

Simon pulls into the estate; kids are everywhere and I'm guessing school has just finished. A little girl is skipping along and falls in the road, making Simon slam on his brakes.

"Holy fuck," I yell.

I get out of the car and see—I'm guessing—her brother is trying to help her get up.

"Ow!" she cries. "It hurts too much, Theo. Ow!" she cries again.

"Can I offer you a lift home?" I ask. Both their gazes come to me and immediately I hold my hands up. "I promise, I mean no harm. Just trying to offer some help." I walk towards them to help.

"Stranger danger! Stranger danger!" she yells.

"Back off, paedo!" her big brother shouts.

I take a step back and hold up my hands, other teenagers walking home and parents with their kids are looking over at us, giving us filthy looks. "I'm not a paedo."

"I'm sure that's what Rolf Harris said," the boy quips.

I fight a smile; this kid has a smart mouth. "Look, I am just offering help. Here, take my phone, and if at any point you feel threatened in anyway, dial nine-nine-nine. How about that?" I offer.

The young lad looks to his sister and nods. He picks her up and carries her to my car. I keep the door open for them and shut it once they're seated. I walk around to the front and sit in the passenger seat.

"How's your leg?" I ask.

"It hurts." The little girl sniffles.

"You'll have to give us the directions to your house. This is my assistant, Simon," I say, pointing to him. He puts his hand up and waves.

"I thought all assistants were girls?" the lad says.

"Theo! That is incest! Girls and boys can do any job they want!" the little girl states.

I choke on my laughter, as does Simon.

"The word is sexist," he snaps back at her.

"That's what I said, incest," she argues back.

He gives up and sighs, pointing us in the direction of where to go. We pull up outside where they say they live. "What level is your flat on?" I ask.

"The third," the lad answers.

"I will carry your sister for you and before you accuse me of anything, you can keep hold of my phone the entire time. There is no way you are able to carry her up three flights of stairs," I say, turning to face him.

He looks to his sister who shrugs. "I like him." She smiles and I smile back at her.

"Jesus, Betty, Mum taught us to be careful when it comes to strangers and now this dude knows where we live and you're okay for him to carry you into our flat? What if he's a bad guy?" he argues.

"He's not a baddie, I can tell. Are you, mister?" she asks sweetly.

"No, no, I'm not," I reply.

"Fine, but Mum's going to go mad and it will be me that will get in trouble for it." He huffs.

"If it helps, I will explain things to your mum, so you don't get into trouble for it?" I offer.

"Let's do that, I think Mum would like him." The little girl smiles, her brother rolls his eyes and gets out of the car.

"Simon, drive back and I will call when I'm ready to be collected. I will have to wait for her another time," I instruct.

I get out and pick up the little girl. She places her little hands around my neck. "I'm Betty and my brother is Theo, what's your name?" she asks.

"Roman," I answer.

"That's a nice name." She smiles.

As we walk through the hallways, the smell of drugs and urine fills the air. Even though I barely know these kids, I feel immediately protective over them. They shouldn't be living in this environment, and where is their mother? This can't be the safest place to live.

Theo stops at a door, but before he can unlock it, the flat next door opens and a tattooed guy in a tracksuit with gold chains around his neck, and clearly smoking a joint, steps out.

"Hey, Theo, my man. Have you thought more about my offer? It could make you some serious money, and that could really help your mum out." He grins.

Theo keeps his eyes fixed on the lock and shakes his head. "No thanks, Drew. I'm good," Theo mutters. Immediately, Drew's face changes, and his mood shifts from friendly to threatening.

He leans in closely. "I don't offer again, it's better that you have me on-side than not, little boy. I'd hate anything to happen to your fit mum. You get me?" he threatens. I place Betty down and push both kids behind me, blocking them from him.

"I suggest you fuck off back inside your shitty flat and stop threatening kids. You have a problem with that, I will happily knock your on your arse. I catch you anywhere near them or their mum, your life will be over," I warn.

He smirks, but I caught the flicker of fear in his eyes. He backs off and walks back into his flat and slams the door shut. I turn and unlock the door, ushering them inside.

"Where is your mum?" I ask.

"She's at work and will be home by five," Theo answers.

"Looks like I'm staying until five then," I state, taking off my suit jacket.

"Yay!" Betty claps.

I help Theo clean up Betty's knee and Theo makes me a cup of tea. I lean against the kitchen counter, drinking the tea. "So, does he often corner you like that?" I ask.

Theo shrugs. "Sometimes."

"Do you ever tell your mum?" I ask.

He doesn't answer, he just puts the milk back in the fridge and stares anywhere but at me. I realise I'm probably sounding like a social worker, I'm asking questions I have no right asking, so I quickly change the subject. "So, what's your favourite subject at school?" I ask then cringe at my question. Jesus, I remember when grown-ups would ask me this when I was his age. The last thing I wanted to talk about was school.

"Computer games, what you got?" I ask.

"Don't own any," he answers and walks into the lounge.

I follow him and notice the artwork on the walls, a gallery of beautiful portrait paintings. They are unusual and have a slight edgy feel to them. "Where did you get these from?" I point.

"Mummy painted them, silly!" Betty smiles. Wow, the woman has talent, these would sell for a small fortune in a gallery.

I take a seat on their sofa and feel the springs dig into my back. It's obvious that money is a struggle, but I can see she has tried make the place nice. She's made it warm and welcoming, a completely different contrast to outside the front door.

I sit with the kids as they watch a quiz show, shouting out their answers. They are both bright kids. Watching them, I smile, they are good kids, they deserve better than this life. I decide in that moment, I am offering their mum a job. Whatever her profession is, I will make sure there is a job available to her and they can stay free of charge in the hotel until she can afford to find a new place.

We hear the lock on the door go and I immediately tense, prepared if its someone breaking in. "Babies, Mummy is home!" is yelled from the hallway. Both kids look to me and I raise my brow in question. They both smirk and wait for their mum to walk in.

"So who fancies a vegetable curry tonight? I promise I wont make it too spic..." She freezes when she walks into the lounge.

I stand stunned, and at the same time feel fucking ecstatic.

"What are you doing here?!" she screeches.

"Same could be said for you," I retort.

"I live here! How did you find out where I live? Did my boss tell you? Because if he did, I will be suing the pair of you for breach of sharing confidential information," she rants. Her cheeks are flushed, and her eyes are alight with rage.

"Mummy, don't be silly, Roman helped me and Theo. I fell over and he drove us home in his really posh car," Betty states, pointing to her knee.

She looks down and her face immediately changes to a soft and caring expression. "Oh, baby, you should have rung me or Nana," she says, cupping her face and kissing her on her head.

"Let's invite Roman to dinner. To say thank you for helping us," Betty says excitedly.

"Oh, honey, I don't think Roman will want to eat our food." She smiles at me and her eyes flare, telling me to decline the offer.

I smile. "I would love to stay for dinner."

"Yay! Oh, Mummy, you haven't said a proper hello to Roman, that's rude, go on." Betty pushes her forward.

"Hi, I'm Roman, it's nice to meet you." I pause, holding out my hand, waiting for her to answer and say her name.

"Cora. Nice to meet you too." She smiles whilst gritting her teeth together. I take her hand in mine, feeling her soft skin.

Theo and Betty are snickering, trying to hide their laughter. Cora turns and gives them a look. "Yeah, laugh it up."

Cora forgets I'm still holding her hand until she feels my thumb stroking back and forth. Her eyes collide with mine and briefly her eyes soften, but she's quick to hide it.

She pulls her hand away. "Right, well, I'm going to make a start on dinner," she states and walks out of the room.

"I will come and help," I yell after her, hearing her growl under her breath along with I'm sure a few choice words, making me laugh.

She bangs around the kitchen, slamming cupboard doors and starts chopping angrily.

"Anything I can help with?" I offer.

"Nope! Everything is just fine, thank you," she says, chopping vigorously.

"Will you slow down before you cut yourself?" I warn her.

She slams the knife down and spins around to face me, her anger radiating off of her. I love seeing her all riled up, I want nothing more than to kiss her right now.

"Listen here, I don't know why you were in this estate and just so happened to run into my children, I don't believe for a second you were on your way to anywhere. There is no way on hell's earth you'd be on this estate. So come on, spill the beans, why are you really here?" she rants.

I instinctively reach out and tuck a stray strand of hair behind her ear. She sucks in a sharp breath at the intimate gesture.

"Truth is, you have me completely spell bound. Simon told me where you lived and what it was like, I had to see it for myself." I sigh.

"Oh, what's the matter, too dirty or rough for you? I have news for you, this is how many, many people live. No savings, no trust funds. They live day by day and count it as a good day if a bailiff isn't knocking on the door, or that they can afford to put the heating on in winter. This, right here, is the real world, this is the reality that people like you are too blind to see because you can't see past your designer clothes and jewellery. You're all in your little bubble, anything happens outside of it doesn't affect you, so there is no need to ever pop that bubble and have a good long look at the reality that surrounds you," she fumes.

I walk towards her until her back hits the wall. "There's a lot of anger there for people you don't know. I will take that we are blind, I will take that some people are snobby arseholes that look down their noses at others, but think to yourself, have I ever treated you that way?" I pause. "No, I haven't. I am not going to justify myself to you or justify my wealth. I haven't judged you, so what gives you the right to judge me?" I fire back.

She bites her bottom lip. "You can't deny you judged me when you offered me that money when you hit me with the door," she retorts.

"I didn't judge you for what you are, I made a mistake reading the situation," I argue back.

She pauses, looking at me, assessing me. She nods. "Okay, I'm sorry for judging you."

Her apology throws me, she said it so quietly and softly with regret. I want to hold her and tell her it's nothing, it doesn't matter, but I can't, not yet anyway.

"Work for me," I blurt out.

Her eyes go wide. "What?" she whispers.

"Work for me. Pack up your stuff and come work for me at the hotel."

I await her answer.

"But I have a job," she says confused.

"I will pay you triple what you earn, there will also be accommodation for you and your children. Think about it. I will come by to pick you up for work in the morning, you can tell me then," I say, grabbing my suit jacket.

"But... But I have to clock in," she murmurs, stunned.

"I will sort it. Tomorrow eight a.m.," is the last thing I say before leaving.

CHAPTER SIX

Cora

I didn't get a wink of sleep last night, I was tossing and turning all night long, weighing up this decision in my head, wondering if he was just after me for a quick shag? Or what if he hated me after two months? Then me and the kids would be homeless. Then what?

My body aching and tired, I get up and get the kids ready for school. The whole time I am clock watching, waiting for eight a.m.

"Mummy, why do you keep looking at the clock?" Betty asks whilst I braid her hair.

"Just making sure we are on time," I say.

"He's coming this morning, isn't he?" Theo queries, watching me for my reaction.

"Maybe." I smile.

"Oh yay! Do we get to go in his posh car to school? I can show all my friends the posh car, maybe offer them rides?" Betty says excitedly.

"No, baby. No rides, he may not even turn up." No sooner have the words left my mouth, there is a knock at the door.

"He's here!" Betty screams, jumping from the chair and running to the door.

"Betty, do not open that bloody door without me!" I yell after her. She completely ignores me and reaches up to open the door. She swings it open and her shoulders sag.

"Oh, hello, Daddy." She sighs.

I immediately pull her back, so she is behind me. "Go help your brother do lunch, Betty," I instruct.

She runs off to the kitchen and I hear the door shut behind her, knowing that Theo would have closed it as soon as she said it was their father.

"I told you to stay away." I sigh.

"I know, I know, but the thing is, I ran into some trouble. It wasn't my fault, honestly. I mean, the horse was a sure thing, it should have won," he says, making excuses.

"Betting? Really? Did you bet the money I gave you? The money that was supposed to help you out of a tight situation, money that I was saving for our kids Christmas presents!" I seethe, feeling my temper flare.

"Its not my fault! I needed more than what you gave to clear the debt, so I gambled some of it, but it fell through.

"You gambled some of it... Right, so what about the rest? What did you use the rest of it for?" I ask.

He looks to the floor and shrugs.

"Drugs, you used the money I gave to help you on drugs and betting. Let me guess, heroin?" I say, beyond frustrated.

He doesn't answer. "I have nothing else to give you, Kyle, I have no more emotion left to give you, no more money to give you. You've killed all that. Go, and don't ever come near me or the kids again. I am so tired of all of your shit, I'm done."

His head snaps up. "Please, Cora, you are the only person I have left, the only person I can trust. The kids, they mean everything to me, I can't live not having them in my life. Please don't take them away from me, please, I'm begging you," he cries.

"Just go, Kyle, please just leave me and the kids alone. If you love them as much as you say you do then go to rehab and sort your shit out, but don't come here until you're clean and can be a proper dad to them, because they don't deserve this," I point out.

"No, you can't stop me seeing my kids, you can't stop me coming round here," he says, getting angry. He gets right up in my face, his hands shaking.

"When was the last time you used?" I ask, seeing the light sheen of sweat across his brow.

"Two days ago. What's it to do with you? You don't give a shit," he snaps, becoming more and more irritable.

"I have no money, Kyle, so just go." I sigh.

"I ain't going fucking nowhere! We are married, that means I'm entitled to half of the shit that's in this flat," he says and storms past me, pushing me, and my back slams against the door.

I go after him. "Stop!" I yell as he rips the wires out of the TV. "You can't take the TV away from the kids!" I shout as I walk over to stop him. He pushes me off, sending me flying backwards. I fall over the coffee table and land on the floor with a thud.

"Put down the fucking TV and get the fuck out," a deep threatening voice bellows across the lounge.

Kyle pauses. I look up and see Roman stood there, dressed in his expensive designer suit, his eyes fixed on Kyle and his hands clenched into fists.

"Who the fuck are you? This is my TV, I'm taking what is owed to me," he sneers.

"What is it you want? Money?" Roman asks.

Kyle nods. He knows just by looking at Roman that he has money. Roman reaches into his pocket, pulls out a wad of cash and throws it on the floor.

"Take the money, fuck off, and don't come back. Believe me when I say take this chance because you do not want to test me. I will make your life a living hell," Roman warns.

Kyle puts the TV down, scoops up the money and doesn't even look back as he runs out of the door as fast as he can, to go and get his next fix. Roman comes to me, holding out his hands, offering to help me up.

"Thanks," I mutter, completely embarrassed by the situation that he has just witnessed.

He takes my shirt and lifts it up slightly. "What are you doi—" I hiss when his hand gently touches my side. I look and see that it's all grazed and feels tender.

"Does he come by here a lot?" he asks.

"Only when he's desperate," I answer honestly.

"Let's get the kids to school and then you and I are talking," he says firmly as he softly tucks a strand of my hair behind my ear.

I swallow nervously and nod.

~

AFTER SPENDING THE ENTIRE JOURNEY TO SCHOOL REASSURING Theo that I was okay, and that his dad wasn't coming back, we head to the hotel. I sit in silence, not in the mood to make small talk and not really in the mood to talk about what just happened either.

The car pulls up outside the hotel and I walk with Roman to his office, his hand placed on the small of my back. I do my best to shut down the warm and fuzzy feeling it seems to be creating.

"Take a seat." He gestures to the sofa in his office and I sit down, feeling anxious.

"Cora, I'm going to cut straight to the point, I am offering you a full-time job here, you will be our head of housekeeping. The pay will be thirty thousand pounds per year plus a bonus on top. I am also offering you residence here at the hotel. There is a suite that has three bedrooms and a communal area. There will be no charge for the room and all room service and food within the hotel will be included. I will have my solicitor draw up a contract protecting you and ensuring your job and accommodation are secure for a minimum of twelve months," he finishes and waits for my response.

"I... Err... I... Err... What?" I ask dumbfounded, shaking my head. "So, I will be earning thirty thousand a year and I don't have to pay for any overheads? No bills, no food, nothing?" I ask in disbelief.

"That's exactly what I am saying. You will have full use of all the hotel facilities including the gym, pool and spa."

"Well, fuck me," I blurt out. I gasp and cover my mouth. "Sorry," I mumble. "You're actually serious?" I whisper.

He smiles and nods. "Never been surer about anything."

"Oh my God, yes, yes!" I screech and lunge myself at him, wrapping my arms around his neck. Tears fill my eyes and I'm too happy to care.

His arms come around me, hugging me back, being careful of my side.

I lean back a little and look into his eyes. "Wait, are you hiring me out of pity?" I ask.

He smiles and shakes his head. "No, I'm hiring you because I know you will work hard, and you will always show up for work on time because you, well, you will be living here." He shrugs.

I sit up and wipe my eyes. "Thank you, I promise I won't let you down and, um, sorry for hugging you. I got a bit over excited. So when do you want me to start?" I ask

"I can have a removal company at your flat within the hour to pack up your stuff and have you here by tonight," he states.

"Tonight? Are you serious? I mean, we haven't talked about times, I will have to talk to the children and work out times for dropping the children off at school, so they aren't late, and then there's telling my parents and I have to work today," I list off.

He laughs and shakes his head. "You're moving twenty minutes down the road, stop getting stressed out about it. I'm here to make it all stress free. I've informed your boss about your new job, I've also taken the liberty of requesting your friend... Sylvia, is it? She will now be employed as a cleaner here and shall answer to you," he states.

"How did you know I would say yes? I mean, it's a little presumptuous," I point out.

"Because I know you're a smart woman and I know you want a better life for you and your kids," he states.

"I can't clean the entire hotel with Sylvia, that's impossible," I point out.

"The company you worked for will continue to clean, you will over see them and make sure they are doing things correctly. Sylvia will be on call for any emergency accidents also. You are to manage them, organise them," he informs me. "Your hours will be ten a.m. to two p.m. Monday to Friday," he adds.

"Are you serious?" I whisper.

"Yes, you need to be available for your children, they come first," he insists. Before I can respond, there's a knock on the door.

"Yeah?" Roman yells.

Simon sticks his head through. "The removal team have arrived," he informs us.

I look at Roman, eyebrow raised. "You really are sure of yourself, huh?"

"I didn't get where I am today by questioning my choices," he answers and stands, doing up his suit jacket. "Shall we?" He gestures to the door.

I stand and follow him, feeling overwhelmed and not really processing it all. It's so surreal. This sort of thing doesn't happen to people like me, we aren't supposed to be plucked from our poor, hard and shitty lives and just given a chance. That just doesn't happen.

I feel the other hotel staff looking at me as I walk with Roman. I feel the questioning glances and I know as soon as we step foot outside the gossip will be rife.

Back at the flat, I try to help the guys box stuff up, but they have everything covered. I decide the best way to help out is to make tea and coffee.

"All your furniture will be put in storage until you decide what you want to do with it. I have already sent an email informing the council of your departure and that it will be vacant from tomorrow." Roman walks in, placing his phone in his pocket.

"You know I am quite capable of doing that... I mean, how do you even know my personal details to do that?" I ask. "You don't even know my surname!" I screech.

Roman walks right up to me and holds my face in his hands, the affectionate and personal action making me hold my breath.

"I know this is happening fast for you, and yes, I could have waited a few days or a week, but the thought of you and the kids living in this place a moment longer than you had to wasn't an option for me. Take a deep breath, Kitten, and enjoy the ride." He winks.

Kitten? Did he just call me Kitten? I stand there, frozen to the spot, my mind feeling like its about to explode.

This is a lot to process in one morning.

CHAPTER SEVEN

Cora

I stand in my empty flat, and it may be a craphole to most, but it was our home. It was where my babies took their first steps. It was my first home away from my parents.

I walk to the wall where I marked the kids heights as they grew each year, right from the moment that they could stand.

"Ready?" Roman says, making me jump. I spin around and wipe my tears.

"Yeah." I sniffle.

As soon as we step out in the communal hallway, the smell and loud music and shouting surrounds us. This is something I won't ever miss.

The van follows us to the hotel and the men unload all of our personal items and take them upstairs to the suite we are staying in. Roman guides me to the restaurant and we take a seat. I hadn't even realised I hadn't eaten and its now past one o'clock. My stomach growls loudly. "Shit, sorry." I smirk, placing my hand on my stomach.

Roman smiles and clicks his fingers in a demanding way. A waiter comes over. "Yes, sir?" He smiles politely.

"Lunch special for two, please, William, and what do you want to drink?" he asks me.

I pause, thinking I could murder a wine or a gin after the unexpected day I've had, and it's as if he read my mind.

"Bombay sapphire and tonic with a lime wedge and I will have the same," he orders. I smile kindly at William and he smiles and winks in return.

"How do you know I like gin?" I ask Roman once William has left.

"I don't, but if you didn't then you would have corrected me, I'm sure," he says arrogantly.

"What if I was being polite? I may not have wanted to appear rude," I retort.

He smiles. "Like you're being now? You may be polite, but you have no problem speaking your mind and you most definitely would have corrected me."

Damn it, he's got me there. I fiddle with the cutlery and bite my lip anxiously. When William brings our drinks, I practically snatch it from his hand and glug back a large amount.

Roman raises his eyebrow. "Better?" he asks and I nod. "William, another for the lady, please," he orders.

William scurries off to get me another. I want to protest, but its my favourite drink and I cannot remember the last time I treated myself to one.

"I have to ask this one question, its being playing on my mind, and well, if I don't say it, it will just fester in my head forever," I say nervously.

"You can ask me anything, Cora," he states.

I let out a long breath. "Are you being nice to me and treating me like this because you want to have sex with me?" I ask bluntly. I look at Roman who doesn't even look the slightest bit phased by my question. His eyes remain fixed on mine as he leans forward on his elbow, his index finger running over his bottom lip as if he's contemplating his answer.

"Yes," he answers honestly. I gasp and swallow nervously.

"If I don't sleep with you, will you take the job and the place to stay away from me?" I ask.

"No," he answers.

I breathe a sigh of relief. "Under no circumstances, Cora, would I ever make a move on you unless you begged me to. Just because I find you extremely attractive, isn't the reason I offered you this job and a place to stay. Will we fuck at some point in the future? Most definitely. When that happens all depends on you," he states arrogantly.

My eyes go wide. "What makes you so sure that I would beg to sleep with you?" I ask.

He smirks. "You will, Kitten. You will be begging me for it. You want to right now but you're too stubborn and too scared."

I feel my cheeks heat as my temper rises at his audacity. "I will never sleep with you. God, you're delusional. There is one thing you should know about me and that is I never beg for anything. I want something, I take it. I. Don't. Beg," I snap.

His eyes alight, much to my irritation. God, he gets me so riled up, I just want to punch the smug look right off his face. William returns with my second drink and I snatch it off his tray, downing it and holding it out for him to take. "Another, please, William," I ask angrily.

I should really slow down, I have a three-drink-limit or I will be tipsy, but at this moment in time, I couldn't care less. He has caused me so many different emotions in just one day. I close my eyes and calm myself down.

"After lunch, I shall show you to your suite. I have arranged for Simon to collect the children from school, and don't worry, I have also taken the liberty of informing the school that Simon will be the one collecting them, giving you time to get settled before they arrive," he informs me.

My eyes spring open and I lean forward. "Do not interfere with my kids, ever. That is my job as a mother, not yours. I barely know you and you have no right making those arrangements without consulting me first," I hiss.

He holds his hand up. "My apologies, I didn't think. I was merely trying to make things easy on you, but I understand how it would appear that I went a little too far."

I sigh. "Thank you for your apology. It's fine, just for future reference, speak to me before you decide anything to do with my kids." I sigh, wishing this very awkward lunch would hurry up and be over. I just want to go and hide away in the suite right now and make sure it's perfect before the children come home from school.

William brings our food on a tiered stand with various little sandwiches and cakes on.

"Afternoon tea?" I ask with a smile. "I, um, never thought you would be the afternoon tea type of guy." I laugh, taking a bite of a sandwich.

"So, what type of person is an afternoon tea type of person?" he retorts.

"I'd say usually an old lady." I laugh.

"Well, I'm no old lady, that's for sure. I ordered this because I wasn't sure what you liked and this way you could choose, plus technically, this isn't afternoon tea as we don't have a pot of tea," he answers, placing an entire sandwich in his mouth.

"Woah, I'm sorry I don't know the proper afternoon tea etiquette," I tease.

He smirks and the awkwardness that was there before eases a little. I will forever have the thought at the back of my mind that he wants to sleep with me, but I can continue to ignore that and push it even further out of my mind with time.

We finish lunch comfortably, and Roman shows me to my suite. He unlocks the door, opens it and gestures for me to enter.

My jaw hits the floor, the suite is huge. It has a large lounge area and there are three rooms off of it; one master, with what looks like a queen size bed, and two more large rooms, both with double beds. I notice how the removal team have unpacked all the personal belongings and placed them in the children's rooms. Betty's bed is covered with all of her teddies and dollies.

"Thank you," I whisper.

"It's nothing. I will leave you to enjoy and relax until the children arrive home," he says softly, leaving me stood there overwhelmed and taking it all in.

I walk to my room and smile. I run and dive on the bed and moan from not having had a bed for the last three years after having to sleep on a crappy sofa. I moan and let out a long sigh, feeling my whole body relax for the first time in an extremely long time.

CHAPTER EIGHT

Roman

I sit in my office, my mind completely consumed by her. It took everything in me not to hold her after seeing her reaction to her suite. She was completely floored. It's not just that moment though, it's all of her. The way she can be so soft and sweet, but you can piss her off in an instant and her claws come out. I admit, I do like pushing those buttons to get that reaction out of her, the way her eyes alight with her anger and the pink flush touches her cheeks. Pure fucking perfection.

I don't know how to be with her. I am trying to be the perfect gentleman, but she makes it incredibly hard. I need to reign it in with her. She is protective over her children and her heart. I need to tread carefully, but I also can't hold back completely. She ignites something in me, lighting a flame inside.

Simon knocks and walks into my office. "Sir, I have the kids from school, but there's an issue, we can't get through to the phone from the front desk to the room, for some reason, she's not answering," he explains.

I jump to my feet and follow him out, grabbing the spare key from the drawer. I wasn't letting anyone else have access to the spare key. I see the kids sat on the sofa waiting, looking around the hotel wide-eyed, taking it all in. I walk to them and smile.

"Hey, kids, your mum's busy, so I'm going to grab her for you. Simon is going to take you to the restaurant where you can order yourselves a milkshake on me while I go get her," I offer.

Betty jumps up. "Do you have banana?" she asks. I get the impression that if I said no, then this would be a deal breaker for Betty.

"Yes, we have banana." I smile.

"Yes! That's my favourite. Come on, Theo!" She tugs at his hand excitedly. Theo follows her, a very slight smile playing on his lips, but being a typical teenager, he can't show too much emotion.

"Stay with them, keep them occupied until I come and find you with Cora," I order.

Simon nods and walks off, following the kids.

I head up to the room, knocking and awaiting her answer.

Nothing.

I enter the room, calling her name, and still no answer. I walk into the master bedroom and see her sprawled out on the bed, fast asleep. I smile. She's led on her front, sprawled out like a starfish. I brush her hair aside from her face and contemplate leaving her to sleep, but I know she would probably have my balls for interfering, and I know she would want to explain to the kids what's going on.

"Cora," I call softly. She groans in her throat but doesn't move. "Cora, wake up," I say a little louder.

"No, I don't want to," she grumbles and shoves her face into her pillow.

I laugh. "Cora, the kids are downstairs, they are back from school."

She jumps up so quick, I have to step back so she doesn't head-butt me. Still half asleep, she stumbles, nearly falling. I reach out to steady her.

"Calm down, it's okay, Simon is with them having a milkshake, wake yourself up first," I say, stroking the hair from her face.

She rubs her face and sits on the edge of the bed. "You alright?" I ask.

"Yeah." She smiles. "I didn't really sleep last night." She yawns. "I haven't slept in a bed for about three years, so I guess I needed the rest." She smiles sleepily.

"What do you mean, you haven't slept in a bed for three years?" I ask.

"Well, as Betty got older, it was obvious she needed her own room and Theo needs his own space, so I gave her mine and I slept on the sofa." She shrugs like it's no big deal that she hasn't had her own bed for three years. A simple thing that every person should have. She's gone without so her child didn't have to. I don't think, I just act as I lean forward and tuck a strand of hair behind her ear and place a kiss on her head.

"Your incredible, you know that?" I say softly. Her eyes go soft and she has a slight blush on her cheeks at the compliment. She clearly isn't used to it. I make a mental note to change that.

"Come on, let's go see your kids, they are probably wondering what's going on," I say, taking her hand in mine.

We walk down to the elevator, her hand still in mine, and the doors slide open. A couple of staff enter the elevator and Cora quickly pulls her hand away. Missing the contact, but not surprised she withdrew her hand, I expected her to do it sooner than that, so at least that gives me some hope.

I guide her through to the restaurant, even though I know she knows where she is going. I still keep my hand on the small of her back. I will use any excuse I can to touch her.

"Mummy!" Betty yells excitedly. I notice she has whipped cream all around her face and I smile. She is adorable. How I didn't know she was Cora's daughter from the moment I met her, I don't know. She is the double of her mum. Her blonde wavy hair, her blue eyes and her button nose. Theo looks like his mum too, although he has his father's dark hair.

"Wow, look what you got! You lucky girl," Cora coos, kissing Betty and getting a napkin and wiping the cream from her face. She leans over and kisses Theo on his head and he brushes her off, scrunching up his face in disgust.

"So, guys, there's something I need to tell you," Cora states, lifting Betty and placing her on her lap.

"I will leave you guys to it," I state and turn to leave.

"No, stay. This kind of involves you too, so stay." Cora smiles.

I nod and pull out a chair. "So, kids..." She takes a deep breath. "Today Roman helped me... Us, helped us leave our flat. And we have moved in here." She smiles.

Both kids look confused. "So, we don't have a home anymore?" Theo questions. "Is it because of Dad?" he asks, getting angry.

I speak up before Cora.

"I offered your mum a job here at the hotel. Better pay, better hours and also with free accommodation. I needed a head housekeeper, and your mum needed a better job, so she's helped me out by taking it and I've helped her out by giving you and your mum a better place to live." I shrug and look to Cora who is looking at me with a soft smile playing on her lips. I want nothing more than to lean over and kiss her, but I can't.

"So, what about my teddies and my dollies?" Betty asks panicked.

"All on your new bed waiting for you." Cora smiles, turning to Theo who is just sat there, staring straight ahead, not saying anything. "Honey? Are you okay with this, because if you're not then we can move back into the flat, if that's what you want?" she soothes.

Over my dead body is my first thought. I would never let them go back there. I'd rather buy a flat for them to live in than have them move back there.

Theo turns to me. "Why would you do this for us?" he asks, clearly not stupid, and he's learnt that nothing comes for free, and I imagine he hasn't seen a lot of kindness shown to him, especially from strangers.

"You want the honest truth?" I ask.

He nods.

"I like you. I like your sister and I like your mum. I think you are all amazing and you deserve a break in life, especially your mum. Your mum works hard, she has earnt this and deserves so much more from life than what she was getting, and that goes for the both of you too." I shrug.

Theo doesn't say anything, he just stares at me blankly. He shocks the shit out of me when he stands and leans over and hugs me. "Thank you," he rasps, the emotion and gratitude in his voice both warms and breaks my heart.

No kid should have to be this grateful for just being given a slightly better standard of living. It's not like I'm making them millionaires, it's a job offer with decent perks. Something that most of us, including me, take for granted. What is nothing to me is completely life changing for them.

Betty jumps from Cora's lap and wraps her arms around me too, both kids hugging me tight. I look to Cora who is smiling, with tears in her eyes. She mouths the words "Thank you." I nod and swallow the lump in my throat.

The kids pull back and both smile brightly at me. I smile back. "Want to go see your new home?" I ask.

"Yes!" they both say excitedly. I almost tell Cora to take a picture because this is the most animated I've seen Theo.

I stand outside their room as Cora opens the door. The kids walk in and I follow. Cora stands smiling, watching their faces. Their eyes are wide, and their jaws are practically touching the floor.

"It's massive!" Betty yells, jumping up and down on the spot excitedly.

"Look at the size of the TV!" Theo yells.

Cora laughs and sniffs back her tears. They run into each of their rooms and we hear screeching as they both come back out. "I have a TV in my room!" Theo shouts, smiling.

"I have a TV in my room too!" Betty squeals back.

Cora lets out a little sob. Without thinking, I place my hand on the back of her neck and give her a gentle reassuring squeeze and kiss the side of her head. Her eyes come to mine and flicker to my mouth.

I know I could make my move now and kiss her, but she would regret it. She would say it was the heat of the moment.

"I will leave you to it and see you tomorrow. Come to my office after you've taken the kids to school, we will sort out your paperwork," I state before turning and leaving.

Everything in me is telling me to turn back around and kiss her, but I don't. It's not the right time. As I've told her before, I won't be doing anything until she is begging me for it.

CHAPTER NINE

Cora

The kids were beyond thrilled. They are in bed, Betty fast asleep, and I expect Theo is led there, watching TV. I drop a text to my mum and briefly tell her what's happened and ask her to come for lunch with dad at the hotel tomorrow, so I can explain more. I yawn and stretch out on the comfy couch. Seeing it's ten p.m., I decide to get myself to bed. Despite having the nap earlier, I still feel exhausted. It's as if years of stress and tension is slowly leaving my body.

I lay in the ridiculously huge bed, feeling comfort like I've never felt before. I set my alarm on my phone and close my eyes, doing my best to ignore the feelings Roman has started to stir within me. Goddamn that pompous arsehole being all sweet and nice, making me feel things I am not prepared to be feeling.

THE NEXT MORNING, SIMON DRIVES ME TO TAKE THE KIDS TO school. I don't miss the looks from the other mums in the playground. As soon as we arrive back at the hotel, I go straight to Roman's office. I take a deep breath and knock on the door.

"Yeah?" he yells.

I open the door and see him sat there, his suit jacket on the back of his chair, his crisp white shirt unbuttoned slightly, showing just a snippet of his chest and his sleeves rolled up to his elbows. He coughs lightly to get my attention. I flick my eyes to him and feel the embarrassment creep up my cheeks for being caught red-handed eyeing him up.

"You wanted me to fill out some paperwork?" I ask.

He nods and stands, gesturing for me to sit at his desk. I take a seat and he places down the documents in front of me. "If you can fill out all of your personal details, bank account and then there's your contract to go over and sign," he instructs, leaning over me, the delicious smell of his cologne surrounding me.

I clear my throat. "Sure, no problem." He moves, giving me space, and I'm relieved because at least now I can try and concentrate.

Once I've filled out the documents he needs, I call him over to go over my contract.

"So your official start date would be Monday, use the remainder of this week to get settled. The contract states one year, but of course you can still leave at any point. If I terminate the contract before the year, I shall pay whatever monies are owed to take you up to the end of that year and also provide you with alternative accommodation. You will also be enlisted in our pension scheme, and the same goes for that if I terminate early, I will pay the remainder. Transport for school run is also included as you have moved away from their schools, and you will also be entitled to five weeks of annual leave. I think that's about it," he states, going over it. "Any questions?"

"No, I don't think so," I answer. He hands me a pen and I sign. He takes the pen from me and leans down and signs. His body cages me and I tense, feeling the heat from having his body so close.

"There, now you're mine," he whispers against my ear.

I suck in a shuddering breath and look to him. He smirks, knowing he is having an effect on me. Bastard.

"Don't just barge in there! He's in a meeting! Don't make me call the police!" we hear Simon threaten.

We look at each other confused, and as Roman walk towards the door, we hear, "Ring the bloody police if you want. They won't rush, it's a Thursday, they are always short staffed on a Thursday!"

"Oh shit." I sigh. Roman looks to me and the door swings open. "Roman, I'd like you to meet my father, Felix."

"Sorry about him, dear, he can get very passionate," my mum apologises to Simon.

"And that's my mother, Margo," I add.

"Don't sign anything! You never know what you're signing away, they bleed you dry and take everything from you, these rich bastards. They just want a peasant to do their dirty work and get paid in scraps," Dad rants on.

"Dad! Stop," I chastise.

"I can assure you, sir, under no circumstance would I ever bleed your daughter dry, nor do I think she is a peasant," Roman defends.

"That's what they all say, mate, I ain't no fool. I've seen a lot, I've protested a lot and I've been there for the poor sods that get shafted from the likes of wealthy dickheads like you. Don't try and play me for a fool, boy, because I won't have it."

I place my head in my hands and groan.

"Felix Edwards, you apologise right now. What is the one thing you hate? You don't fight, you don't make war, you make love and peace. Now do as you preach or so help me I will... I will... I will go and purchase a new item of clothing from that store that you protested outside of over allegations of child labour," Mum threatens.

"You wouldn't?" Dad gasps in horror.

"Oh, I would, Felix, and do you know what else I would do? I would wear it once then bin it, that's right, bin it. Not donate it, not recycle it, but bin it," Mum continues to threaten.

Christ, any moment now, Dad will have a panic attack or file for divorce, although I'm not sure he would do that as it would cause an unnecessary carbon footprint in printing the divorce papers. At this point, I have given up hiding my face in my hands, now face planting Roman's desk seems like the wisest thing to do. I could knock myself unconscious, that would definitely take me out of this situation.

I feel a hand on my neck, giving me a gentle squeeze. I sit up and Roman smiles at me. He leans forward and kisses my forehead, still keeping his hand on the back of my neck, his thumb moving in a soothing motion.

"Felix," Mum practically growls.

"Fine, I apologise for jumping to conclusions. Please, I meant no offence in what I said," Dad apologises then turns to Mum. "There, is that acceptable?" he asks. Mum just gives him a nod.

"Why are you guys here? I told you to come for lunch and we would talk," I point out.

"Well, yes, but see, because you were so vague, we were worried you were being held here against your will, so we figured we would arrive a little early and catch everyone off guard." Mum shrugs.

"Jesus Christ." I sigh. Roman gives me another gentle squeeze and I look up to him. He is smiling widely, trying hard to contain his laughter. I give him a don't you dare look which just makes him cough, trying harder to contain it.

He clears his throat. "Why don't you take your parents upstairs, show them around and explain all to them, and I will meet you up there in a little while. Then we can all have lunch together and I can answer any questions you may have. How does that sound?" Roman offers.

Mum speaks before Dad. "That sounds like a perfect idea."

"Great, Simon, could you show Mr and Mrs Edwards up to Cora's suite while I finish business here. Cora will be up in five minutes, it wont take long," Roman orders.

Simon's lips twitch and he nods, leading my parents out of the room. Roman walks and closes the door behind them. I stand confused as I thought we were done.

"What else is it you need to talk to me about?" I ask.

He turns to me and stalks slowly towards me, stopping just in front of me, his eyes searching mine. What they're searching for, I don't know. He reaches out and tucks my hair behind my ear, something I've noticed he does a lot. For a brief moment, I think he's going to kiss me, but something changes in him. He closes his eyes and shakes his head.

"It's nothing that can't wait, I will see you at lunch." He sighs, giving me a tight smile.

Feeling I don't know what... Disappointment? A part of me wanted him to kiss me, he looks like a walking model from Men's Health or GQ magazine. Do I want to start a relationship with my new boss? Probably not the best idea. What if it's not a relationship he wants? Can I do just the one night thing then carry on as employee and boss? I know he's made his intentions clear that he likes me, but apart from that there has been nothing. The flirting, the little intimate touches, I can't read if this is a normal thing for him. Maybe he is this way with certain female staff that he likes? I won't know until I start work on Monday and get to know a few of the other staff members.

I was so inside my head with my own thoughts, I hadn't realised that I was stood outside of my room door. I shake my head and take a deep breath, ready to face the questions my parents will no doubt throw at me.

CHAPTER TEN

Cora

I sigh and pinch the bridge of my nose as the onslaught of questions come flying at me regarding Roman.

"Oh, honey, he isn't helping you just to be nice, he likes you more than that, I can assure you. I saw the way he looked at you. You just be careful with that big heart of yours. When you fall, you fall hard, just like your mother, and unfortunately, you fell hard for the wrong guy before. Make sure you know he's the right guy. If he is then you deserve all the happiness he brings you." Mum smiles, cupping my face.

Dad on the other hand has walked around the suite, looking at all the electrical appliances and taken note of the manufacturer and how much energy each item uses and what the carbon footprint must be for just this room alone.

"Mum, for the millionth time, he only offered me a job and accommodation, nothing more. Does he like me? I don't know. All I know is I would have had to be a complete idiot not to take this job.

This is a better life for the kids and for me. You know, I may even have time to paint, I haven't painted in years." I sigh.

"This room alone is using more power than our entire flat, Margo. Honestly, I'm fighting a losing battle here." He sighs.

"Oh, Dad, give it a rest, will you? It's a hotel. I'm sure you can chew Roman's ear off at lunch about your ideas to make the hotel greener," I snap.

Dad pauses and looks to Mum. She shakes her head and he comes to sit next to me. "You know we love you, and we only ever want what is best for you and for the kids, right?" he asks.

"I know that, Dad," I mumble.

"Then if you're happy, we are happy. That's what we've always told you, it's how we raised you. We raised you to be happy in whatever path you take, whether that be painting or your cleaning job, here or back at the flat. One thing I know Mum and I are happy about is that you've distanced from Kyle. There's nothing you can do for him anymore and he is heading down a dark and dangerous road. Now, my little warrior, lets go get some lunch because I'm starving, and I have a peaceful march at three p.m. for same sex marriages in churches," he states, looking at his watch.

I smile. "Another day another fight for the people, hey, Dad?"

"You know it, standing together and getting yourselves heard. Jason and Barney are meeting me there with a rainbow flag and I'm in charge of the megaphone." He smiles proudly.

I laugh. "Well, as long as you remember to say the correct things this time, not like when you were protesting for... What was it?" I ask.

"For the Communities Unite Nationwide Trust." Dad sighs.

"And what was it you kept shouting?" I ask.

"C.U.N.T's are coming together, you will not destroy our C.U.N.T," he mumbles under his breath.

Mum and I are laughing. "How did you not hear what you were saying?" Mum shakes her head.

"I was in the moment," Dad defends. "I didn't realise until Mike and the boys showed up and arrested me for disturbing the peace." He shrugs.

"Surely the children that were crying was a giveaway, or even the nun that got on her knees and started praying for you," Mum points out.

Still laughing, I stand, grabbing my phone and purse. "Come on then, let's go get some lunch, and please be nice to Roman, Dad," I warn.

He holds his hands up in defence. "Hey, best behaviour as always," he promises.

∼

WE SIT DOWN AND ORDER OUR DRINKS WHILST WAITING FOR Roman. I notice him across the lobby, talking to a very pretty, very well-dressed woman. She laughs at something he has said and touches his arm affectionately. Roman smiles and reaches forward, tucking a piece of hair behind her ear. I immediately feel the kick in my gut. I have clearly misread the situation between Roman and I. Not that I would have done anything anyway, but I guess I thought, in the very least, that affectionate gesture was just for me.

Roman leans forward and kisses the woman before she turns and leaves. My eyes are glued. I know I should look away.

Roman looks my way, our gaze connecting. His smile falls and his jaw tenses slightly. I look away and keep my gaze focused on my menu. I don't dare look up, not trusting what my expression will read. I don't have to look up to know he is stood right there, I feel his presence immediately.

"I apologise for my lateness, I had some business to take care of," he says as he takes the seat next to me. How I wish I had my parents sat either side of me.

"Oh, no bother, lad. Can't be helped." Dad smiles.

"Have you chosen what you are having?" Roman asks as he places his hand on mine. I move my hand away like he's burnt me.

"Yes, I think I will have the salmon, please." I ignore Roman and smile politely at the waiter.

Everyone else places their order and I don't miss the side glances coming from Roman, probably wondering what's crawled up my arse. I'm not admitting it to myself, so I certainly wont be admitting anything to him.

Roman tells my parents about my duties and what it will entail. "Of course there is also the prospect in the future of becoming my housemaid at my private home," he states.

My head whips up from staring absently at my lunch. "What?" I ask in shock.

His lips twitch, the bastard only said that to get me to face him. "It's a possibility. Greta is coming to the end of her contract with me and it may be something you're better suited to, but we will cross that bridge when it comes to it," he says arrogantly.

I feel heat rise in my cheeks. I would love nothing more than to tell him where to shove his job, up his arrogant arse. But of course, he knows I can't. He seems to love to push those buttons that make me want to smash his face in my salmon.

I smile sweetly whilst biting the inside of my cheek. "Well, if that is what sir wishes, then I suppose it's something to consider," I reply.

Mum and Dad's eyes flit back and forth between us, my Mum's are probably popping out of her head at my reaction, I have always had my Dad's rebellious streak. While my mum added calmness and stability, my dad taught me to fight for what I believe in and never let anyone take your kindness and good nature for granted. Only one person I let do that was Kyle, and I did that for the children. Just look at how that worked out. I know I will never be making the same mistake twice.

Roman's eyes alight, enjoying the fact he's making me angry. "It's good to know you're acceptable to change, especially if your skills are inadequate for the hotel, you may be better suited for a much smaller scale job." Roman smirks.

I grip hold of my fork so tight in my hand, fighting the urge to stab it in his leg. "Excuse me a moment, I need to use the bathroom," I grit through my teeth.

I storm off, feeling my blood boil. Why did I take this job? From the moment I met him, he has gotten under my skin. I can see this job making me take up smoking. Hell, I've not even officially started yet.

After pacing up and down like a rabid caged animal in the ladies, getting some peculiar looks from customers, I swing the door open to head back to the table, but my hand is grabbed and I'm pulled back so I'm practically pinned to the wall... by Roman.

"What the hell do you think you're doing?" I fume.

"Why are you so angry at me?" he asks.

I decide to ignore him as I have no right to feel angry at him, I'm not even sure why I feel angry at him. So, therefore, I feel really angry because I shouldn't be feeling this way.

"Was it Camila?" he asks. I keep my face neutral, showing no signs of emotion. I can't figure what's going on in my own head. I am sticking to my decision in not letting him become aware of my thoughts.

"I'm fine, thank you. My parents can be a little draining. I also just want to start work, I am not used to having time off like this," I lie to him, hoping it's enough to mask what's really pissed me off.

"Right, well, you can start work any time you would like, call your friend up and have her come in with her I.D. and you can get started straight away," he states, stepping back. I let out a long breath. I had purposefully been holding my breath so not to breathe in his heavenly scent.

We walk back to the table, his hand placed on the small of my back, and I try my hardest to ignore the fact that I like his touch. My mum and dad are sat whispering as we approach. Mum shushes Dad and gives him the eye in warning.

"Everything okay?" Mum asks.

"Yep, I have decided to start work tomorrow, you know how I get irritable not working." I smile tightly at my mum.

"Well, look at the time! It's been a pleasure, but I have to go protest. Thanks for lunch, Roman, I'm sure we will see you around," Dad says, shaking his hand. He pulls me in for a hug before leaving and waving over his shoulder.

"I have to get going, I'm teaching a life class at the community centre in an hour and I have to put the heating on to warm up the place for poor old Derrick's todger or it will shrivel up. Not that it shrivels up much, I mean the man maybe under five-foot in height, but he doesn't get the nickname Nelly the elephant for nothing, if you know what I mean." Mum winks and I die a little inside.

After Mum leaves, I turn to Roman. "Thanks for lunch and for putting up with my parents," I say politely.

"My pleasure, I will escort you back to your room," he offers.

"No, thank you, I'm going to go for a walk, I think, get some fresh air." I smile politely and walk away, leaving him stood there.

This tornado has swept in and my life has changed in the blink of an eye, for the better. I just need to make sure my heart doesn't get swept up too and become damaged in the process.

CHAPTER ELEVEN

Cora

I walk through the busy streets, people are forever rushing in London and I'm never sure why. I mean, what is so important you have no time to say hello or good morning to anyone? People just push past each other, not paying the slightest bit of attention to the world around them, the beauty that London holds or the history. But also, it's when people are blind to things that are happening right under their noses, too wrapped up in their own lives to care or to help others.

I spot a little old lady waiting patiently to cross the road. The crossing isn't working and not one car has bothered to stop and let her cross. I walk up to her and offer my help.

"Oh, why thank you, dear, but be careful, these busy bastards don't stop for nobody. If my lovely Jack were still with us, he would have given them what for, for not having any manners," she rants.

I laugh at her blunt response. "No worries, I know just how to stop traffic." I wink.

I let go of her arm and lift my shirt up, exposing my bra. The taxi that was approaching slams his breaks on. I laugh and hold up my hand.

"Well, if I had known that's all it took, I would have lifted up my skirt and flashed the old girls off. Of course, they are currently tucked into my knickers, so would have been a little difficult." She cackles.

I laugh, helping her over the street. Once over the other side, she thanks me for my help and gives me a pound for helping. No matter how much I refuse, she wont hear of it, so I relent and accept it.

I carry on walking, not too sure where I'm going. I take a seat on a bench and just people watch, rather than focus on my own thoughts, I'd rather watch the lives of others.

A man who must be in his fifties is sat, begging for food. No money for food and everyone is just walking on by, stepping over him as they go. I walk to the nearest café and get as much food as I can with the last of my money in my purse. It's not much but hopefully it will help. I walk up to him and crouch.

"Would you like some company?" I ask.

His weary and tired eyes come to mine, and he nods, obviously a little sceptical of my intentions. I hand the bag over.

He opens it and smiles.

"I'm, Cora, and you are?" I ask.

"I'm Terry," he answers. "So, what's a pretty thing like you doing, sitting on a dirty street floor with the likes of me?" he asks.

"I was just out for a walk when I saw you and I figured you could use some company, and I know I could, so I thought, why not?" I shrug.

"Darling girl, I could be anyone, why on earth would you approach a man like me? I could be dangerous, I could have made off with your wallet, anything could have happened," he adds, taking a bite out of the sandwich I got him.

"You can have my purse if you want it, there is no money in it. Even my bank cards wont get you anywhere as they are empty too." I shrug. "But I want the photos of my children, the rest is yours." I smile.

"You just spent the last of your money on this dithery old tramp?" he asks, looking at me dumbfounded.

"Yes, but I'm okay, I have a roof over my head, I have food. My parents taught me there is always someone worse off than yourself. It's not like I'm handing you loads of money, but it's what little I can do to help." I shrug.

"You, girl, are a crazy, kind-hearted woman." He shakes his head.

"So, can I ask how long have you been sleeping rough?" I ask.

"Well, let's see, it will be five years next month, I believe," he states.

"Wow, and what caused you to end up here? I mean, in the nicest way, you don't appear to be drug or alcohol dependant."

He sighs. "I lost my job that I had been in for nearly thirty years. No redundancy money, the company went bust. At my age, I'm not exactly prime hiring material. The wife tried her best working and trying to keep our spirits up, but I lost a part of me that day, the day I lost my job. I got into a deep depression and the wife couldn't take it anymore, so she up and left me. Of course, I couldn't afford the house, so I lost that too and now here I am… Have been ever since," he says sadly.

"Your wife left you?" I repeat, shocked and saddened.

"Yeah, I don't blame her. I was a shit to live with, pushed her away. She deserved better." He shrugs. "Anyway, that's enough depressing stuff. What's the real reason you're out here, sat with a tramp." He smiles.

"Well, I have a new job offer… Well, it's a whole new life offer, really. And I've taken it, I would have had to have been really stupid not to. It's just that my boss is messing up my head a lot. I like him, I mean, he's great looking, but I don't like him because he can be an arrogant and pompous arsehole, and sometimes, I just want to just punch him in his beautiful face," I rant.

Terry laughs. "My, dear, for a man to stir that kind of emotion in you is definitely a matter of the heart. Whether you chose to listen to your head or your heart is on you. I imagine he is completely smitten by you, and if he isn't then he is bloody well blind."

I don't say anything, I just nod, knowing he is right. "I think as the job is new, I shall be sticking to following my head. I mean, he is extremely good looking so it's probably just a crush that will pass on by. You know, because where I used to live, you'd be lucky if the best-looking guy on the estate had all his teeth." I laugh. "Yeah, definitely a crush, I'm just not used to seeing that kind of beauty," I add.

Terry nods and continues to eat. I look at the time and jump to my feet, brushing myself off. "I have to go and pick up my children. Will you be here in an hour?" I ask.

"Ain't got nowhere else to be, darling." He laughs.

"Okay, good, I will be right back." I rush out and run back to the hotel and find Simon waiting for me with the car to pick up the kids from school.

"Sorry, I got distracted," I say, jumping in.

Once we pick up the kids, I drop them at the hotel and explain Terry to them. They agree to have Terry over for dinner to offer him a shower, and he can crash on the sofa in our suite.

"God, I love you kids, do you know that?" I smile and kiss them.

I leave them in the hotel and run back outside to find Terry where I left him.

"Come on, Terry, I got you a sofa to crash on for a while," I state.

"Girl, you do not want to be offering a strange man you don't know your sofa for the night." He shakes his head.

"Terry, come on, if you were a bad guy, you would have stolen off me earlier, now, come on. Plus, I live in a hotel, so one scream and everyone will hear.

He sighs but eventually caves. I guide him through the hotel, and I don't miss the disgusted looks from others. Once up in our room, Terry lets out a whistle. "Woman, you've definitely landed on your feet."

"Hello, Mr Terry, I'm Betty and this is Theo, we've run you a nice big bubble bath with my special stuff that won't sting your eyes." Betty claps happily.

He smiles down at her. "Thank you, I look forward to it."

"I have put some clothes in there for you, they were my ex-husband's. I just used to wear them for decorating, so they are a bit worn but will do whilst I get your clothes washed," I offer.

"Sweet girl, you have no idea." He sighs. I see the emotion behind his eyes, and I swallow a lump and nod.

"I will order us room service for dinner," I suggest.

"This way, Mr Terry, your bath is waiting." Betty ushers him into the bathroom.

I pick up the phone to ring down to reception. "Hello, this is, um, Cora, room number—"

"Hello, Miss Edwards, we know what room you're in, how can I help you?" she asks.

"Oh, right, can I order our dinner for room service to be put on tab, please?" I ask nervously.

"Absolutely, what can I get you?" she asks.

I breathe out a sigh of relief, I worried for a moment that I would be charged. "Um, can I order four cheeseburgers and fries, all with cokes, please?"

"Sure thing, they will be with you shortly," she says before she disconnects.

Whilst I remember, I message Sylvia and tell her to be in work for ten a.m. tomorrow.

"Mummy, it's sad Mr Terry doesn't have a home or family," Betty says, cuddling in to me.

"It is, baby. Maybe we can find a way of helping him more? But for now, we can help him with some food and a warm place to sleep," I say, kissing the top of her head.

There's a knock at the door. "Oh, that was quick," I say, getting up to answer the door.

I open it and see Roman stood there, looking pissed off. "Can I have a word?" he states, walking back a few steps.

"Kids, it's Roman, I will be just outside for a moment," I yell and shut the door behind me.

I brace and cross my arms over my chest. "What's so important?" I ask.

"You have a visitor and are using my generosity to feed them. If I had known you would be inviting men around, abusing my good nature, my hotels services, there is no way I would have offered you this position," he seethes.

My will power has gone, the whole control-my-temper-for-the-job is out the window.

"So, let me get this straight? Are you calling me a slag or a freeloader? Also, it would have been good to know that a cleaning job required me to remain single. I mean, can you hear yourself right now?" I hiss angrily back at him.

"Do not put words into my mouth, you've been in the job for less than forty-eight hours. Technically, you haven't even bloody started yet, and already you've got a man in there, ordering room service. That is taking the piss and you know it," he bites back.

"I put that room service on my tab, that I will pay when I get paid from here, not that it's any of your business! And why are you following what I am doing? It's creepy. It has nothing to do with you if I was up all night having a shagging marathon! I can shag all day and all night with whoever I damn well choose as long as it doesn't affect my job. It has absolutely nothing to do with you!" I yell, getting in his face.

He grits his jaw tight; I'm surprised it hasn't snapped. He doesn't say anything, he just turns and storms off, leaving me stood there in a ball of rage. I want to scream at him to come back, but I don't, I just watch him walk away. I take a long breath and go to turn back into my room, seeing chambermaids and other hotel residents stood there gawping.

"Oh, just piss off." I sigh as I walk back into the room.

Thankfully, the kids and Terry are sat watching TV. Terry looks like a new man all cleaned up and I smile. Roman can go fuck himself, the pompous arsehole. If he had just spoken to me normally, he would have met Terry. Instead, he chose to jump to conclusions.

I shake my head to rid it from my mind and spend the evening relaxing with my babies and a lovely homeless man called Terry.

CHAPTER TWELVE

Roman

I pour myself a whiskey as soon as I get back to my office. God, that woman infuriates me. As soon as I saw her walking in with that guy and the way she so brazenly took him up to her room then ordered room service, I snapped. I may have played down my feelings, and I know I haven't made my intentions clear, but I thought she would have more respect for me than that.

I down my whisky and pour another, trying to calm my anger. There's a knock at the door. "Yes?" I yell and Simon sticks his head in.

"Sir, you wanted a daily report of Cora?" he asks.

"Fine," I snap, even though I know how it ends.

"After she left here for her walk, she helped stop traffic by flashing them her, um, her, err, you know, and then escorted an old lady across the road."

I spin around to face him. "She did what?" I ask in disbelief.

"She, err, flashed her bra, sir, to stop the traffic, because no one was stopping to let the old lady cross. It was quite effective." He smirks.

"I bet it bloody was, then what happened?" I ask.

"Then she walked around for a while, purchased some food in a café, which she then proceeded to give to a homeless man, then she sat down and talked to him for a while," he informs me.

Jesus, the woman has absolutely nothing, and she still gives away her last penny.

"Then after picking up the children, she returns to the homeless man and brings him into the hotel, I presume as somewhere for him to stay." He shrugs.

My head snaps up. "What?" I ask.

"She brought the homeless guy into the hotel, he's still up there now," he repeats.

I sigh. Fuck, I have been a fool. I accused her of bringing men back to her room, I accused her of taking liberties, when in fact, it was someone in need that she is helping out. I have been a complete arsehole. I have judged her, the one thing she accused me of in the very beginning, the one thing I am trying to prove... that I'm not a judgemental arsehole, and here I am, being just that. No wonder she was pissed at me.

"Shit!" I slam my glass down.

"What is it, sir?" Simon asks.

"I may have accused her of having men back and abusing my kindness," I state, cringing at my own stupidness.

"Oh, sir, even after you saw her in the supermarket carpark take her own food and give it to that homeless guy and his dog? Not only that, but she still paid for the shopping, even after I had paid for it, rather than keep it and have extra money for herself," Simon states.

"Yes, alright! Shit! I know I've been an idiot. How in the hell am I going to make it up to her now?" I ask.

"Well, sir, I'm just saying, she's probably the most caring and giving person I have met, so the only way you are going to get her forgiveness is by being just as kind and caring," Simon points out.

"Good idea. Simon, do we have jobs available at the moment?" I ask.

Simon smiles. "We actually do need a gardener for the roof top garden and to manage all the plants around the hotel," he states.

"Who the hell did it before?" I ask.

"It was a job you so kindly bestowed onto me, sir." He smirks.

"Ah, shit. Right, tomorrow morning, you're with me. We will be offering this guy the job, and also, is there a room he can stay in until he finds his feet?" I ask.

"Yes, sir, no problem. I will get on that right away." I nod and Simon leaves. I just hope it's enough to win Cora back over.

~

THE NEXT MORNING, I ACTUALLY HAVE NERVES IN MY STOMACH. I don't get nervous about anything, but for some reason, she seems to bring out everything in me. Simon comes with me, along with a waiter and a trolly full of a breakfast selection. It's seven a.m., so I know she will be up and getting the kids ready for school.

I take a deep breath and knock. The door swings open and Cora smiles at the trolly of food, but her smile soon falls when her eyes land on mine.

"Breakfast," I state as the waiter pushes the trolly past her into the living area.

"Cora, I want to offer my sincerest apologies to you and to your visitor. I appear to have judged you unfairly and I cannot apologise enough. There is one thing I would like to discuss with you and your visitor, if I may?"

She just stands to the side to allow me in, not saying a word. I swear, she would make an excellent poker player. She can mask her emotions perfectly, which I hate as I want to always know what she is feeling.

As we enter, I see an older gentleman with grey hair and a beard, wearing clothes that appear to be far too small for him. His eyes come to mine. "What's this? The old tramp not allowed in your fancy hotel? Came to escort me off the premises, have ya?" he asks sarcastically, eating some fruit.

"Not at all, I have come with a job offer for you and temporary accommodation." I smile.

I hear Cora gasp. "I need an onsite gardener, I have a rooftop garden that needs to be ready for next year, plus the plants around the hotel need to be maintained. What I am offering you is not just the job of the gardener but also free accommodation until April next year. While you are working, you will not have to pay towards any living costs. You can use this time to save for your own place. The salary you will receive will be twenty-three thousand pounds per year. Included, will also be a private pension. I need you to start Monday. I will also give you a business card for you to go out and purchase any tools, plants, and of course you will need clothing and safety boots. Do we have a deal?" I ask.

" I... I... But you don't even know my name or who I am," he points out.

"What's your name?" I ask.

"Terry Wilkens," he answers.

"Now I know your name. So, are you interested or not?" I ask.

"Yes, yes, of course." Terry smiles, his eyes filling with tears.

"Excellent, Simon here has your contract to go over and also the business card, and he will show you to your room." I smile and leave.

I walk out of the room, a warm feeling settling in my chest at doing something good, something that clearly meant a lot to Terry.

"Roman!" Cora yells from behind me. I stop and turn round.

She runs at me full force and wraps her arms around my shoulders and hugs me tight.

"Thank you," she whispers.

I wrap my arms around her, careful not to scare her away. She leans back and smiles, tears in her eyes. "Thank you," she says again before kissing my cheek and running back to her room. I smile, determined to make her smile like that more often. This woman has me completely under her spell and I can't deny that I'm loving every minute of it.

WORLDS APART

I have to do more to win her over, me just being around and offering her kindness isn't enough. I need to step up my game and prove to her I'm not the pompous arsehole she thinks I am.

∽

I DECIDE TO GIVE HER SOME SPACE FOR THE NEXT COUPLE OF weeks, let her find her feet with the new job. I have instructed Simon to still keep a close eye on her and report back to me.

I decide to stay at home and work from there, that way, I won't be tempted to go to her. She's like a siren, any time she's near, I have to go to her.

I read through the notes that Simon dropped off. I'm sure she would probably go insane at the fact that I've asked Simon to watch her, but at this moment, I don't care. They are giving me an insight into what she is like and how to approach her. She is a completely different woman to anyone I have ever dated before. I am ashamed to say that anyone before now have come from some of the wealthiest families. It's not that I picked those on purpose, it's that we all moved in the same social circles. Sure, some were stunning, but most were stuck-up snobs. They were only ever interested in going to the higher end bars, it was all about being seen in their designer dresses. I may have been lucky and had a privileged life growing up, but I wasn't from old money. My father worked his arse off to get where he is now, and I have done the same.

My phone rings and I look down. Seeing it's Camila, I roll my eyes and answer it.

"Yeah?" I answer bluntly.

"Oh, Ro-Ro, sweetie, that's not how you answer a phone. Did your parents never teach you any manners?" She sighs.

My skin crawls at her name for me, I hate it.

"What do you want, Camila?" I ask.

"I am wondering if you will be going to the charity ball in two weeks' time? When I spoke to India, she said that you were invited but that she hasn't had a response from you," she says.

I roll my eyes. I hate these charity balls, it's just a chance for each family to show off their wealth, and although they make money for charity, it's more of a 'look how much I have given' statement, and of course they mainly use it for tax break reasons. I normally avoid them like the plague, but this time I will invite Cora along with me. It's for charity and I will treat her to the full-gown and beauty treatments. I smile to myself.

"Put me down for two tickets. I assume my parents will be there?" I ask.

"Yes, of course, and may I ask who is the lucky lady that you are bringing on your arm to the event?" Camila asks.

"None of your business, have the tickets sent to my assistant. Goodbye, Camila." I disconnect, not giving her a chance to respond.

I have to tolerate Camila because I do a lot of work with her father and he has made it clear—on more than one occasion—how he would like us to be together. There is one problem with that... I can't stand her. She is a spoilt brat and has never worked a day in her life. Her father on the other hand, is like my father and works hard, but the mistake he made was giving his daughter everything she ever wanted rather than making her work for it.

I have two weeks to win Cora over and convince her to come to the ball with me.

I always did like a challenge.

CHAPTER THIRTEEN

Cora

Since I hugged Roman in the hallway, I haven't seen him, he hasn't been in work and when I asked Simon if he was okay, the only answer he gave me was that he is working from home.

I am trying to not think too much about it and focus on work. The kids have never been happier, and Terry has shaved and bought new clothes for his job. He looks like a new man. I wish Roman was here to see the good he has done by giving Terry a lifeline.

"What you daydreaming about now? Is it Mr Boss Man?" Sylvia says next to me.

I shake my head. "No, I was just miles away. Why would I be dreaming about Roman?" I ask.

Sylvia rolls her eyes at me. "Fine, you're not into him, so why don't you go on a date with William then?" She nudges me.

I shake my head. "No, he's not into me like that. I mean, he has to be, what, like five years younger than me?" I point out.

"So what if he is? You're a MILF, a cougar! Go all Mrs Robinson on his arse, enlighten the boy on how to make a woman climax. You will be Mr Miyagi and he is your Daniel LaRusso, you know, wax on wax off. You are like the professor and he is the student, all forbidden and naughty." She pants, fanning her face.

"You alright there? I think you need to calm down, maybe take a cold shower." I laugh.

"Yeah, yeah. Well, you may think I'm insane, but William is heading straight for you now and he cannot keep his eyes off of you." She winks.

I look up, and sure enough, William is making a beeline for me.

"Hey, Cora." He smiles, tucking his hand in his front pockets, all nervous.

"Hi, William, you okay? Anything you need?" I ask.

"Oh no, no, just thought I would say hi. So, um, hi." He smiles nervously.

"Alright, hi. Is that it?" I smile.

"Yes," he says and starts to walk away but then spins back around to face me. "I mean, no, that's not it. Um... Would you like to get a drink with me sometime?" he asks.

"I, err, um..." I stutter.

"She would love to. Tonight at seven, meet in the lobby. I will babysit the kids." Sylvia smiles.

"Great, I will see you at seven," William says happily and walks off.

I turn to Sylvia, eyes wide. "What the hell, man?!" I exclaim.

"What? You need a break, a night having a couple of drinks with William will be harmless, he's a nice lad. Go have a drink or two and enjoy yourself." Sylvia shrugs.

"I don't even have any money," I point out.

She shoves her hand down her bra and pulls out a twenty pound note. "Here, take this, you can pay me back on payday. You haven't had a night out since your twat ex-husband left. So get your arse upstairs and make yourself look all hot, and maybe just a little bit slutty, but not too much, you don't want to be scaring the poor boy." She smiles.

"You're younger than me and talking like my mother," I point out.

"Yeah, well, you've done it enough times for me over the years and now it's my turn. Go on, it's four-thirty now, go have a nice long soak in the bath and send the kids down to me, I will take them for dinner." She smiles.

I want to protest but she isn't giving me a chance and she practically shoves me into the elevator. I know she's right, it will do me good to get out and actually have some adult time.

~

I'm heading down in the lift to meet William in the lobby. I am really nervous, and it took me forever to find something to wear. Not that I had a lot of choice, I live in jeans and a basic top most days, so I made a little effort and put on my only skirt, which is a chord plum button-down that comes mid-thigh, with my thick black tights and my only heeled boots I own. I found a black long sleeved V-neck body, which I decided would do, and I left my hair down as it's always up for work.

I head out of the lift and look for William, finding him stood in jeans and a nice jumper, waiting for me by the fireplace.

I walk to him and smile, he smiles back. "You look beautiful," he greets and kisses me on the cheek.

I smile, feeling myself blush slightly. "Thanks, it's the only clothes I own that aren't jeans." I laugh. "So, where are we going?" I ask.

"There is a nice pub just across the street that I thought would be good." He gestures as we walk out of the hotel. He wasn't lying, it is literally across the street, which I don't mind, I don't want to be too far from the kids and possibly if I need to make a quick escape.

He buys me a gin and tonic and we sit by the open fire. We talk and it's nice. He tells me his dreams and where he plans to be with his five-year-plan. He has everything thought out, it's a little overwhelming. He asks me mine, but of course, I don't have one. I look at the clock and see its near ten p.m., time to bail.

"Oh, wow, I, um, better head back, poor Sylvia is still sitting with the kids," I say, standing.

"Oh, right, of course. Let me walk you back," he offers.

We stop outside the hotel and William smiles. "Well, goodnight, and thank you, it was a nice night and good to get out." I smile.

"Yeah, I had a great time." He leans in to kiss me, but I turn my head, so he kisses my cheek instead.

"Oh, um, right, okay," he mumbles, embarrassed.

I rest my hand on his arm. "William, you're a handsome guy, a lovely guy, you're just a little too young for me and I just see you as a friend, nothing more, a great friend actually. Are you good with that, being friends?" I ask.

He smiles and nods. "Sure, we can do that. Night, Cora," he says and leaves.

I turn and walk up the steps of the hotel, feeling like I've just punched a puppy.

I walk up to the room and being as quiet as I can, I creep in so as not to disturb the kids. Walking into the lounge area, I nearly scream, because sat there instead of Sylvia is Roman.

"What the hell are you doing here?" I hiss.

"I relieved Sylvia. She had to go on a date or something," he states, his eyes roaming over my body.

"Well it would have been nice to have been informed, I could have come back sooner." I sigh.

"She did, she sent you a text. You have a nice time with William?" he asks. I don't miss the way he says William's name like it's left a bad taste in his mouth.

"Yes, thank you, I had a lovely time. Now, I hate to be rude, but I am really tired, and I just want to go to bed and get some sleep," I snap, walking to the door and holding it open for him.

He gets up and walks towards me. I avoid looking at him and focus on a spot on the wall instead. He stops directly in front of me, giving me no choice but to look at him.

His eyes drop to my lips and my heart starts racing in my chest.

His hand cups my face and his thumb runs along my bottom lip. I suck in a breath. This is it... he's going to kiss me.

"Come with me to a charity ball in two weeks," he says.

"What?" I whisper, confused.

"Be my guest, say yes," he says, leaning in so his lips brush against my ear.

"Yes," I breathe.

He moves and kisses my forehead, his lips lingering just for a moment. "Goodnight, Cora," he rasps and then goes, leaving me stood there, wondering what the hell is going on and wishing that he would just kiss me.

CHAPTER FOURTEEN

Roman

It took every bit of willpower to leave her that night. I had to use every ounce I had not to march across to that pub and drag her back to mine. I pace my office, I want to run upstairs and kiss her, I want nothing more than to have her in my bed. Jesus, the woman has me so tied up in knots it's ridiculous.

I need to be with her, I need to wear her down. I know if I had kissed her tonight then she would have kissed me back, but I want more. I don't want any doubt creeping into her mind. I don't want her to ever second guess herself when it comes to me.

I sit down in my chair, different ideas coming to my mind.

One idea sticks, and it's one idea I'm going with. It will take a lot of willpower from me, but it will have to work.

I pick up my phone and call Simon.

"Sir," he answers.

"Have arrangements made for me to take Cora out to lunch, book us in at that restaurant on the Thames. Also, I will be offering Cora a position as head housekeeper at my house as well as the hotel, her accommodation will be in the annex at my property. Can you make the necessary arrangements should she accept my offer?" I ask.

"Sure, boss," he answers without complaint.

"Great. Goodnight," I say and disconnect.

I write a note to put under Cora's door for her to see in the morning.

CORA,

Be ready for midday, I am taking you out for lunch. There is something important we need to discuss.

Roman x

I FOLD IT UP AND SMILE TO MYSELF, KNOWING SHE WILL BE stressing about this note and wondering what is so important that I need to talk to her.

I walk up to her room and slide the note under her door. I stand there, just for a moment, at war with myself if I should knock or not. I step away, deciding I need to head home. If I act too soon, she we will use our differences in class as an excuse not to be together. I want her feeling like I am now, captivated and completely owned.

Once I am home, I pour myself a whiskey and I sit in my lounge by the open fire. I watch the flames flicker and dance, sitting alone night after night in my big empty house... now the time is right for that silence to be drowned out.

∼

I WALK UP TO HER ROOM AND KNOCK ON THE DOOR. I'D BE LYING if I said I wasn't a little anxious about today. I know she will be mine, but I don't want her to say no, I need her with me, and this is the only way I can get her there now.

She opens the door, and she looks stunning. She is wearing a black fitted jumper dress that hugs her figure with tights and heeled ankle boots, her hair is loose, flowing down in natural waves.

"Wow," I compliment.

She blushes. "Do I always look that bad when I'm working?" She laughs.

"You never looked bad, you always look beautiful, but right now you look exceptional," I point out. I lean forward and kiss her cheek, and I catch the way her breath hitches at my touch.

"Let's get to our reservation," I say, clearing my throat.

As we walk through the lobby, I don't miss the whispers or the questioning looks coming from the other members of staff. I grit my teeth to stop myself from yelling at them to mind their own damn business.

The car ride is pure torture, the smell of her perfume, being so close to her and I can't do a thing about it. I practically jump from the car when we arrive. I walk around the car and open the door for her and escort her inside. Her eyes are wide at the opulence of this restaurant.

"Wow." She breathes.

"Mr Nash, how good to see you again, we have your table ready for you, please follow me," the waiter greets.

While Cora is bewildered, I take full advantage and take her hand in mine, leading her through the restaurant.

We sit and I order a bottle of wine, Cora's eyes still everywhere.

"This place is something else," she states, her eyes wide. "I mean, the cutlery probably cost more than what I earn in a month."

"Money isn't everything," I point out.

Her eyes flicker to mine. "It is when you don't have it," she answers.

"Good point." I smile.

The waiter pours our wine then leaves. Cora drinks some, clearly nervous. "So, what is so urgent you needed to speak with me?" she asks.

I smirk. "Quick to dive in there, not going to enjoy our meal first before we talk business?" I question, sipping my wine.

"Nope, I'm an impatient person and I like to know things upfront." She smiles.

I lean forward, my eyes never leaving hers. "I want to offer you a promotion."

"A promotion?" she asks confused.

"Yes, well, it will be a promotion for you and Sylvia, actually."

"Go on," she urges, intrigued.

I knew that would be the way to get to her, she is never about herself, and if it means someone else could benefit, then she is more inclined to do it. Always thinking of others.

"I want you to be head housekeeper," I state.

"But I'm already a head housekeeper," she says confused.

"I mean, head housekeeper of my personal home, and to oversee the hotel too."

She goes to protest but I hold up my hand, halting her.

"I'm not asking for much more hour wise. Sylvia will run the hotel, pretty much by herself. It will only be you calling and checking in with Sylvia, making sure all is running smoothly. Then at my house you will be the main—and only—housekeeper. I will give you a pay rise, and Sylvia too, but there's more than that." I pause.

"What?" she asks.

"You will live at my address. I have an annex in the basement. It has two bedrooms at present, but that is being modified as we speak. It has a kitchen and a living space, and doors onto the garden. It would be more of a home for you and the kids. It's fully-furnished, so you don't need to worry about any of that. Your contract will be extended and the new terms added." I finish and sit back, watching her intently, wondering what she is thinking.

She's quiet, I don't like it.

"What are you thinking?" I ask.

"Um, you want me to live with you?" she asks.

"Yes, in a professional way, of course. You will have your own living space, even your own access, so you don't have to walk through the house to get to it," I reassure. I catch a slight glimmer of disappointment in her eyes, but she quickly hides it.

She smiles. "Then, great, I think we have a deal."

"Great, champagne to celebrate." I click my fingers and call the waiter over and order a bottle of champagne. We finish our meal, and the entire bottle of champagne. As the meal went on, the alcohol definitely relaxed her and she spoke more freely.

I call Simon to come and collect us as I have had too much to drink to drive safely. In the car on the way back to the hotel, I realise she is slightly drunk. She leans and rests her head on my shoulder.

"Hmm, you smell delicious," she says, burying her nose into my suit jacket and taking a deep inhale.

I laugh. "Ooo I like that too. Do you know, I don't like rich men, but you, sir, are rather scrummy!" She smiles, pinching my cheek.

"Is that so?" I smile.

"Yes, your face is beautiful, so handsome I could paint it. I miss painting. I miss art." She yawns, laying down and resting her head on my lap before falling asleep. I gently brush her hair from her face and smile to myself. This lunch couldn't have gone better.

"Simon, book me in at the portrait gallery, private viewing for tonight with food, make sure it's suitable for kids too. Also, when we get back, get me the architect on the phone... Apart from the third bedroom, there's another thing I would like to discuss," I tell him.

"Sure thing, sir." He nods from the driver's seat.

She has given me a small window into her heart, and I am taking that and smashing my way right through it.

CHAPTER FIFTEEN

Cora

I feel my face being stroked and I open my eyes, feeling a warm lap beneath my head. I jump up and see Roman fighting back his laughter.

"Oh God, did I fall asleep on you?" I gasp, mortified.

"You did, but don't worry, I quite enjoyed the cuddle." He winks.

I feel heat burn my face as embarrassment takes over and I mentally die inside.

"Oh God. I'm sorry, I should have said that wine makes me sleepy, including champagne. I didn't sleep well last night so that wouldn't have helped," I apologise.

"Like I said, I enjoyed it. Go inside and freshen up, Simon will pick up the children. Be ready for four p.m., I will come and get all of you then," he states and leans forward, kissing my cheek. I freeze at his touch.

Simon opens my door and I walk up to my room, even more confused about my feelings for Roman than I was before.

I make myself a strong coffee and try and wake myself up a little.

There's a knock at the door and I open it to find Sylvia stood there with her hands on her hips.

"Hi." I smile.

"Hi? Is that all you're going to say? What about, 'Oh, I've taken a promotion and you get one too, Sylvia!'" she exclaims, pushing past me into the room.

I shut the door and follow her. "I have literally been back all of twenty minutes, give me a chance." I sigh.

"Oh I know, I watched you come back all loved up," she states.

"I am not loved up," I defend.

"Oh really? You're so loved up you practically have heart-shaped eyes, and don't even get me started on him because he has it bad for you," she says, pouring herself a coffee.

"He does not." I snort.

"Oh no, of course not, he just happens to offer a woman he barely knows a job and a home purely based on her credentials. He likes what he sees, and he wants a piece of your pie." She nods.

"He does not want my pie." I sigh.

"Okay sure, he doesn't want your pie, just like I don't want to sit on Jason Momoa's face," she says sarcastically, rolling her eyes.

I give her an exasperated look. She holds up her hands. "Fine, fine, I'm wrong. So, do you want to go get some dinner with the kids later?" she asks.

I bite my lip. "Um, I can't, Roman is taking me and the kids somewhere at four," I admit.

She bursts out laughing. "Oh my God. He so wants your pie, he wants to eat your pie and shag your pie senseless." She snorts with laughter.

"Eww, I hope you're still referring to my vagina, because now I'm just thinking of Roman shagging an actual pie," I say, scrunching up my face.

"So you were thinking about him shagging your spasm chasm?" She giggles.

"Oh for God's sake, yes! Okay... Yes, I think he's good looking, very good looking, who wouldn't think that way?" I admit.

"Well, girl, no judgement here. He is a hot piece of arse, but just saying, if you're thinking of going there, you need to, um, hit the salon," she says, pointing with her finger.

"What do you mean? I shave!" I bite back.

"Oh, babe, I bet you have a lovely little landing strip there, or in the very least a trimmed bush. Am I right?" she asks.

"Well, yeah, I maintain the garden, if that's what you mean?" I shrug.

She shakes her head and tuts. "You have a mum bush, which is great, go retro!" she says, giving me the thumbs up. "But times have changed. Now it's all about the smooth, it's all about being completely bare," she informs me.

"No hair?" I clarify.

"Nope."

"As in, bald like Bruce Willis? Bald like Patrick Stewart? But it will look like Uncle Fester, or worse, a naked mole rat!" I screech.

"Oh yeah, honey, bald, I promise it will not. Only women over fifty with bald cooters resemble a naked mole rat, believe me, I've seen them. Yours will probably look a lot prettier than that, think more along the line of one of those little flowers that look like vaginas. What can I say? The guys dig it. Even guys are getting their balls waxed now," she states.

I wince, thinking that must hurt a lot. "Well none of this matters because there is nothing going on with me and Roman. He is just being nice and charitable, I guess. Probably makes him feel good, helping out us less fortunate. You forget, we are from completely different worlds. I could never be a part of his world. I mean, could you imagine me trying to fit in with all those wealthy people? They would hate me." I snort.

"No one can hate you, you're too nice. But seriously, we should go to the salon. You need a pamper and clearly a little refurbishment," she states, pointing to my vagina.

"Gee, thanks, can't wait for that." I roll my eyes.

"So, when do you move into the new digs?" she asks.

I shrug. "No idea. You good with the new arrangement?" I ask.

"Sure, I get more money, free access to the gym and beauty spa. Plus, have you seen some of the guys working here? I'm all set." She wiggles her eyebrows. "And who knows, Mr rich and wonderful could walk through that door at any moment and sweep me off my feet."

"Very true," I agree.

"Well, I am heading off home, I have a hot date tonight. Enjoy yourself later, and stay out of your head a little, enjoy it," she says before leaving.

~

I TOLD THE KIDS ABOUT THE MOVE AND THEY WERE MORE THAN happy. They said they would miss the hotel but are happy for a more homely place.

Right at four, Roman shows to pick us up.

"You all ready?" he asks.

"Yes!" Betty claps excitedly.

He smiles down at her. "Well, let's go," he says, walking to the elevator. Betty takes his hand and he doesn't pull away or flinch. He turns and smiles at me, and my heart does a little flip at the sight of them.

When we arrive at the car, Simon isn't driving us, Roman is. The kids sit in the back and I notice he has purchased a booster seat for Betty. I shake my head at all he's doing, and I try to control and shut down my feelings.

I sit in the passenger seat, next to Roman as he drives relaxed and with ease. He has hung his suit jacket off his seat and has rolled his shirt up, exposing his forearms. I can feel myself getting hot. I know Sylvia said to listen to my heart more and not my head, but she didn't say anything about whether I should listen to my libido?

He parks up at the back of a big building. I frown, looking out the window, wondering where it is he has brought us.

We walk up to big metal doors and Roman knocks. A woman

opens the door and smiles at us. "Welcome, Mr Nash. Please follow me." She smiles.

We follow through what looks like a warehouse. She stops at the door and hands Roman some keys. "If you could lock up before you leave and post them through the door when you are done. The alarm is automatic, so you don't need to worry. Everything is here ready for you. Please don't worry about cleaning up, I have a crew ready for an early morning clean before opening tomorrow. Have fun and enjoy." She smiles and leaves us.

"Where are we?" I ask.

Roman smiles and takes my hand in his, leading me through the doors. I gasp when I see where we are. "Portrait gallery?"

"I know how much you love art, especially portraits." He smiles.

I let go of his hand and walk around, looking at the amazing artwork displayed.

"Oh my God... Philipp Weber!" I gasp.

"It's beautiful, looks like a photograph," Roman states standing next to me.

"That's him, his attention to detail is exceptional. He literally brings a painting to life." I sigh.

I walk a little further and then I spot it, an Anika Tunstall portrait. I stand there just staring at it. Roman comes up and stands behind me.

"A favourite?" he asks.

"Yeah, she is one of my inspirations. This painting is my favourite of her work. You know, this is actually of her daughter. The attention to detail she puts into her pieces makes them look like a photograph and this one in particular is just beautiful, yet haunting. It's truly breath-taking."

Roman squeezes the back of my neck. I turn to look at him and smile. "Thank you for this. It's... It's amazing," I say honestly. He smiles warmly and his eyes flicker to my mouth. I lick my lower lip and he leans in closer.

"Mummy! Look!" Betty yells, breaking the moment. I cough a laugh.

"What is it, baby?" I ask, walking away, leaving Roman stood there.

I walk around the corner and freeze. There is a table with food and drink laid out, but that's not what has me frozen to the spot, it's the four easels set up for painting.

Roman comes behind me and whispers in my ear, "For you."

I turn and face him. I don't say anything, I just place my hand over his heart and let my eyes do the talking. I try to convey just how much this means to me, and if truth be told, if the kids weren't here right now, I would most definitely be kissing him. Roman takes my hand and places a kiss on my palm. I smile brightly and practically run to an easel and help set up the kids, then dive on my own. I know the instant I sit down who I am painting, the only person on my mind right now, the only person who is consuming my every thought.

We spend hours there, the kids are laughing at Roman's attempts at painting. I smile whilst watching them as I paint. I can't explain the feeling I get, it's not euphoric, it's more like it's second nature to me. Like breathing, it fits, the flow of each stroke of the brush, each line I draw. It's therapeutic to me, my outlet.

Roman stands behind me. "Wow," he breathes. I look over my shoulder at him and smile. "That is stunning, Cora," he compliments.

"It's just a little painting. If I had space, time and paints, I could paint a proper canvas, but that would take... I don't know how long, days probably. Never really had the chance to try that." I shrug.

My painting is of him and the kids laughing, it's not a photorealism painting, it's my emotion and what I see and feel.

"I'm sorry, Cora, but we have to get going," he apologises.

I smile and nod. "It's okay, I have had the best time. What time is it?" I ask.

"Nearly ten p.m." He smirks.

"Oh my God, Betty, baby, it's way past your bedtime and you're covered in paint." I gasp.

"Cora, relax, it's fine, no panic. This was a nice treat, the children had fun and so did you. I will get all our pictures sent to the hotel," Roman states, calming me. He is right, it's a one-off treat.

On the drive back, I feel relaxed. For the first time in my life, I don't have any worries, I can't remember a time when I felt like this.

Roman parks up at the hotel and he smiles and points to the back seat. I turn around and see Betty fast asleep with paint smudged all over her little face.

"I will carry her up for you," Roman offers.

We walk up to our room and I pull back Betty's covers and Roman lays her down in bed, tucking her in. We walk back out to the lounge and Theo has his hands in his pockets, which is something he does when he gets embarrassed or shy. "Roman," he calls.

Roman turns to him. "Yeah, Theo?"

"Thanks for today, and, well, for everything. It's good to see Mum smile again." He shrugs and then walks off to his room, shutting his door.

I place my hand over my heart at my sweet boy's words.

Roman coughs. "I better get going," he states, walking to the door.

"Sure, it's late." I nod and walk with him.

He stands there, facing me, I really want him to kiss me. I know it will just confuse everything, but I've gone past caring.

"Good night, Cora," he says.... and leaves.

Leaving me stood there, my heart lurching. I almost run after him and force him to kiss me, but I don't, I just stand there leaning against the door, feeling like I've been kicked in the gut, deciding I've been stupid for letting my hormones take control over my rational thought. He is clearly just offering me friendship, I should take what he's offering and not ruin it.

CHAPTER SIXTEEN

Cora

It's been three days since Roman took us to the art gallery and we had that amazing night. I've seen him in passing, he has been busy working. I find myself purposely walking past his office door in the hope he will walk out, any time I hear someone mention his name my head snaps up, looking for him. He's managed to get under my skin and I cannot shake him.

Simon walks up to me and smiles. "Hey, Simon, everything alright?" I ask.

"Yeah, here are the keys to your new place, go finish work early and pack up, I will take you there in two hours." He smiles. I hug him tight with excitement and run off to pack the few things we do have.

Once all packed up, I head down to find Simon. Walking around the corner and straight into a hard chest, arms come around me and steady me. I don't need to look up to know who it is. Just by his scent alone, I know it's Roman.

"You alright?" he asks.

I look up at him, my palms on his chest, his arms still around me, his beautiful eyes searching mine. I lick my bottom lip. "Kiss me." The words leave me on a breath.

"What?" he asks.

"Kiss me, Roman," I repeat. His eyes flicker from my eyes to my mouth, and he leans in slowly, his hand coming up and cupping my face, his thumb stroking across my bottom lip.

"You want this?" he asks, his voice low and gravelly.

"Yes," I whisper.

"Say the words," he says. For a moment I am confused, then I remember what he said at dinner.

"Kiss me, please, I need you to k—" My words are cut off as Roman crashes his mouth down on mine. I moan as his tongue sweeps against mine, I grip his suit jacket tightly in my hands and he stops suddenly, his eyes hooded.

"I'm sorry, I have to go," he breathes. He kisses my head then walks away, leaving me stood there, wondering what the hell has him running off like that.

I hold my hand over my beating heart and try to calm my breathing. That kiss was incredible, but why would he just leave me like that? I try not to let it get to me, I shake my head, refusing to let myself think about it too much.

Simon appears a moment later, smirking, almost as if he knows Roman and I have just kissed. "Ready?" he asks.

"Um, yup, was just coming to find you."

Simon raises an eyebrow, giving me a look. I completely ignore him and hold my head high, acting as if nothing happened.

∼

We pull up outside a beautiful huge white town house in the prime location of Chelsea.

"Wow!" I breathe.

"Come on, let me show you around," Simon offers.

We get out of the car and Simon takes me straight down to the side of the house where—as promised—my own private entrance is located. I unlock the door and step inside. The place is cute, freshly decorated with an open-plan kitchen and living space, and large patio doors that lead to the garden. I follow Simon into the rooms, each fitting a double bed easily, all furnished beautifully, and I notice purposefully that Betty's room is decorated in soft creams and pinks and Theo's is in blues and grey. The place is perfect, I can see us living here happily. I wipe a tear that has fallen and sigh.

"Thank you, Simon." I smile at him.

"Isn't me you need to thank," he states.

"Um, where is he? So I can say thank you to him." I say.

"He's working away for a while, but I will show you the entrance to the main house and alarm system for while he is away," Simon offers.

Why didn't he say that he was working away? Why did he just run off like that earlier? None of it makes any sense.

I follow Simon up to the main house and my jaw hits the floor, the house is out of this world incredible. It screams wealth. "Is that a chandelier?!" I screech. "A grand piano?!" I breathe, turning to see the painting on the wall. "Oh Christ, is that an original Monet?!" I am almost having a panic attack.

"You alright?" Simon asks.

"Yeah, it's just, holy shit, this place is like something you see on MTV Cribs," I point out.

Simon laughs and continues to show me the rest of the house, including its nine bedrooms! I may have lingered slightly in Roman's room, his smell still present. We walk back down to the annex and I look out to the garden, seeing something being built at the end.

"What's being built?" I ask.

Simon looks up and shrugs. "Not sure, a home office I expect."

"What, because one of the eight spare bedrooms wouldn't do?" I snort.

"You okay?" Simon asks and I nod. "Good, there's my number

and the alarm number. I will shoot now and pick up the kids for you, give you some time to unpack," he offers.

"Thanks, appreciate it." It's on the tip of my tongue to ask him for Roman's number, but I stop myself.

He leaves and I go about putting our things away. I open the fridge and notice its been fully stocked as have the cupboards. I notice a card on the fridge, I take it off to read it.

Cora, if you need me, here's my private line. R x

I type the number into my phone and place the card in a draw as I hear the kids come running down the steps.

"OH MY GOD, THIS PLACE IS AMAZING!" Betty screams, running around the place over excited, like she ate a bag of sugar and drank a can of red bull on the way home.

The kids settle in and I cook us dinner, which I am surprised to say I missed doing at the hotel. I bathe Betty and get her to bed and Theo shuts himself in his room to watch TV. Finally sitting down, I pull out my phone, deciding to text Roman.

THANK YOU FOR THE BEAUTIFUL ANNEX AND THE FOOD. YOU REALLY DIDN'T HAVE TO DO THAT. CORA. x

I CLICK SEND AND PLACE MY PHONE DOWN, ANXIOUSLY awaiting a reply. Only a couple of minutes later, my phone vibrates with a message.

NO THANKS NEEDED; I AM GLAD YOU LIKE IT. R x

HE REPLIES, KEEPING IT BRIEF. I BITE MY THUMB NAIL AND text my response.

. . .

C: Your house is insanely pompous.

R: Why thank you, that was the look I was going for.

C: Where are you?

R: Currently sat at hotel bar in Scotland, trying to understand what the barman is saying to me. Where are you right now?

I pause for a moment, wondering if I can play a little. I bite my lip and reply.

C: In the bathtub.

It takes a little while for his reply to come through which makes me nervous.

R: Really? You're going there while I'm sat in a very public bar?

I laugh and type my reply.

C: Oh yeah, I'm going there, you left me hanging earlier, it's only fair I get some payback. Brace yourself, posh boy, this council estate girl is about to show you how dirty us commoners can get.

R: You have no idea what this posh boy is capable of, Kitten.

C: Oh, then let's play, posh boy. I'm getting out of the bath, the water and bubbles are cascading down my very naked body, I am now wrapping a very small towel around myself and walking straight to your bedroom.

R: I'm in my hotel room now, led across my bed. I have my thick and painfully hard cock in my hand, thinking about your wet and naked body in my bed.

C: Touché, posh boy. I'm now led on your bed, my hands travelling over my body, my breasts aching for your touch, my hand keeps travelling south until its between my legs, circling my clit while my other hand rolls my nipple. I don't stop, too turned on thinking about you fucking me.

I feel myself getting incredibly turned on. He doesn't reply and I start to panic, thinking I have gone way too far. Maybe I've scared him off? My phone vibrates and I sigh, relieved.

R: Okay, you win, I am ashamed to say I just came in my pants like a teenage boy. You win, Kitten, you win.

. . .

I laugh at his reply. Anxiety kicks in at what I'm actually doing.

C: I can't believe I just wrote those things, and you're my boss! God, I'm sorry.

I need to reign it in, he is my boss after all, and if this ends badly then I lose everything, and me and the kids are without a home, I'm without a job and without money. As much as I want to kiss him and more, the reality is, if I do, I'm playing with fire. There is a lot more at stake than just my heart and that is something I need to remind myself of.

R: Don't be sorry, don't ever be sorry. They were the best texts I've ever received.

I smile at his reply. God, why does he have to be so nice? If he was an arsehole it would make my life a lot easier.

C: Well, I can't let it happen again. The kiss was a mistake, I just got swept up in the moment. It won't happen again.

R: It wasn't a mistake, and it will happen again.

. . .

I stare at his response, taken aback by his bluntness.

C: Are you threatening me?

R: Most certainly.

I don't know what to reply back, I am surprised by his response, he always carries himself in a professional way. I gave him the way out, to go back to being professional. I'm not sure what to say or do at this point. The hot and cold, him being my boss is a complete mind fuck.

R: You've gone quiet because I am guessing you're inside your head. I will repeat, no matter what, your job and living arrangements are safe. I am not about to write a long text message about my intentions. Just take this message as a warning.

C: A warning for what?

I await a reply and get nothing.

C: Hello? A warning for what exactly?!

C: Roman! Answer me!

. . .

C: Really?! You're just going to ignore me and behave like a dick?! Fine! I'm off to clean your toilet with one of your toothbrushes.

I chuck my phone down feeling infuriated and frustrated being left in limbo like this. Deciding I can't sit here any longer going over the million thoughts running around my head, I go to bed and curse him for buying this ridiculously comfy bed.

CHAPTER SEVENTEEN

Roman

I switch my phone off, so I won't be tempted to text her again. She has no idea what she has done to me. The kiss, the texting, I nearly jumped right back on the plane to be with her.

When those words left her delectable mouth, begging me to kiss her, all resolve was lost. Trying to keep myself contained after the evening at the gallery has been hard, I could see that night she wanted to kiss me. I just needed to hold off. I had set the charity ball as the date that she would kiss me, want me, without any doubt. But she literally crashed into my arms, of course I was going to take what she was offering.

The texts threw me completely off guard, in a good way. The plan of her being so wound up, so consumed by me that she wouldn't have any doubt, that by the charity ball she would be desperate for me is back firing. It's me that is becoming desperate for her, needing her. Just being here in Scotland, I miss her, miss seeing her in person, even if it was on my CCTV.

Coming to Scotland wasn't part of my plan, it's an inconvenience

I could have done without, but a hotel I have had my eye on for some time has finally come up for sale. I wasn't about to let it slip through my fingers. Luckily for me, the owners are old family friends. I just have to get them to sign on the dotted line and the place will be mine. Unfortunately, because they are old family friends, I can't just fly in for the deal and fly back again.

I stand looking out the window at the beautiful Scottish landscape, the moon reflecting in the lock. I smile, because as soon as I'm back it will be the ball, and what Cora doesn't know is I have plans for her that night. Plans I have been looking forward to for a very long time.

I look at my watch, it's near midnight, and in six hours the first package will arrive to surprise her. I wish I were there to see her face, but instead I will have to make do with Simon telling me, and maybe a text... if she decides to text me that is.

I climb into bed, thoughts of Cora wet and in my bed fill my mind. I groan, she is killing me. "Just two more days," I remind myself.

After a restless night's sleep, I switch on my phone and drink my coffee, awaiting the message from Simon to say the package has been delivered.

Six a.m. on the dot, Simon rings.

"Yeah?" I answer.

"I have just delivered the package and I am currently just waiting on her to open the door and see it, sir," he says.

"You well hidden? She can't see you?" I ask.

"Yep, oh! Hold on, the door is opening, she's seen the package, she is opening it and looking around for anyone that delivered it. And she's crying, sir, she's holding it and crying," he informs me.

I smile, I knew she would. Little does she know it's just the start for her.

My phone beeps with an incoming call and I look at the screen, surprised to see it's her.

"Simon, I have to go, it's her," I say before disconnecting.

"Hello," I answer.

"I can't believe you brought me my own easel, and paints." She sniffs.

"Did you read the note?" I ask.

"Yes, it made me cry. *To Cora, a gift for you to start making your dreams a reality. R x.* Thank you so much," she whispers, fighting the emotion that is thick in her voice.

"For you, anything," I say honestly.

"Roman, I... I don't know what's—"

I interrupt her. "Don't say anything, just enjoy the gift. As I said before, save it for when I return. Goodbye, beautiful," I say, cutting the conversation short. I had to or I would have said so much more.

A simple inexpensive gift to most, meant the world to her. To her that gift is me giving her part of her dreams. What she doesn't know is that it's only the start, and by the end of the ball, I will have made all her dreams come true.

I need to get my head in the game and get this deal signed and done, I just want to be back there with her now.

I get ready for the day, determined to get business done and get back to her.

As I enter the main restaurant area, guests are enjoying their breakfasts. I find Alec, the owner, sat by the roaring open fire, reading the newspaper. I take a seat opposite him and set down the contract next to his breakfast tray. He bends the corner of the newspaper over and peers at me then the contract.

"It's a bit early for business, son," he points out.

"It is for some, not for you or me, have you looked over my proposal?" I ask.

He sighs and puts down his paper. "Look here, son, I know you're young and you live for getting those deals, and I'm sure you have another hotel deal you're waiting to dive onto after this one, but let me give you a piece of advice. At my age, I've learnt there is more to life than business—"

"Alec, just hear me out," I interrupt but he holds up his hand to stop me and continues talking.

"You spend your whole life making money. Who are you going to share that good fortune with if you're working all the bloody time? No one because, laddie, you'll be too busy working to find that special someone to share it with. Then you wasted your entire life for money, and money ain't no fun when you're old and on your own," he adds.

I sigh and pinch the bridge of my nose. "Alec, I have met that someone. I am trying to get this deal done up here so I can fly back down to her," I point out.

"Well, why didn't you say so, laddie?" he exclaims and snatches the contract up and signs then chucks it down.

"Did you go over my proposal at all?" I ask stunned.

"No, son, I was always going to sell it to you. It was your daddy that said I should make you work for it like I would anyone else." He shrugs.

"Figures." I smile and shake my head, picking up the contract.

"No point in delaying now, not when there's matters of the heart involved. I won't ever stand in the way of that. Now fuck off and let me enjoy my breakfast," he says, picking up his paper.

I laugh and stand. "Always a pleasure doing business with you, Alec," I say, patting his shoulder.

"Oh, laddie, I expect to meet this fine lassie that has your attention," he yells to me. I just give him a smile and go to my room and pack as quickly as I can then head straight to the airport.

∽

"I AM SORRY, SIR, THE FLIGHT IS ALREADY BOOKED UP AND THERE are no other flights today. I can book you in tomorrow afternoon?" the lady at the check-in desk offers.

"Shit. No, no, I want to get to London as quickly as I can," I state.

"May I suggest the train then, sir? I believe there is a train leaving at ten a.m. which arrives in London by three p.m... Well, providing there is no delays." She smiles.

I look at my watch and see its nine-thirty. "How far from here to the train station and ticket office?"

She smiles. "If you run you would get there in about ten minutes."

"Great, thank you." I grab my bag and run.

I spot the train station up ahead and see the queue for the ticket office. "Shit," I hiss.

I stand and wait anxiously, checking my watch. I'm now next in line. Unfortunately, the guy in front of me appears to be a first-time train traveller that needs to know the answer to every question.

"So if I get on the train and someone is sat in my seat, what do I do then?" he asks.

"Fuck me," I mutter. He turns around and raises his eyebrow at me, then continues asking the ticket guy twenty questions.

"And what if I need to use the lavatory? But I don't feel safe leaving my stuff, or what if the lavatory isn't fully functional and can another train see in through to the lavatory window as they pass?" he asks.

"Oh for goodness sake!" I yell.

"I beg your pardon?" he says, turning to face me.

"Will you just move out of the bloody way? Some of us want to get a ticket and get on a train that is in fact leaving in eight minutes time," I seethe.

"I shall have you know, under railway handbook section five, paragraph twelve, I am allowed to ask such questions to any member of the railway staff, and as a paying customer, I would like to know in its entirety what I am to expect on my journey," he states, pushing his glasses further up his nose.

"I will give you one hundred pounds to move out of my way," I offer.

His eyes go wide. "Well, of course, do get your ticket, but please, do not see this as a bribe. Bribery or gambling should not take place on any rail establishment."

"Oh, do shut up!" I snap.

"One way ticket to London, please. First class, if you have it?" I ask.

The woman behind the counter smiles and prints off my ticket. I pay her and shove the one hundred pounds at the annoying customer as I run to catch the train.

"Thank you, sir, please do not run unless there is a clear emergency," he yells after me.

I finally find my train and jump on. Sitting in my seat, I sigh, wiping the sweat off my brow. I pick up my phone and ring Simon.

"Sir," he answers.

"Hold off on the other gift, I want to give it to her myself. I'm on a train now and should arrive in London around three p.m. I will get a taxi straight to the house, just keep her there," I order.

"Yes, sir," he confirms and I can hear the smile in his voice.

I disconnect and smile. Five hours and counting, I'm coming for you Cora.

CHAPTER EIGHTEEN

CORA

TODAY HAS BEEN A STRANGE DAY, BUT IN A GOOD WAY. THE surprise gift from Roman this morning blew me away, literally. It was so unexpected and after worrying about last night's texts, it put me at ease a little.

Every time I go to leave the house, Simon shows up, saying to not leave, that I am to stay put. He says its for a delivery, but I am not so sure, he is acting all weird and looks really stressed.

With the cleaning done and my parents taking the kids out after school to an arts and jazz festival over in Ealing, I decide to sit and do some painting. I hit play on my phone and start painting, smiling to myself.

There's a knock at the door and I jump, noticing its dark outside. I must have lost track of time whilst painting. Mum and Dad must have brought the kids back. I stand with my brush still in my hand and open the door, but it's not my parents and the kids stood there, it's Roman. He looks dishevelled, his suit is all crumpled.

"Roman, are you o—" He doesn't say anything, he cuts me off, taking my mouth and kissing me. His hands cup my face as his lips caress mine, and then he breaks the kiss, leaning his head on mine, both of us panting.

"Fuck, I've wanted to do that for so long," he breathes.

"Roman, I... I don't understand what's going on," I whisper honestly. I may be dumb, but I need clarification. I need to hear him say what's happening because I just don't trust my own instincts anymore.

He smiles and shakes his head. It's at that moment I realise I still have hold of my brush.

"Oh shit, Roman, um, I may have gotten paint all over your suit." I gasp.

He looks over his shoulder as do I, and all over his jacket is green paint. Shit.

He just shrugs off his jacket and chucks it on the floor, taking the brush and putting it on the palette. He takes my hand and leads me to the sofa, not saying a word, he pulls me down so I am sitting right next to him. He tucks my hair behind my ear and smiles.

"You need clarification," he states.

I nod. "Yeah. It's a lot for me to risk, I need to know I'm right in what I am feeling, in what I think you feel for me."

He smiles and cups my face, his thumb stroking along my cheek. "Cora, you have nothing to worry about when it comes to your job or your home, it's in your contract," he states and pauses for a moment.

"The moment I met you, when you went unconscious from being behind the door..."

"You mean when you opened the door, knocking me out?" I point out.

He laughs and shakes his head. "Easy, Kitten. Anyway, from that moment, I haven't been able to get you out of my mind. You completely captivate me, the way you would take food from yourself and give it to the needy, the way you helped Terry even though you didn't have to. Through all of it, you have nothing to give yet you always find a way of helping someone and giving them something, even if its food from your own bag," he says with sincerity in his eyes.

"Simon told you about that, huh?" I shrug.

He shakes his head. "No, I was there, I watched you. I told Simon to help you, to drive you home. All the times I have been with you, I have watched you on hotel security footage or Simon has been giving me notes. I know I sound insane and borderline stalker, but it wasn't to spy on you, it was to see when it was the right time."

"Right time for what?" I ask.

"Right time for this, for me to make my feelings known. I knew you would question yourself and worry about losing everything. I had to wait for you to beg me, for you to come to me. The last thing I wanted was for you to be running scared or back tracking on your feelings," he confesses.

"Wow," is all I can manage to say.

"I have another gift for you, this one I wanted to gift you personally," he says standing.

I frown in confusion. He opens the door and pulls in a large present covered in a brown paper with a note attached.

"Read the note," he instructs.

I get off of the sofa and read the note.

Cora, thank you for loving my work, I hope you will enjoy my painting in your home. Anika x

"You have to be shitting me!" I gasp.

Roman smiles. "Open it," he orders.

I rip off the paper, and there, on a very large canvas is an original Anika Tunstall portrait. He bought this. Tears fill my eyes and I look up to Roman.

"You got this for me?" I whisper.

He nods and moves the painting carefully to the side and walks towards me and cups my face. "There is nothing I wouldn't do for you, Cora, nothing. For all the years you've had to go without, for all the years you've dreamed, it's now my honour to make sure you never have to go without ever again, and I vow to make your dreams a fucking reality," he says sincerely, wiping away my falling tears.

"But I have nothing to give you." I sob.

His lips brush mine. "That's where you are wrong. You... All I need is you. Just you being you gives me so much. You continue to give me more and more of yourself each and every day, and when you give all of yourself to me, that is when I will be complete," he says before his lips kiss mine softly and slowly.

He breaks the kiss, letting out a deep groan. He trails kisses on my cheeks and down my neck. "I need to stop, tell me to stop," he says in-between kissing.

I don't answer and he cups my face and runs his thumb across my bottom lip. "Tell me to stop," he rasps, his eyes searching mine.

I step back out of his embrace and lift my top over my head and slowly walk backwards towards my bedroom. "Sorry, boss, I'm not very good at taking orders." I wink.

Romans lips twitch and he stalks towards me. "I can correct that." He smirks, unbuttoning his shirt.

I sit on the edge of the bed and he kicks the door closed. His shirt hangs open, exposing his ripped, toned body. His eyes never leave mine as he takes it off, chucking it on the ground. My eyes roam greedily, his broad chest has a light dusting of dark hair. I bite my lip as I take him in.

He stands in front of me and I reach out, slowly grazing my nails along his toned stomach to his belt. His fingers run through my hair and grip it tight, tilting my head back, making me gasp. He crashes his mouth down on mine, taking control, laying me on my back. Gone is the slow and teasing pace, instead it's heated and desperate. My hands are touching every inch of him, he grinds his hips and I moan. His hand travels down, unbuttoning my jeans, dipping beneath my panties, his finger slowly grazing over my clit. I gasp at the contact. He continues to circle my clit, causing jolts of pleasure to surge through me. My nails dig into his back as I can feel my orgasm starting to build.

"Oh God," I moan. As soon as the words have left my mouth, he stops and slides his finger inside me, expertly stroking my G-spot.

"Oh Fuck!" I cry, feeling my orgasm hit me from out of nowhere. Roman takes my mouth as I ride out my orgasm.

"Mummy?!" I hear Betty scream. I freeze.

"Shit," I hiss. Roman smiles.

I push him off me and run around looking for my top, remembering I had taken it off in the living room. I grab one from the wardrobe and chuck it on. I turn to Roman who is sprawled out on the bed, smiling at me.

"Get dressed!" I whisper-yell, throwing his shirt at him.

He slides on his shirt, stalks towards me and kisses me. "Tomorrow night after the ball, it's happening, no interruptions." He takes his finger and places it in his mouth and moans. "A delicious preview." He smirks at my shocked face as I feel my cheeks heat.

He buttons up his shirt and I shake my head to snap myself out of my Roman-daze. I open the door and walk into the lounge.

"Hey!" I greet over-enthusiastically.

"Mummy!" Betty hugs me. "You feel very hot, are you poorly?" she asks.

"No, I'm fine, everything is fine!" I rush out.

All eyes flicker behind me and I see my mum smirk, and my dad shakes his head.

I feel his chest press against my back and his arm snakes around my waist. I freeze, my body going rigid. "Yeah, everything is fine, I was just helping Cora move some furniture. Isn't that right, kitten?" he states before kissing my cheek.

The kids stand there staring, and I catch Theo smiling. "Come on, Betty, let's put the TV on for a bit before it's your bedtime," he says, pulling her away.

"Yes! We shall join you, come on, Felix." Mum ushers dad away to the living room.

I spin and practically growl at Roman. "What do you think you're doing? Acting that way in front of my parents and kids!" I hiss.

He smirks and his eyes alight with a playful sparkle. "No point hiding it, I made it clear that you're mine and that wasn't a chat up line. I'm serious about this. Now I will go, and I will be back to pick you up at six p.m. tomorrow for the ball," he states before kissing me briefly and walking up the stairs to his house.

I stand there feeling a little bewildered. "Well, I can't say I'm surprised," Mum says from behind me, making me jump.

"What? Really?" I stumble.

"Yes, blimey, we could see it from the moment we saw you together. I think you've done good there, honey. Also, I've seen the Tunstall portrait in the living room. Definitely a keeper!" Mum claps excitedly.

I shake my head and take a deep breath. It's all out of my control now, I guess everything is out there, feelings and all. I need to let go and dive in with both feet and enjoy where this takes me.

CHAPTER NINETEEN

Cora

I awake the next morning to knocking on the front door. I groan and roll over, looking at my phone and seeing it's only seven a.m. The knocking continues, so I roll out of bed and shuffle myself sleepily to the front door.

"What?" I squint through my nest of hair that is covering my face.

"Well, good morning to you too, sunshine," Sylvia sings.

"Ah?" I say frowning, sweeping my hair from my face.

"Get some coffee in you and get dressed, we leave in one hour," she says, pushing past me.

"Leave to go where?" I ask, shutting the door.

"To the salon, so don't worry about shaving, we shall have you waxed from head to toe, not a hair will be left on your body. Well, apart from your head of course, but not the 'tache, the 'tache has to go," she says, pouring us a coffee.

I touch the top of my lip. "I don't have a moustache!" I exclaim.

She looks at me and smiles. " Of course you don't, just some peach fuzz is all," she states, handing me my coffee.

"Hang on a minute, did I tell you about the ball?" I ask.

"Oh, honey, I'm here from orders of boss man. He said to book you in for all the treatments, make sure you get pampered and part of that bonus means I get treatments too!" She claps happily.

"But it's Saturday, who is going to have the kids?" I ask.

No sooner have the words left my mouth, there is a knock at the door. "Who in the hell is that now?" I ask.

I open the door and see Simon stood there, smiling. "And why exactly are you here?" I ask.

"I am here to sit with the kids for a while, then I am taking them out for the day whilst you get ready for the ball, your parents are staying over night with them in the hotel. Roman has everything all arranged," he informs me, still smiling.

"He sure does," I mutter under my breath.

I down my coffee and jump in the shower quickly while Sylvia and Simon wait. I get dressed into jeans and a jumper and walk into the lounge.

"Oh no, honey, go change into something else," Sylvia states.

"Why? What's wrong with what I am wearing?" I ask.

"Oh nothing, just trust me, soft cotton is the way to go, believe me, you don't want no chaffing afterwards." She winces and Simon coughs in his coffee.

I roll my eyes and walk back into the bedroom and put on a pair of black leggings with my boots instead.

"There... Better?" I ask, twirling.

"Yes, comfort all the way. Now, let's get going before London traffic starts getting heavy," Sylvia says, standing.

"Simon, you sure you'll be okay with the kids? I have my phone on me if you need anything," I say as Sylvia practically drags me out of the door, Simon waving us off.

Walking up the steps to the street, I pause. There, parked waiting, is a limousine. "Did you know that was here for us?" I ask Sylvia.

"Of course, it brought me here, now come on, let's go get our wax on!" She cheers, jumping into the limo.

I follow and thank the driver. "You know, you may be the only person I know who is excited about getting waxed, it's not supposed to be an enjoyable experience, you weirdo," I point out.

"Oh, Cora, the place Roman has booked us in is the best of the best. I wouldn't be surprised if the wax isn't gold, blessed by Buddhist monks and created in an ancient waterfall." She sighs.

I snort with laughter. "Well, if the place is as posh as you say it is, we are going to stand out like a sore thumb," I point out.

"Well, you might, but I can blend beautifully with the upper class, it's where I belong, they are my type of people," Sylvia says, lifting her chin.

"Oh, sure, yeah, totally your type of people. So that wasn't you on your Instagram, drunk, falling asleep, face planting your kebab?" I ask, raising a brow.

"I drank Jager bombs that night, I cannot be held responsible when Jager is involved. Even the queen would do crazy shit on Jager bombs," Sylvia retorts.

We take around an hour getting to this amazing beauty retreat, a beautiful big manor house with vast land.

As we enter, a woman dressed all in black greets us. "Welcome to Serenity. We have your treatments all scheduled. If you would follow me, I shall take you to our dressing rooms where you will change into your organic cotton robes. Once you are robed, I shall take you to your first treatment," she says in a calming voice, opening the door to our very own private changing rooms. Our robes have our initials on them.

"This is insane," I whisper, shaking my head.

"I know, it's amazing." Sylvia claps excitedly.

Once dressed, we follow her to our first treatment. "Here we are," she says, opening the door. "Please lay on the table and our consultants will be with you shortly to begin your wax treatments." She smiles and closes the door behind her.

Two women enter the room and smile. They don't ask what we

want waxed, they just get to work, not talking or making eye contact. I'm not sure if I'm thankful for this as she pulls my legs apart to wax my most intimate part or if I feel more awkward. Like knowing her name would be nice before she goes downtown on my vagina.

She spreads the warm, soothing wax and I moan. "Oh, that feels lovely." She smiles at me and soothes the strip over the wax.

"Do you know what Sylvia, this feels kind of nice, I was expecting it to be a lot more pain——Ahhh, holy motherfucking labia!" I scream as she rips the strip off.

"Shhhh, please, Miss, you will disturb other members," the waxinator warns me.

"Don't shush me," I snap.

"Cora, relax, it will get easier," Sylvia says with her feet by her head and her arsehole in the air.

"What are you doing?! Do you have a hairy arsehole as well as a hairy doo-dah?" I ask, stunned at the sight before me.

"Girl, we all do, nothing a wax and a little anal bleaching won't fix." She smiles as the woman rips away the strip from her ring piece. She doesn't even flinch.

"Anal bleaching? Oh God, is that what you were on about when you said about changing your ringtone?" I cringe. "I stood there and gave you a list of the best ringtones to buy and you didn't correct me!" I point out.

The waxinator rips away another strip. "Holy flappers!" I hiss in pain.

"Ha-ha, yeah, that was funny. I didn't want to correct you and corrupt your poor innocent mind." Sylvia chuckles.

"Miss, hold this and pull tight, please," the girl says, handing me my thigh.

She adds more wax and I brace for the pain. She rips the strip off and I swear my clit came off with the hair. "Ow, mother tucker. Jesus, you just tore my clit off, why? Why would you do that?!" I cry.

"Oh, Cora, chill out, she is just doing her job." Sylvia shrugs, reading a magazine calmly as her arsehole is being bleached.

"Chill out? Chill out?! I feel like my lips are on fire and my clit has been torn from me. My poor, poor little button of joy taken out in cold blood by the waxinator, not a thought or any sympathy spared," I cry. "It's okay, Perl, my little liquorice allsort, it will be okay." I sniff.

After what felt like I had been locked in some kind of torture chamber for nearly an hour, we finally moved on to our second treatment of the day, a full body massage. We walked up the curved stairwell... well, I tried my best, but I was walking like I had just been fisted by the hulk. All I wanted to do was sit on a bucket of ice and rest my poor vagina.

We enter a room filled with scents of what seems to be every essential oil. We both lay down and wait for our masseuses to come in.

"This better be a lot better than the wax," I grumble with my head in the hole.

"Oh shut up whining, you've just had a first class wax treatment, believe me, you go cheaper and you wont be able to sit down for days," Sylvia points out.

We hear the door open and the masseuses enter. I see a pair of shoe-clad feet and I frown. They are big feet for a woman, then I feel warm, strong, oiled hands move over my back and I swear my eyes roll into the back of my head and I let out a deep moan.

"Cora, look up, you might moan louder." Sylvia sighs.

I lift my head and look up and in front of me is a broad muscled chest. "What the hell?" I mutter.

"We are here to give you a full Swedish massage, please lay down and relax, Miss."

"But why are you topless?" I question.

"For the love of God, Cora, shut up and let Sven do his job," Sylvia moans.

I shrug and lay back down, I'm guessing this treatment is a popular one with the ladies. I have to admit, he really does have magic hands, it feels incredible.

He moves the towel, so it is literally just covering my behind, his hands massage my thighs, moving up dangerously close to my now-silky-smooth vagina. "Whoa, steady there, Sven. Any closer and we will be in porno territory," I warn.

"Ain't nothing wrong with that," Sylvia murmurs.

He moves down my legs to my feet. "Err, no, thank you," I request.

"No, no, you like it, it is good." He ignores me and continues. I can't help what I do next, it's like a reflex. I kick out as soon as he touches my foot. There's a crack sound and then a sound that is a lot like a ten-year-old girl screaming, but of course it's not, it's Sven screaming, holding his nose.

I turn around. "Oh my gosh, I am so so sorry. I hate my feet being touched, I can't help but kick out. Let me see," I say, reaching out.

He flinches away and wails, running out of the room. I look over to Sylvia who is just sat there with her towel wrapped around her shaking her head.

"What?" I ask. "In my defence, I told him no, he chose to ignore me," I say nervously, biting my nail.

We put our robes back on and wait to see what's happening. The lady that has been showing us around comes to us and she doesn't look so peaceful and surreal as she did when we arrived.

"I am so sorry, I told him no, but he just continued to touch my feet," I ramble my apology.

"It's fine, he is no longer with us," she says sternly.

"Oh my God, is he dead?!" I screech. "I didn't mean to kick him that hard!" I defend.

"No, fired," she clarifies, looking at me like I'm stupid.

"Oh, please don't fire him because of this, he was doing brilliantly before that moment. A real top notch massage." I smile.

"Come, I shall take you to your next treatment." She ignores me and continues out the door with Sylvia and I running behind her to try and keep up. The running isn't helping my poor vagina.

Thankfully, the next treatment was a manicure, something normal and something I could do without screaming in pain or ruining it in anyway.

After our manicure, which was a success, we stop for lunch. I am starving, so when they place down my tiny portion of salad, I'm close to blowing my top.

"Is this a starter? I mean, I need meat, I need carbs. I need substance," I complain.

"No, this is our food, this is healthy, they aren't about to serve us a big fat greasy burger and chips. This isn't your local greasy spoon, it's a health spa. Stop your whining and enjoy your salad," Sylvia whispers angrily, shovelling her salad in her mouth.

I mutter and grumble under my breath and eat the pathetic excuse for a salad.

"I'm not comfortable in places like this," I point out.

"What do you mean places like this? What, a spa?" Sylvia asks.

"No, you know, monied places. Wealthy places. It's so obvious I don't belong here," I state, taking a sip of the green tea they've given us then quickly spitting it back out into the cup. "God, that's disgusting, it's like drinking algae," I complain.

Sylvia looks at me and smiles, shaking her head. "No idea why you would think that you don't fit in here. What ever gave you that impression?" she says sarcastically, rolling her eyes.

I sip my water and choose to ignore her. I look around at the other women here, they all clearly have plenty of money with their designer purses, and I even saw a woman carrying her dog in a handbag. The dog had more bling than Mr T!

We finish our lunch and go to our next treatments, hair and make-up. I will say one thing, the beautician and the hairdresser were fabulous. I stare back at the mirror in complete disbelief. Looking back at me was like a whole new woman. The soft make-up made my eyes pop, my tired bags under my eyes had disappeared, I didn't look tired and stressed, I looked like I was ready for the red carpet.

My hair was curled into soft loose waves, there was no frizz, nor was it over sprayed in hairspray. It was perfect.

"Holy shit, you look hot. So hot, I'm even questioning my sexuality right now." Sylvia winks.

I laugh and slap her arm. "It's good to know I looked so much like shit before all this," I retort back.

"Oh, honey, you were one foxy, hot mama before but now you're Hollywood hot, like sexy pin up. Full wank bank material to all men and teenage boys. Roman is going to be all over you." She smiles.

I smile and thank the ladies for their witchery at making me look so amazing.

On the limo ride home, I'm anxious to see Roman. I'm now worrying the dress I have to wear to the charity ball is going to look crap against my flawless make-up and hair.

CHAPTER TWENTY

Cora

I walk through the door and drop my bag and keys down and head straight to the fridge to grab a sausage roll. I moan when I take a bite.

I notice a note on the fridge from Mum.

Cora, we have the kids. Have a fabulous time and enjoy yourself, we'll keep them until lunchtime tomorrow. So have a drink enjoy yourself and have a lie in.
Love you lots!
P.s Parcel for you on your bed.

I smile and head to the bedroom and there on the bed is a box. There is no note. I shrug and open it, gasping when I see what is inside. A beautiful pair of strappy heels. There is a note at the bottom of the box, and I rip it open.

. . .

Hope you like them, they will match your dress perfectly, or so the sales assistant assured me. Check behind your bedroom door.
   R x

I smile, turn and go to my door, and there, hanging on the back is a large clothing bag. I bite my lip and unzip it. There is a stunning burgundy A-line V-neck floor-length chiffon dress with lace sequin bodice and an extremely high split.

I run my fingers over the delicate sequins. I look at the time and see I have literally thirty minutes until Roman arrives to pick me up. I can't wipe the smile from my face. I go to my draw and pull out the only nice underwear I own, black lace bra and thong. I spritz my perfume and slip on the dress, the bodice clings to me, and the split exposes right up to the top of my thigh. I put on the heels to go with it and stand and look at myself in the mirror.

For the first time since I can remember, I feel beautiful. I've never really given my looks much thought. I haven't had time to, my life has always been running around for other people. But at this very moment, I not only feel beautiful, but I feel sexy. I feel like a woman, not just a mum who has jobs to do.

There's a knock at the door that makes me jump. I smile and take a deep breath.

I open the door to a very handsome looking Roman, his black slimline suit and crisp white shirt with the top few buttons undone. He even has the same colour as my dress pocket square.

My eyes finally reach his, and he has the same hungry desire in his eyes that I know is in mine.

He steps forward, I don't step back. I tilt my head up to look at him, he slowly cups my face and leans in, placing his mouth to mine, torturously kissing me softly and slowly.

"You look unbelievably stunning," he rasps across my lips.

I smile and open my eyes. "Thank you, sir, you don't look so bad yourself," I tease.

He lets out a deep throaty growl and pecks me on my lips. "Come on, let's go and get this over with. The sooner we leave, the sooner I can get you back and peel that dress off of you." He winks.

The same limo is waiting for us to take us to the ball. The entire way there he holds my hand, keeping me close. "I should warn you about my parents," he states.

"Oh God, they're going to hate me, aren't they?" I cringe.

"No, not at all, they are... Well, let's say, big characters, like your parents but less of the hippy side. They are loud, they will most certainly be drunk at some point of the night and will most likely say something highly inappropriate," Roman warns.

I laugh and kiss him. "Look, you've met my parents, they are anything but normal and if you can handle them, then I can handle yours. I would rather they be that way than stuck up snobs," I point out.

He smiles. "Well, there will be plenty of other people like that. Some are still decent people, others not so much, but don't worry, I will look after you," he promises.

I nod, feeling the butterflies swarm in my stomach. I don't handle rich people well. Apart from Roman, they have always been stuck up and looked down their noses at me, but I've made myself a promise to keep my mouth in check whilst I'm around people like that.

We pull up at an expensive hotel and Roman helps me out of the limo, holding my hand the entire time as we make our way into the hotel. I may be gripping his hand tightly as nerves swarm my stomach.

We walk into the ballroom and my jaw practically hits the floor, it's like something I imagine the Royal family would attend.

People smile and nod their heads in greeting to Roman, they don't offer me the same greeting. I get a flick of a gaze or a sweep from head to toe then they carry on with whatever conversations they were having.

A waiter with a tray of champagne offers us a drink and I gladly take one, practically downing the entire thing.

Roman stands in front of me, leans forward and whispers in my ear.

"Easy, I want you fully awake and mobile for when we go back home and I have you in my bed," he says, nipping my ear, making me gasp.

"Roman! Darling, I'm so glad you could join us this evening," I hear exclaimed from behind Roman. He steps back, putting his arm around my waist. I look up and see it's the woman I saw kiss him at the hotel a couple of weeks ago. Her eyes flicker to mine, assessing me.

"Camila," Roman greets.

She leans in, kissing his cheek, her lips lingering a little too long for my liking.

"Oh, you're Camila, nice to meet you," I interrupt, making myself known.

"Oh, Roman, have you been talking about me?" she flirts, gently slapping his chest.

"Oh, yes, he mentioned your name when we were watching that documentary. Oh, what was it?" I pause. "Oh, yes, that was it, African Warthogs." I smile bitchily. Roman coughs a laugh, and Camila looks like she is about to explode with rage.

I can tell she is about ready to snap at me with a bitchy retort when Roman's name is called from across the room. "Excuse us," he says politely to Camila as he walks us around her.

"That was naughty," he whispers in my ear.

"She deserved it for the look she was giving me and practically groping you," I mutter.

He kisses the top of my head and laughs. "Kitten's claws are coming out to play tonight I see."

Up ahead are an older couple, waving us down excitedly. The couple I am guessing are his parents. I take a deep breath and brace myself.

"Darling boy! Give your mother a kiss," she says, grabbing his face and kissing him loudly.

"Son!" his dad exclaims, pulling him in for a hug and slapping his back.

"Mum, Dad, let me introduce you to Cora. Cora, this is my mother and father, Audrey and George Nash," Roman introduces.

I hold out my hand in greeting but his mum bats it away and grabs me, pulling me in for a hug.

"None of that here, my darling girl, we are all about the hugs in this family," she says, squeezing me. She steps back and smiles. "Isn't she just beautiful, George?"

"Certainly is, nice to meet you, my darling." He smiles kindly at me.

"Come sit down, let us get to know you a little better, how did you two meet?" his mum says excitedly, patting the chair next to her for me to sit on.

I look to Roman for assurance. He nods, pulling out a chair and taking a seat next to me.

"I, um, was working my shift at his hotel, I'm a cleaner," I mutter, feeling embarrassed at my career. Comparing it to everyone here this evening, I have more in common with the waiters and hotel staff than the guests.

"Oh, that's lovely, so how long have you two been an item?" she asks.

"Audrey, enough of the twenty questions, let the girl be." George tuts.

"I'm just trying to get to know her a little, she could be our new daughter-in-law, do you not think it would be good to get to know her?" she defends.

"Mum, seriously, this is our first official date, so just put the brakes on a little." Roman smiles, shaking his head.

"I'm sorry, my girl, it's just that he never brings a girl to these things, so I'm a little excited," she apologises, squeezing my hand.

I smile. "Don't worry, it's all okay," I assure.

"So, Cora, come on, sweetie, tell us about yourself before all this pompous rich stuff starts up," she says, waving her hand around. I laugh, feeling myself start to relax a little. I feel at ease with her.

"I, um, have two children, Theo is fifteen and Betty is four. I am a cleaner and that's all there is to it." I smile and shrug.

"That's not all of it, she is a very talented artist too," Roman adds, squeezing the back of my neck. I blush at his compliment.

"Oh, that's amazing, I wish I could paint but I don't think drawing stick men is a talent." She laughs.

"Where is the damn wine for this table?" his dad bellows, clicking his fingers at a waiter to bring us wine.

"Ladies and gentlemen, please take your seats as we prepare for our meals to be served," a voice announces over the speaker.

They bring out the food and it's amazing, nothing like I've ever had before. I'm careful not to stuff my face or spill anything down my dress. I'm already an outsider, don't need to make it worse with the commoner with soup down her dress.

I am surprised at how relaxed I feel with Roman's parents, they are down to earth. His dad explains to me about how he started this business by purchasing an old run-down hotel, which he did up from scratch and it grew from there.

An auction starts and the bids are way out of my price range. I thought I might be able to bid on some bath sets, but no, these are designer bath sets. I mean, I didn't even know you could buy designer bath sets.

"Woohoo, George, your paddle is number sixty-nine." Audrey giggles, downing more wine.

"Well, my darling, I knew it was your favourite number." He winks.

"Stop it, you naughty beast." She giggles.

"Christ," Roman groans, making me laugh.

"Oh shush, boy, you should be ecstatic your parents are still very active lovers. You know, when we spoke to Dr Phil, he said we were an inspiration to other married couples, even featured us in one of his books." Audrey nudges me.

"Dr Phil... as in Oprah?" I ask.

"Oh yes, dear, lovely man. Oprah is too, salt of the earth. True gems."

"Do you know any other celebrities?" I ask.

She leans in closer and whispers. " Well, yes, dear, I know a few, and a few secrets too. They have all come to stay at one of our hotels at one time or another. But of course, I am sworn to secrecy. We all sign an NDA, that way the celebrities feel comfortable and safe at our hotels, and boy do they let their inhibitions go. There was a certain man of power shall we say who had three women up in his room." She pauses to take a drink. "Now three women you say, that's not too bad... Well, what if I told you they left things from their personal adventures... This certain pres... I mean, powerful man, liked to dress as a baby and have these women change his diapers, the lot. It was a real eye opener," she states.

"Audrey, you naughty minx, keep that waggling tongue quiet." George tuts.

Audrey giggles and I laugh. Roman takes my hand in his and kisses it. "I can only apologise for the emotional damage my parents are causing you right now." He smiles.

I laugh. "I love them, they are great fun," I say honestly. He rolls his eyes. "I'm just nipping to the ladies," I say, standing.

"Oh, sweetie, I shall come too," Audrey adds.

We walk together and Audrey links her arm with mine as we make our way through the ballroom. Someone calls her over. "You go on ahead, I will meet you there in a moment." She smiles.

I nod and continue to the ladies. I take care of business and wash my hands. I check my hair and make-up, all still perfectly in place. I hear the door open and expect to see Audrey there, but instead, I see Camila. I curl my lip in disgust, ready for whatever she is about to throw at me.

"Come on then, let's hear it, what is it you have to say?" I sigh. It throws her that I am not intimidated by her. I imagine she uses her status, money and power to intimidate a lot of people and use it to get her own way.

She smiles, all fake and it's sickly sweet. "I don't know what you mean, I simply needed to wash my hands. I think it's lovely that Roman has extended the invite for you to be here tonight. Seeing such opulence must be a real novelty to you." She takes a paper towel and dries her hands. "Yes, Roman's always been extremely giving. Being selfish isn't in his nature, treating 'the help' is so Roman. He doesn't have a selfish bone in his body, he's always been so giving, so selfless." The way she says the last part, I know she's meaning sexually. I bite the inside of my cheek to try and contain my reaction.

She sighs. "Look, Cara—"

"It's Cora," I bite back.

"Right, Cora." She waves me off. "Listen, this place isn't for you, these people aren't for you. You come from an entirely different world. You don't belong in this world. Well, you do, but only when you're cleaning up after us. Everyone has their place in the world and this place isn't for you. Roman just wants a ride on the wild side, a bit of street pussy, to say he's lived life on the edge. I mean, he will need a full medical after going anywhere near you. Who knows what diseases you're carrying," she spits.

I have my fists clenched, and I'm ready to snap.

I click my neck and lean in close. "Yeah, you can't be too careful, what I might be carrying, but I mean, I'm from the streets, right? So, I know how to take care of myself. I mean, who is to say what I'm capable of?" I threaten. I catch the hint of fear in her eyes.

"What's going on here?" Audrey announces loudly as she enters. I immediately step back.

"Nothing, Audrey, Camila here was just reminding me how we are so different. She was just extending her welcome to me," I say, smiling.

"Hmm, Camila, if I hear of you being anything but kind to Cora, I wont remind you of what I am capable of. I can quite easily create a rumour about you sleeping with Mrs Kelemen's husband for your degree. Oh, I forget, that's not a rumour, it's the truth. Now go sink your fangs into someone else," Audrey snaps.

Camila doesn't say anything else; she flounces out of the

restroom. I turn to Audrey who is re-applying her lipstick in the mirror.

"I'm so sorry, Audrey, she just said some things and I lost it and may have threatened her a little." I wince.

Audrey laughs. "Oh, honey, I know, I heard every word from her and you. Her face was brilliant. But you're no more street than she is. I grew up in Brentford, dear. I've seen the side of the tracks you're from, but Camila can't see it, she is blinded by her money goggles. She just sees you as lower class." She shrugs. "Now, let's go drink some more champagne and enjoy the rest of the evening," she sings, linking my arm, and we return to our table.

CHAPTER TWENTY-ONE

Cora

The rest of the evening went by without any more drama. Roman's parents were well and truly drunk by the end of the evening, but they weren't the only ones, I was surprised to see how drunk people with wealth could get. Roman pointed out that things can get a little wild.

"Let's get you home," Roman whispers in my ear, sending shivers down my spine.

I nod and stand. We hug his parents and promise to go to dinner with them soon.

The whole journey home, I feel the sexual tension build. Roman's hand is on my bare thigh, his thumb circling slowly.

"Keep driving until I say otherwise," Roman orders and closes the screen partition.

"Where are we—" my words die as his mouth crashes down on mine, his mouth hungrily owning mine. I run my fingers through the back of his hair, gripping tightly. He moans. I move so I am straddling his lap, his lip trails kisses down my neck and along my collarbone. I can feel his arousal and I shamelessly move, rubbing myself against him. I moan.

"Fuck," he grits.

His eyes are hooded as he watches me move. He slides his hand up my thigh and his thumb slides into my thong, rubbing my clit. I gasp and continue to move my hips, feel myself build.

"Shit, I'm coming," I moan. I cry out as my orgasm hits.

"Fucking beautiful," he rasps.

I kiss him. "What about you?" I whisper across his lips as I move my hips teasingly.

"I will get mine, don't you worry about that. The night is young, and I am no where near done with you yet." He smiles, nipping at my lip.

"Driver, take us home now, please," he instructs.

I bite my lip, excited and a little nervous, it's been a long time since I've had sex. I just hope I remember how to do it.

∽

ROMAN TAKES MY HAND AS HE LEADS ME UP TO HIS BEDROOM. Once inside, he switches on a lamp, lighting the bedroom in a soft glow. He sits on the edge of the bed and removes his shoes and socks. Not saying anything, he stands and unbuttons his shirt, leaving it hanging open. I stand there like a stunned deer. His eyes never leave mine as he removes each item of clothing, leaving himself only stood in his fitted black boxers.

I swallow, taking him in. He steps back and takes a seat in the armchair, his eyes watching me. "Take off your dress," he orders in a low but authoritative tone.

I bite my lip and slowly unzip my dress. Letting it go, it falls in a pool at my feet. His eyes hungrily sweep my body.

"Remove your bra," he orders.

I reach around and unhook my bra, chucking it to the side. I'm just stood there in my heels and my thong. He runs his tongue along his bottom lip. "Now lose the panties," he rasps.

I take in a shuddery breath and run my thumbs under the lace material. I slowly slide them down and step out, picking them up I throw them at him, he smiles and catches them.

I consciously hold my hands so they're covering my private area. Roman notices and frowns. "Hold your hands up above your head, and slowly turn around," he orders.

I take a deep breath and do as he asks, his jaw tenses as he takes me in and I turn slowly on the spot. "Stop," he orders.

With my back to him, I feel the heat of him before I feel his touch. He glides his hand slowly down my spine to the curve of my behind. His hands slowly move around my hips, gently grazing my skin, making my skin prickle with goosebumps. His lips brush along my shoulder to my neck, placing feather-light kisses. My arousal is building, I want him to touch me, I need him to touch me. His hand moves up to my breast and lightly teases my nipple, causing me to shudder.

"Turn around," he whispers as he nips my ear. I turn around, my hands automatically go to reach out to touch him, but he grabs my wrists, stopping me.

"Not yet, I will tell you when you can touch me," he orders. I nod and he lets go of my wrists.

He starts placing soft kisses along my collar bone, slowly moving down to my breast. His tongue teases my nipple, I roll my head back and moan as he moves across to the other breast. He keeps going, trailing soft gentle kisses down my body.

He reaches the tops of my thighs and he kisses everywhere but where I want him to, where I need him to.

"Roman," I pant.

"Yes," he says softly.

"Please," I beg.

"Please what? Tell me what you need. Let me hear you beg for it," he says right before he lightly glides his tongue over my clit. I gasp.

I look down at him on his knees before me, his lust-filled gaze fixed on mine. "Please, Roman, kiss me, lick me. I need you to. Please, sir," I beg.

He smiles and lifts my leg over his shoulder, his hand cupping my behind helping me balance. "Good girl, brace yourself, I'm hungry."

He places his mouth on me, licking and sucking my clit. I moan and grip his hair tight in my hands. He moves one hand around and slides his finger inside me, all while continuing the delicious torture. I feel my orgasm build, but suddenly it hits me hard and fast. I cry out and nearly buckle. Roman holds me up, he moans tasting my orgasm. He places my leg down and slowly stands, wiping his mouth.

"Fucking spectacular." He leans in, kissing me. I moan tasting my arousal on his tongue. Backing me to the bed until I'm sitting in front of him, his long thick, hard erection presses against his boxers. I lick my lips, eager to taste him and have him in my mouth.

"Remove my boxers," he orders.

I do without hesitation as I drop his boxers to the floor, setting his hard length free.

"What do you want to do now?" he asks.

"I want to taste you," I answer.

He nods. I open my mouth, taking just the tip, licking off the drop of pre-cum. I moan at his taste. I take him deeper, sucking and swirling my tongue, his deep growling spurring me on. He grabs my hair tight in his grip and thrusts his hips forward, hitting the back of my throat. I look up at him through my lashes and take what he's giving me. He's close I can feel it.

"Going to come, you're going to swallow every last drop I'm going to give you," he grits through his teeth. I moan and suck harder, showing him I'm ready and wanting it. He throws his head back and moans, his cum spilling down the back of my throat. I swallow all of it, every drop. I've never been so turned on in all my life at giving head before.

His gaze comes to mine and his thumb runs along my bottom lip, wiping away his cum. I take his thumb in my mouth, sucking it clean.

"Lay on your back in the middle of the bed, hands above your head," he orders. I do as he's asked and move to the centre of the bed.

He gets up and walks to get something and walks back to the foot of the bed.

"Open your legs," he orders. I do as he's asked. "Wider," he adds. I move my legs further apart.

"I can see your tight, wet pussy waiting for me. Did sucking my cock turn you on?" he asks.

I nod.

He smiles and crawls up the bed until he is over me. He has a tie in his hands and wraps it around my wrists, tying them together. "Keep your hands up there, until I say."

I nod and bite my lip. He nestles himself between my legs and I feel his erection pressed at my entrance. He doesn't say anything, his gaze intently watching me, then without warning he thrusts inside me. I arch my back and cry out as he fills me.

"Look at me, baby," he rasps. I open my eyes and look at him.

He moves slowly, rocking his hips in and out. He lifts my thigh, hooking it over his hip, making it feel deeper. "Oh God," I moan.

"Fuck, you feel incredible," he grits. It takes everything in me not to move my hands so I can touch him.

Each stroke of his cock inside me has my orgasm building. "I need more. Please," I beg.

"As the lady wishes," Roman grunts. He thrusts harder and faster, our bodies slapping together. I feel myself start to clamp tightly around him.

"Oh fuck, oh fuck," I cry out as my orgasm hits.

"Yes, fuck, take me, baby, fucking milk me." He moans, reaching his climax. He buries his face in my neck as both of us try to get control over our breathing.

He lifts his head and kisses me. "That was… There are no words." I smile.

"That was only the beginning, I'm nowhere near fucking done with you yet," he says winking.

"Wow, who would have thought? You're a gentleman on the street but a dom in the bed. I've definitely hit the jackpot," I tease.

He nips my neck and thrusts forward, my giggle dying in my throat, making me gasp.

We don't get to sleep until the sun starts coming up. I lay in his arms and his fingers glide up and down my back. I lift my head. "Go to sleep, woman, you've killed me, I have nothing left," he grumbles with his eyes closed. I laugh.

"Not that, I, um, just thought we didn't use any protection," I state.

He peers at me through his eyelashes. "You got anything?" he asks.

"No, of course not," I defend.

"Then we are good. I don't want anything between us, I want to feel every part of you, no barriers," he states.

"But it's not just STI's, I don't want a baby right now," I state honestly.

"That won't happen, you have the coil fitted," he states.

I gasp. "How did you know that?"

"Saw your appointment card on your fridge," he points out.

I pinch him, he jumps and laughs. "That's private," I yell.

"Oh right, I must remember that when I want things that are personal to be kept private, I shall place them on my fridge for all to see," he says sarcastically. I laugh and slap his chest.

"Now let me sleep," he grumbles.

"Yes, sir," I say smiling as I feel my eyes becoming heavy.

CHAPTER TWENTY-TWO

Cora

I awake late morning. Stretching, I feel aches in places that I haven't felt in a really long time... In fact, I don't think I've felt like this ever.

I open my eyes and see the other side of the bed empty. I get up and grab Roman's robe off the back of the door, heading to the bathroom to take care of business before going in search of him. I walk down the stairs, the waft of food cooking greets me, so I head to the kitchen. Stopping in the doorway, I take in the view in front of me. Stood at the stove in jeans and a T-shirt is Roman, next to him in a chef's hat stirring something in a mixing bowl is Betty and to the side chopping is Theo, all laughing and talking. I walk into the room and cough. All eyes come to me and I smile.

"Mummy! You're awake. We are making you lunch. Homemade vegetable soup and fresh rolls!" Betty says excitedly. I smile and kiss her floured cheek.

I walk to Theo and squeeze his neck. He smiles and continues chopping, the whole time I can feel Roman's intense gaze on me. I bite my lip and walk to him.

"Smells good," I whisper.

He pulls me into his arms and kisses me. "Hmm, you taste good," he whispers across my lips.

"Roman, the kids," I hiss.

"They know about us, your mum told them." He shrugs.

I roll my eyes. I look to the kids who are both grinning like Cheshire cats. "You guys okay with this? Roman and I?" I ask.

They both nod their heads excitedly. I laugh, shake my head and shrug. "What time is it?" I ask.

"Nearly one p.m.," Roman answers.

"You can't be serious? I never sleep in this late ever! Why didn't you wake me when my parents dropped the kids home?" I ask.

You had a late night, I figured it was best to let you sleep in." He winks. "Now go shower, lunch will be served in thirty minutes," he orders before kissing me briefly and practically escorting me from the kitchen.

Not one to argue, I walk back upstairs into the ensuite bathroom. I turn on the powerful and large shower and step under the spray. I moan at how good it feels, I could get used to this. I use Roman's shower gel and shampoo as my stuff is still at mine. I sniff and close my eyes at the scent of him. Once finished, I get out of the shower and wrap myself in one of his big fluffy towels.

I rummage through his draws and find a T-shirt and a pair of trackies, I have to pull the drawstring tight to stop them falling down.

With my hair wrapped up in a towel, I head back downstairs. I find them all in Roman's extremely large living room, sat on the floor around his coffee table with bowls of soup and a plate of warm crusty rolls in the centre. I immediately feel anxious at the kids not having placemats on Roman's expensive table. Not to mention if the kids spill something on the rug. Lord knows how much that thing cost!

I take a seat next to Roman who kisses the side of my head. "Why are we sat in here? Why not at the table?" I ask anxiously.

"It's a Sunday, soup, crusty rolls and a movie. Thought it would be nicer." He shrugs.

I lean forward and kiss him. "It's perfect," I whisper across his lips. "What about your table and rug?" I point.

"What about it?" He shrugs.

"I don't want spillages, I dread to think how much it cost." I wince.

"I don't care, anyway she's only four, it's to be expected." He shrugs.

"I'm not on about Betty, I'm on about me, I always manage to spill soup down me or on the floor. I'm a little clumsy," I point out.

Roman laughs. "Shut up and eat your soup. You spill any, I can get creative with a way for you to pay me back."

I shrug and tuck into the delicious soup and warm bread rolls. I warned him, I'm also a little intrigued in what he would do to make me pay for it.

We spend the next few hours all curled up on the sofas watching old family movies, from Hook to Jumanji. The kids look happy and relaxed, I haven't seen them this content in a long time. They are not alone, I haven't felt this content in a long time either.

After we've had dinner, reality sets in, with baths and getting kids settled ready for school tomorrow.

"Stay here," Roman states.

"I can't, it's not fair for the kids to sleep in a different bed again." I sigh, wrapping my arms around his neck.

"Fine, then I'm sleeping in your bed," he answers.

"What if I didn't want you there?" I raise my eyebrow in question. He laughs and kisses me.

"Yeah, that's not happening. Go down and bath Betty, I will grab my phone and be down in a minute," he says before kissing me.

I don't argue, because I do really want him with me. I bath Betty and settle her in bed. After reading her a story, I kiss her goodnight and go to shut her door.

"Mummy," she calls out.

"Yes, baby," I reply.

"Can Roman come in and say goodnight to me too?" she asks.

I smile and nod my head. "I will get him," I say.

"Roman, Betty wants you to say goodnight," I inform him. He looks a little surprised but smiles and goes into her.

I walk into the lounge to see Theo. I sit next to him and nudge him.

"Are you sure you are okay with this? Me and Roman, I mean?" I ask. He shrugs, continuing to look at the TV.

"You can be brutally honest with me. Please, I need to know you are okay with this. You and Betty are my world, you know that. If you guys aren't happy then I'm not happy. So tell me honestly, are you good?" I ask.

He sighs and looks up at me. "I'm good with it, Mum, it's nice to see you happy. Roman seems like a cool guy. I just... I just..." he pauses.

"What, baby, what is bothering you?" I ask.

"I don't know, I feel guilty that we are getting all this, and I wonder where dad is living, if he's okay... Which I really hate because I hate him for what he does. For picking drugs over us," he admits.

I pull him into a hug. "It's okay to feel for your dad, you love him regardless. Would it make you feel better if I went to see him? Make sure he's okay. Put your mind at rest a little?" I ask.

"I don't want you going near him, Mum, he's dangerous if he needs a fix. I don't want you getting hurt," Theo points out.

"I will go with your mum, keep her safe, how about that?" Roman interjects, standing in the doorway,

Theo smiles and nods. "Yeah, Mum, let Roman go with you."

I sigh. "Okay, baby, we will go tomorrow. Now go get showered and organised for school," I say, kissing the top of his head.

Roman comes and sits next to me, pulling my legs across his lap. "You know you don't have to come with me to see Kyle. I can go on my own. I can handle him," I offer.

"I promised Theo I would be there, so I will be there," Roman states. "You're going to have to get used to me being around and helping out, you're not on your own fighting these battles, you know

I'm with you every step of the way," He says, leaning forward he kisses me.

I smile. "I think I could get used to that."

~

The following day we drop the kids at school and drive around my old estate in search for Kyle. People look at the car, some run from the car thinking its undercover police.

I spot one of my old neighbours—one of Kyle's dealers—stood by the shop, selling blatantly to a kid that can't be more than fifteen. I feel my blood boil.

"Pull over," I instruct.

Before the car has even stopped, I jump out and head straight to him. His head flicks up and he smirks. The young lad freezes, clearly nervous about getting caught buying drugs. He should be, I know his mother and she would kill him if she found out.

"Frasier, give him back the drugs and piss off home. You want your life to be over then carry on down this path. Now go before I speak to your mother," I threaten.

He nods and runs off. I stand in front of my old slime-ball neighbour with my hands on my hips.

"What the fuck do you think you're doing selling to kids?!" I fume.

"Man got to make a livin' init." He shrugs.

I sigh and roll my eyes. "Where's Kyle?" I ask.

"What makes you think I know?" He shrugs, lighting a cigarette.

"Stop dicking around and tell me where he is," I say getting frustrated.

"What's it worth? I'm thinking of ways you could pay me for this information," he says smiling, his eyes sweeping my body.

"You touch her, and I will fucking end you," Roman growls from behind me. I lift my chin and raise my eyebrow at the dealer.

"What the fuck you going to do rich boy, slap me? Imma' bang you out, dick'ed." He smirks.

Roman throws his head back and laughs. "What the fuck was that? Shit, did you even go to school? Was that English? Listen, whatever you think you're going to do, you're not. You are going to behave like a normal civilised human fucking being and answer her goddamn question," Roman says angrily.

"Rich boy has no clue." He tuts. "Kyle is over Wentworth street, back of the flats. Some advice, Richie Rich, don't go throwing threats like that round here or you will get yourself a blade to the chest," he threatens.

Roman doesn't respond, he just takes my hand and leads me back to the car.

"He is right, you know? You're already different to them and stand out. You threaten them, you will get stabbed. More to the point, you may get robbed. You scream money, there are lot of desperate people, your watch alone would feed a family," I point out.

"Don't hate on the Rolex," he teases. "If someone who truly needed it asked me for money, I would happily help them," he points out.

"I know, but these people don't ask, they take. So just watch your back, rich boy," I tease.

We park up. "Stay here, just wait ten minutes then if I'm not back, come and get me?" I ask.

"No. I'm coming with you," Roman argues back.

"Okay, five minutes then? He will probably kick off if he sees you. Please, just five minutes. If there's an emergency I shall scream. How about that?" I offer.

He sighs, clearly not happy but relents. "Fine, five minutes, not a minute longer," he warns.

I smile and kiss him. "I promise," I say before jumping out of the car.

I walk around the back of the block of flats and see a few bodies huddled together in sleeping bags. Rubbish and discarded needles litter the area. Being careful where I step, I approach the first guy I come to.

"Kyle?" I ask. The man looks up, it's not Kyle. He stands, his eyes assessing.

"What do you want?" he snarls. He has a busted lip and rotten teeth, his stare is cold with no emotion.

"I'm, err, looking for Kyle, I was told he was here," I stutter nervously.

He grunts and turns and kicks the person led on the floor. "Kyle, get your arse up, someone here to see you," the man snaps. Kyle doesn't move so the guy kicks him harder. Kyle groans and rolls over. "Get up," he barks.

Kyle moves rigidly to his feet. He turns to face me and his eyes go wide. I gasp. His face is a mess, his nose is swollen and busted, he has a bad black eye and bruises on his face.

"Oh my God, Kyle, what happened?" I ask.

He shoves his hands in his pockets and looks away. "Nothing, all part of living on the streets." He shrugs. "Living the fucking dream."

"Jesus, Kyle, what happened to where you were staying?"

"Lost it, had debts to pay. Still do." He looks me up and down. "You look like you've landed on your feet, is that because of Mr Money Bags? Bet he deposits more than his normal load, doesn't he?!" he sneers.

"Don't you fucking dare!" I snap back.

"What? Does the truth hurt? You open your legs and suddenly you're living this amazing life. You're a real-life pretty woman, aren't you? If I had known you'd be so valuable on your back, I would have pimped you out long ago," he spits.

I don't think, I slap him hard across the face, making his head whip to the side.

"Do you know why I came here to find you? Do you? For your kids. Theo asked me to check on you, to see that you're okay. I realise now that was a huge mistake, I shouldn't have bothered, I should have just told him you were dead because then at least he could move on and stop worrying about his junkie of a father!" I yell.

Kyle moves quickly, his hand wrapping around my throat, pushing me hard so my back slams against the wall. His eyes are dark, evil almost. "You'd like that, wouldn't you? Make it easier on your new rich lifestyle. Be easier if I was dead in the gutter somewhere. You always did want more, I was never enough for you. You pushed me into this life, it's your fucking fault why I am living like this," he says angrily.

"How exactly is it my fault? I never gave you any drugs, I never told you to gamble all our money so me and the kids would starve!" I yell back.

"It was your high expectations, this life living on this estate was never good enough for you. You always wanted more, and the truth is, I couldn't give you that. Do you know how hard it is to see that kind of disappointment in the eyes of the one person you love? Do you?!" he bites back.

I am about to snap back when Roman's voice booms loudly. "Get your fucking hands off of her now!"

I turn and see Roman storming towards us, looking pissed. I shake my head, warning him to not get too close. I wouldn't put it past Kyle—or any of them for that matter—to attack and steal from Roman.

"Oh look, Mr Money Bags is here, how nice," Kyle says sarcastically. He releases his hold on my neck and turns to Roman.

Determined look on his face, he walks straight up to Kyle without hesitation and swings, hitting him square in the jaw. Kyle falls to the floor.

"Touch her again and I will fucking kill you," he seethes.

Kyle groans and nods, holding his face. Roman takes out a large wad of money from his pocket and chucks it down to Kyle. "There, do everyone a favour and OD. You decide this isn't the life for you, you come to me and I will help you. You do not contact her or the kids. Only me. I am giving you one chance, a lifeline, it's up to you which path you chose," Roman says before taking my hand and dragging me away from Kyle and back to the car.

Once inside the car he turns to me, cupping my face and checking my neck. "Are you okay?" he asks concerned.

"Yeah. You know, you being all manly like that was kind of hot." I smile.

Roman bursts out laughing, shaking his head, he starts the car. "Only woman I know that would be okay and say something like that after that shit-storm. How long until the kids finish school?" he asks.

"Four hours," I state, wiggling my eyebrows.

"Best put my foot down then." He winks and accelerates off at speed, making me laugh.

CHAPTER TWENTY-THREE

Roman

The woman is insatiable. I thought I had a high sex drive but clearly it is nothing compared to hers. Not that I am complaining much.

I sit at my desk, my mind on her, it's only ever on her. Christmas is only six weeks away and I know my parents will expect me there, but the truth is, I'm not going anywhere without her.

There's a loud commotion at the office door and it bursts open. Kyle is stood there, if possible, looking worse than when we saw him a few days ago.

"Sorry, sir, I tried to stop him," Simon apologises.

I hold up my hand. "It's fine, give us a minute, please," I instruct, my eyes never leaving Kyle.

Simon shuts the door, leaving us. "What is it, Kyle? Why have you come barrelling into my office causing a scene?" I ask.

"Your offer, I want to take it. If it still stands?" he says shaking, his eyes are looking everywhere, his entire body is twitching.

"I will make the call, but my offer comes with conditions. You go to rehab, you do not contact Cora or the kids until you are clean, you stay there, you do not leave early. You give up and quit, then that's it, this is a one time offer. I wont do it again. Deal?" I ask.

He nods, his teeth starting to chatter.

"Good, take a seat, I will make the call," I state.

I arrange for him to be picked up within the hour. He will start a six month rehabilitation program. I have promised him a job and a place to stay should he stick to it.

"Why are you doing this for me?" he asks.

"I'm not doing it for you, I couldn't give a shit if you died. I'm doing it for the kids. They don't need to see their dad like this, they deserve better," I grit through my teeth and stamp down all the anger and rage that I feel.

He looks at his hands, knowing I am right, knowing he chose drugs over his own family. That shit is on him and he has to come to terms with it.

I walk with him to the back of the hotel for the car to take him to rehab. The air is tense, Kyle cannot stop fidgeting. "You'll look after them, yeah?" he asks, his entire body jittering.

"Of course," I answer sharply.

The car pulls up and I open the door. For a moment, I think he is going to change his mind and run, but he surprises me and gets in. I don't say anything, I just slam the door shut and watch it drive away.

I meet Cora after he's left, I don't tell her. I won't unless he shows up at the door six months from now, clean and sober. I don't want to give her or the kids false hope.

"So, I was thinking about Christmas," I state.

Her beautiful blue eyes connect with mine. "Yeah?" she says hesitatingly.

"I was thinking about you and the kids coming to my parents with me?" I ask.

She smiles, but it's not a happy smile, it's a sad one. I immediately feel it in my gut. Jesus, since when did I become dependent on a woman? Not that I'm complaining, I am enjoying every second of it.

"We would love to, but I can't leave my parents on their own at Christmas. We are all they have." She shrugs.

"They can come too, I go up there Christmas eve and stay until the day after boxing day, what do you say?" I ask.

She smiles wider, her eyes light up and I feel that in my gut too, her happiness. Warmth spreads through me. To be rewarded with her beautiful smile, I will be forever doing what I can to receive it.

"Okay, let me talk to my mum, maybe not so much my dad, because, well, let's face it, he will be happier in a tent." She rolls her eyes.

I take her hand in mine and kiss her palm. "I think for the first time in a long time, I am actually looking forward to Christmas. You'll have to give me a list of what to get the kids and I will send Simon out to get it," I offer.

She throws her head back and laughs. "What?" I ask.

"You are not sending Simon out for any shopping, we shall go together and do it ourselves. With my money, not yours. Okay, rich boy?" she teases.

"Call me rich boy one more time, I will have you over my knee," I threaten.

Her lust-filled eyes sparkle at my words and she bites her bottom lip seductively. I stand and chuck my napkin down on my plate, take her hand and drag her away.

"What are you doing? We are in the middle of lunch," she asks, shocked.

"It's your fault looking at me the way you were. Now, now I have to have you," I state, leading her into my office and slamming and locking the door shut.

She smiles and perches on my desk. "So, sir, what will you do to me?" She smirks with a sultry tone.

"Oh, Kitten, patience to those who wait." I smile as I walk to her and spread her legs, standing between them.

I unbutton my trousers and free my already desperately hard cock. I run my head up and down her covered entrance, making her moan.

I rip her tights and move her panties aside quickly. Catching her off guard, I thrust inside her to the hilt. She cries out, her nails digging into my shoulders.

I lean forward and take her mouth hungrily, easing her onto her back across my desk, sweeping everything off and onto the floor. I run my hand over her white T-shirt and up to her neck. I grab the neck of the T-shirt and rip it apart, exposing her beautiful full-lace-covered breasts.

"Roman! Oh my God, I can't believe you just ripped—" her words die in her throat as I slam in and out of her hard.

"Fuck," I grit, the feeling of her tight pussy already beginning to clamp around me.

"Oh God, Roman, don't stop," she cries.

"Not fucking planning on it," I pant as I continue my hard and relentless pace. I reach forward and grip lightly around her neck. I watch as she arches her back, and I feel her walls clamp tightly around me as her orgasm hits.

"Roman! Fuck!" she screams.

I don't stop until my climax hits. "Fuck, Cora. Fuck," I groan. I slump forward, resting my face in the crock of her neck. We are both panting like we've run a marathon.

Lazily I trail kisses along her neck. She moans softly, and just at that moan I feel myself beginning to harden already. I don't know what she's doing to me, but I cannot get enough of her.

She wiggles slightly, feeling me harden inside of her. "Ooo, is sir not done with me?" she goads.

I smile and bite her neck, making her gasp. "Oh, Kitten, sir has only just fucking begun," I growl.

∼

"MUM, LISTEN TO ME, DON'T GO CRAZY, SHE HAS TO HEAR BACK from her parents first, okay?" I try to reason with her.

After our extended lunch break that turned into an extended phenomenal session of fucking in my office for two hours, Cora returned to work whilst I was on the phone to my mother, who was to say the least excited about the possibility of all of us there for Christmas.

"Oh, I know, sweetie, but to have children in the house at Christmas again, oh their faces will be such a picture. And to have you all here would just be magical. I am writing a list for decorations, no expense spared this year. I shall make sure every bedroom is decorated. Oh, Roman, this is going to be so much fun!" she exclaims before she disconnects.

"Mum? Mum?" I yell down the phone. "Jesus Christ," I say, dialling Cora.

"Hello, super sex maid here at your service, sir," she answers.

"Don't start," I groan.

She laughs. "What can I do for you, sir?" she asks.

"That's a dangerous question to ask," I tease back. "And believe me, as much as I want nothing more than to fuck you again, I can't right now. My mother just called about Christmas, I told her that there is a possibility about you, the kids and your parents coming too. And to say she was over excited would be an understatement. She is already writing lists, and by the sounds of it Santa's grotto will have nothing on their house by the time she is done with it." I sigh.

Cora laughs. "Well, I have spoken to Mum and she's good with it, she said she will work on my dad later, so your mum can get all excited," she says happily down the phone.

"That's great news, but just saying, I wouldn't be surprised if there aren't real reindeers in the back garden. Knowing her and her excitement, she will probably have hired dwarves to be elves." I sigh.

"No she wouldn't." She tuts.

"Never say never when things come to my mother, she wants to do something, she will always go big. Take this as your warning. Brace yourself for whatever we may be walking into because six weeks is more than enough time for her to go way over the top," I warn.

"The kids will love it. Now, I have to get back to work or my strict arsehole boss will have me up on a disciplinary," she teases.

"Will he now? You best get to work." I smile into the phone.

"Yes, sir," she breathes before disconnecting.

I put down my phone and sigh happily, I will give her twenty minutes before having her escorted into my office. I smile to myself at the thought. She may kill me, but fuck it, I will die happy.

CHAPTER TWENTY-FOUR

Cora

"Oh God, yes," I moan as Roman takes me from behind.

"Shh, Kitten, or the kids will hear you," he warns, right before he pounds into me harder. I bury my face into the pillow to smother my cries. My orgasm hits me hard, my entire body shudders. Roman grips my hips tight as he buries himself to the hilt as he comes.

He places tender kisses up my back and I moan. "I swear, if I could fuck you all day and all night, I would," he says between kisses.

"Oh, sir, I don't think you could handle me," I tease.

Without warning, he flips me on to my back, pinning me. I squeal and giggle. He slides back inside me, making me moan. "Oh, Kitten, you know I am always up for the challenge," he says as he thrusts forward.

Just as Roman starts moving, Betty bounds through the bedroom door. "Mum! Wakey, wakey, sleepy head, it's so late," she yells, running to the bed. Roman rolls off me quickly, pulling the covers up over us.

"Shit," he mutters under his breath.

I laugh and pat his chest. "It is? Well, I best get my lazy bones up and make us all some breakfast then, hadn't I?" I smile, kissing Betty on the cheek.

"Yes, I am starving. And Theo is being grumpy and wont make me breakfast." She huffs.

"Okay, baby, go in the lounge and wait for me, let me spend a penny and put my robe on, okay?" I say.

"Okay, Mummy, but don't take all day about it, I'm wasting away," she says dramatically, placing her hand across her forehead.

I laugh and shake my head as she walks out the door, closing it behind her. Roman rolls back on top of me, still hard.

"So how long do we have until she comes back in here for you?" he asks.

"I'd say, like, less than ten minutes." I sigh.

"I can work with that," he says and reaches for the draw next to his side of the bed. He pulls out a small bullet vibrator and switches it on, placing it on my clit. The sensation causes me to gasp as pleasure builds within seconds.

"Oh God," I moan.

"Yeah, I know, hold it there, Kitten, because I'm going to fuck you hard and fast," he says, handing me the vibrator.

He wasn't lying as he grabs hold of my hips and fucks me relentlessly. I place the vibrator on my clit, and with Roman fucking me and the sensations it's causing, it's almost too much.

"Oh fuck, Roman," I moan.

"Open your eyes, watch me fucking you," Roman pants.

I open my eyes, watching as he fucks me. My orgasm hits me without warning. I arch my back and I feel my walls clamp tightly around him.

"Fuck, I feel you, fuck, feels incredible," he moans. He continues to pound into me, finding his release. I watch him as his muscles tense, and he throws his head back.

"Mummy! Come on," we hear Betty shout from outside.

We laugh. "Well, moment is definitely over now," I say.

Roman kisses me as he slides out of me, and we both moan at the lost connection. "Duty calls." I smile as I get out of bed.

I get cleaned up and put on my robe and go in search of Betty. I find her dancing around the living room, watching kids cartoons. I put on some toast for her and start the coffee machine up. I feel Roman's arms come from behind and wrap around my waist. He buries his face in my neck and kisses me.

"You didn't have to get up, you could have stayed in bed," I suggest.

"Don't want to be in bed if you're not in it with me," he whispers.

"Roman! You're awake too! Yay. Come see my bestest cartoon." Betty claps excitedly.

Roman smacks my behind and then turns to Betty. "Let's go, beautiful, show me the bestest show ever." He smiles at her.

She takes his hand and leads him to the lounge. I make the coffees and toast and carry them in. Curled up on the sofa, they're both glued to the TV, watching Betty's favourite show. I sit the other side of Betty with the plate of toast and hand Roman his coffee.

I've never felt this before, not even with Kyle. It was never like this. Even if you were to take away all of Roman's money, I don't think this feeling would go. I look across to Roman, Betty cuddled into him and it's in that moment I know a million percent that I am completely head over heels in love with him.

~

"OKAY, SO THIS IS LIKE THE FIFTH STORE WE HAVE BEEN IN NOW, and you still haven't picked anything for Roman. I mean, do you even know what he wants for Christmas? Did you ask him?" Sylvia questions, picking up aftershave and sniffing it.

"I don't know, I mean, what do you buy the man that has everything? He could literally buy himself anything he wants, so what in the hell am I going to get him for Christmas?" I stress.

Each shop is the same thing, designer scarfs, designer clothes, even designer money clip for crying out loud. I mean, come on, if having a money clip because you have enough money to fill one isn't pretentious enough, you can buy a designer one just to rub it in people's faces that little bit more.

"Oh, I know what you could get him, some sexy lingerie," Sylvia sings, shaking her arse.

I laugh. "It's an option, but I still think he needs something that he can unwrap in front of the kids and his parents."

"Good point. Maybe you can be his personal present to unwrap later? So clothes is a no, aftershave too cliche, and he definitely isn't into football or supports a team of anything?" Sylvia asks.

"Nope." I shake my head.

"Right, while we know one thing he will like, let's hit the sex shop and get you all kinked out," Sylvia says, linking her arm in mine and dragging me to the seediest shop I have ever been in.

"I'm afraid to touch anything in here," I whisper to Sylvia.

"Oh shush. Berny regularly disinfects the place. Just don't go through that curtain at the back." She points to a red velvet curtain at the back of the shop.

"Why? What's behind there?" I ask.

"Just don't go in there, okay? Even I won't go in there." She shudders.

"Okay," I mutter, my eyes glued to the now-tempting red velvet curtain. I now more than ever want to see what's behind the curtain.

"What about this?" Sylvia holds up what can only be described as a chain bra and thong set.

"What? No!" I reply, feeling grossed out.

"This isn't what I had in mind when getting kinky underwear. I meant, like a lacy bodice, or satin. You know, suspenders and heels, that sort of thing," I explain.

"Fine, let me just go over there and grab some more lube and handcuffs, my last pair got ruined by the fireman." She sighs.

"You handcuffed a fireman?" I ask.

"Oh no, I lost the key and had to call them to cut Tim free. I found it hilarious, Tim did not." She shrugs. "Still, the fireman that got him out gave me his number, so silver lining and all that."

She wanders off to get her stuff, and I find myself in front of the red curtain. I look around me, making sure no one is looking, and peek inside. It's a dark corridor. I decide to go and have a better look, my curiosity getting the better of me.

As I walk down the corridor, the air has a funky smell to it, and I can hear moaning and groaning. I start to worry that I'm about to walk in on a secret gang bang or a live sex show.

As I walk around the corner, I see a large screen playing a porno, and I sigh with relief.

I hear a noise coming from beside me and I turn to look to see an older gentleman jerking off to the movie. I scream and he jumps, turning his body towards me. It's unfortunate in that very moment that the gentleman climaxes. I try to move out the way, but its dark and he seems to ejaculate like a super soaker three thousand. I cannot dodge it, and it's then that I feel it right on my cheek.

"Oh my God!" I screech.

"Shh! Can you keep it down over there? I'm trying to get off over here!" a guy yells, followed by the horrific sound of him furiously beating his meat.

"Oh my God! Cora, I told you not to come back here," Sylvia hisses.

"I have jizz on my face, I have that man's jizz on my face!" I panic.

"If that's what you're into love, I can add to that!" the guy yells.

"Jesus, it's turning into a damn bukkake party," Sylvia mutters.

"Sylvia, jizz on my face!" I flap.

"Right, here." She hands me a face wipe from her bag.

I snatch the entire packet and begin to scrub at my face. "Yeah, that's it, love, scrub it harder," another guy calls out.

"Sylvia, get me out of this fucking place," I cry.

She snaps out of her porn-induced daze. "Right, right on it," she says, grabbing my hand and pulling me out of the shop.

I continue to wipe at my face. "Sweetie, I don't think you should keep scrubbing at your face, it's looking a little red and sore," she says.

"It's still there, I can feel it. Damn, bleach, I need bleach!" I cry.

"Come on, I will take you for an emergency facial." She snorts. "Not that you haven't already had a little facial."

I stop scrubbing and give her a look. "Keep talking and I will kick you in the crotch," I threaten.

"Okay, fine, too soon for jokes." She holds her hands up in defence.

She drags me into the nearest beauticians. "We need a beautician stat! Accidental bukkake, she needs a face mask and a possible chemical face peel," Sylvia yells while I die that little bit more inside.

A beautician runs to me. "Oh, honey, I have just the treatment, although they do say semen is good for the skin. What I tend to do is just massage it around the wrinkle-prone areas. I find it helps, just don't get it in your eye, it stings a bit," she says, escorting me through to a room.

"Did you just tell me to massage sperm onto my face?!" I ask.

"Yeah, honestly, it's the best kept secret." She smiles.

"This was an accident because my friend took me to the sex shop down the road," I exclaim.

"Oh, you went behind the red curtain, didn't you?" she asks.

"Yes!" I screech.

"Oh, was there a bald guy with glasses?" she asks.

"Yes! He is the sperminator!" I say, laying down.

"Oh, that's my Uncle Barry. Don't worry, he's a good guy, clean. Proper church goer." She smiles, lathering stuff onto my face.

"Well, he may want to pray for forgiveness at what he was doing in there, definitely wasn't very holy and I'm pretty sure they don't have that sort of thing in the bible," I point out.

After the facial treatment, I feel a lot better. I return home and flop onto my bed. How did a Christmas shopping trip for Roman end up in me being jizzed on by a stranger?!

CHAPTER TWENTY-FIVE

Roman

"So, how long for the electric and heating to be installed? When will it be done?" I ask.

"Looking at another two weeks." Giles sighs.

"Fine, just get it done in time for Christmas," I say, shaking his hand and returning back to my work.

I want to make sure everything is perfect for her. After what happened on her shopping trip the other day with Sylvia, she deserves a treat. I don't think I've ever laughed as hard as I did when she told me. I then fucked her because of the thought of her in sexy lingerie.

My phone rings and I smile when I see it's Cora.

"Beautiful," I greet.

"Hey, handsome. So, come on, I need you to give me some ideas on what to get you for Christmas," she says, frustrated.

"I told you that you are enough for me, you are all I will ever want or need," I remind her.

"Ughh! Will you stop being such a gentleman and just tell me what you want?" she practically growls at me down the phone.

I laugh which only infuriates her further. "You're so bloody annoying, do you know that? Do you know what? I know exactly what I'm getting you. I am hitting the pound shop. I bet you've never stepped foot in there before, have you? Be prepared to get some serious tat, lots of crap you shall never use and possibly some cheap chocolate," she mocks with an evil laugh.

"I will love whatever you get for me, you know that," I say sickly sweet purposefully to piss her off more.

"Oh just bugger off!" she snaps and disconnects.

I laugh and send her a text straight away.

R: Keep those claws out for tonight, Kitten, you know how I like it when you're all fired up. x

C: Ha, try all you want but you wont be getting any. X

R: Challenge accepted; I have talents that will soon have you caving in. X

C: We shall see, now will you politely piss off, I am trying to do some Christmas shopping and you sex challenging me is not helping.

R: Fine, can you at least send me a kiss to keep me going? X

She doesn't reply, so I text her again.

. . .

R: Just one kiss. x

R: All I want.

R: Is it that hard to send your man a kiss?

R: It's just clicking one letter.

Eventually my phone pings with a message and I throw my head back laughing.

C: Jesus Christ, stop! XXXXXXXXXXXXXXXXXXXXXXXXXXXXXX There, will that do you? Now piss off and let me shop for you!

All I can think about now is her all riled up and I'm hoping she gets back before the kids finish school because I want nothing more than to fuck her right now.

There's a brief knock at the door and in storms my mother, not waiting for my answer to come in.

"Mum, come on in," I say sarcastically.

She sighs and sits down, pulling an entire folder out of her handbag. On the front it is titled 'Family Christmas.' I sigh and roll my eyes.

"Right, I expect you all to arrive at three p.m. on Christmas eve, I shall have Nora prepare the welcoming mulled wine, orange juice for the children and mince pies. Once you have all settled and presents placed under the tree, I shall put all of Father Christmas' presents in your father's office and keep it locked, so as not to spoil the magic of Christmas. We shall enjoy a light salmon dinner then we shall all wrap up warm and head into the grounds for the Christmas eve spectacular!" She claps.

"Christmas eve spectacular?" I ask.

"You'll just have to wait and see, I won't have you going all scrooge and ruining it." She points her finger at me.

I pinch the bridge of my nose. "Mum, you know just a simple Christmas will be fine," I remind her.

She waves me off like I'm talking nonsense. "After the Christmas Eve spectacular, we shall all retire and get the children in their Christmas pyjamas which will be placed on their bed ready for them. And we shall allow one present to be opened by them before bed—"

"Mum, Theo is fifteen, he isn't going to want to wear Christmas pyjamas," I interrupt her.

She thinks on this for a moment. "Fine, I have another idea. I will go with that. So Christmas morning, everyone will get up and go downstairs in their Christmas day robes that I have provided, and we shall enjoy fresh coffee or tea while the children open their stockings. And then after breakfast we shall do our presents around the tree. While I am preparing Christmas dinner, you, your father and Cora's father can assemble any toys that require it."

"I need to take Cora away for an hour or so. To give her her Christmas present," I state.

Mums eyes soften and smile. "Of course, you're excused of Christmas assembly. Then I shall serve Christmas Dinner for approximately three p.m. The evening shall continue with drinks and family friendly games. Then there is boxing day—"

"Mum, you don't need to list off everything. I'm sure what you have arranged and planned will be just exceptional." I smile at her.

She smiles back and sighs, looking at her watch. "Oh my goodness, I have to go, I have a meeting with the council about having a livestock licence," she rushes out.

"Wait, what? What do you need a livestock licence for?" I ask.

"Bye, darling, have to go!" She leans forward, kissing my cheek.

"Mum?" I repeat. "Mum?!" I yell after her.

God knows what she has planned, but all I know is it's definitely going to be a Christmas we are never going to forget.

∼

"What about this one, sir?" the older gentleman asks behind the counter.

"No, it's too gawdy for her. She isn't flash. She needs something that is classic, elegant and a little unusual." I start looking through the display case.

"Well, well, well, as I live and breathe, Roman Nash is looking at engagement rings." I recognise the voice immediately.

"Camila." I sigh.

"Roman, darling, please tell me you're not going to ask that cleaner to marry you?" she mocks. I tense my jaw, not in the mood for her snobbery.

"You want something, Camila? Because if you don't mind, I'm busy," I snap.

"Oh, Ro-Ro, chill out. All I'm trying to say is be careful. I mean, she has nothing and you have everything, she could take everything. At least do a prenup, be sensible about it. Remember you both come from very different worlds. I mean, can you honestly say hand-on-heart that she wouldn't try and take everything from you if it didn't work out?" she sneers.

I grit my teeth to stop myself from retaliating. She leans in and kisses my cheek softly. "Bye, Ro-Ro, remember, I'm only ever a phone call away," she whispers and leaves.

Her words float around my head, a prenup. Do I really need a prenup for Cora? She wouldn't take everything from me, would she?

"Sir?" the guy calls, snapping me out of my thoughts.

"Err, not right now, thanks, I will come back another day," I say, walking out of the shop. I'm pissed, I'm pissed that Camila's words have managed to invade my mind.

I get in the car and drive straight home to see Cora. I need to get what Camila said out of my head.

CHAPTER TWENTY-SIX

Cora

I'M IN THE KITCHEN COOKING DINNER WHEN I HEAR ROMAN come through the door. He's spent more time in our little annex part of his house than his own home. I'm not complaining, I love having him to curl up with at night, and of course the amazing sex is a bonus too.

He comes up behind me and wraps his arms around my waist and kisses my neck. "Something smells good," he mumbles, his face buried in my neck.

"It's just a prawn stir fry." I moan as he nips my ear.

"Wasn't talking about the food, Kitten." He smiles, spinning me around to face him.

He crashes his mouth on mine. "I see you've calmed down," he teases.

"I have, but only because I found the perfect present." I smile.

His eyes alight. "Oh yeah?"

I nod "Yup." I turn back around to turn the heat down and stir the vegetables.

"Oh, that reminds me, Mum popped by earlier, she has a full itinerary planned right from three p.m. Christmas eve through to the day after boxing day," Roman states, pulling a beer from the fridge.

"Oh no, we can't do from three p.m. on Christmas eve," I state.

"Why not?" Roman asks.

"Because it's a Christmas tradition that me, the kids and my parents go to the local shelter and serve them Christmas lunch, we are there all day until five. Dad wears his Santa clothes and the kids help and play board games with everyone," I inform him.

He pauses drinking, his bottle in front of his mouth.

"Are you okay?" I ask.

He places down his beer and walks back towards me and kisses me. "You amaze me, each and every day," he says across my lips.

I smile and kiss him back. "It's only volunteering at the shelter, it's not like I'm giving up a kidney." I shrug.

"It's more than you realise. One question, if I lost everything, the house, hotel, the lot, and I had to work in a low paid job, and we had to live back where you lived before, what would you do?" he asks.

I frown in confusion at where this question has come from. "I don't understand what you are saying. What's all this?" I gesture to the house. "Got to do with us?" I answer.

Something crosses Roman's face. "I love you," he blurts. My eyes go wide.

"What?" I whisper.

"I said I love you. You have no idea how much, but I promise I will show you every damn day. Even if I lose everything tomorrow, I will always prove that I am worthy of your love. Because to be loved by you is an honour no man should ever fucking take for granted. Say you love me back, Cora, give me your heart and give me that honour of your love," Roman declares.

Tears fall down my face and I nod. "I love you, Roman, I love you so much, and not for your wealth. I love you in spite of that. I love the man you are—" I don't get to say anymore as Roman's mouth crashes down on mine, kissing me, possessing me. Our hands are frantic, our mouths are desperate with our tongues colliding.

"Mum! What's burning?" is yelled.

We break the kiss, both of us panting, and we both laugh. Roman kisses me briefly before moving the pan containing the burnt stir fry. I touch my lips, swollen from our kiss.

"Kids, get your shoes and coats on, we are going out for dinner!" Roman yells, smiling. He pecks my lips softly.

"Yay!" Betty yells excitedly.

"Tonight, when they are asleep, I am showing you everything I love about you, and I will make sure you are screaming just how much you love me," he says, his voice low and almost threatening.

I bite my lip, loving the sound of that threat.

The kids soon kill the spark in the room and Roman piles them into the car while I grab my coat. I can't help the feeling of elation coursing through me, a feeling I have never felt. This feeling is the stuff of fairy tales, this is what it must feel like to get your happily ever after. Now I know why they sang and skipped with the animals. Now I truly understand their happiness, because I may just start breaking out in song at any moment.

We end up at a Chinese restaurant, kids already stuffing their faces with prawn crackers.

"Hi there, what can I get you?" our waitress asks.

"We will have the share selection for four, please," Roman orders.

"And drinks?" she asks.

"Make mine a vodka, I've had a hell of a day." Betty sighs. We all pause and look at her. She shrugs. "What?" she asks.

"Just four cokes, please," Roman says to the waitress, fighting his laughter.

"Betty, sweetie, you can't have vodka, that's grown up juice. Now why don't you tell me why your day has been so bad." I laugh, kissing the top of her head.

"Suzie Platte was being mean today, she said that I am a stupid stinky head all because Brendon kissed me, which was gross. Boys are gross," she says, poking her tongue out in disgust.

"Sounds like this Brendon needs to be taken aside and taught some manners on how to respect a lady," Roman adds.

I look to him and raise my eyebrow in question. "They are four-year-olds," I point out. "You never played kiss chase or tried to kiss a girl at that age?"

"What I did is not important, no boy is to touch you without your permission, understand Betty? They do, you tell me, and I will deal with them," Roman says seriously.

"You're weird." Betty giggles. "But you make me laugh."

I snort with laughter and kiss his cheek. "I love that you're so overprotective," I whisper.

I sit back and swiftly change the subject. "So, Theo, how's school?" I ask.

The smile drops from his face immediately at the mention of school. I hate that, I hate that school, but I've suggested moving schools and he just wont hear of it.

"Honey, what is it?" I ask. He looks away and doesn't answer.

"Those bullies pick on him every day, they call him names and one said he was a loser junkie just like his dad. What's a junkie?" Betty asks.

"Shut up, Betty," Theo grits.

"Hey, enough. She's only looking out for you. Why didn't you tell me? You know I could sort it out," I offer.

"I don't want you to sort it out, it just makes it worse. I only have one more year and then I am out of that place. Just leave it and let me deal with it," Theo snaps.

I look to Roman who looks pissed. I grab his hand and squeeze. His eyes come to mine and I shake my head in warning not to say anything.

Roman nods. "So, you guys looking forward to Christmas? I have to warn you, my mother has gotten a little over excited at us staying with them. Theo, I talked her out of matching Christmas pyjamas for you and Betty. You owe me." Roman winks and smiles. Theo smiles back and I'm thankful for him changing the subject.

The rest of dinner goes smoothly and without a hitch. When we get into bed later that night, Roman leans over me, caging me in his arms.

"I will sort Theo's issue at his school. Leave it with me," he states.

"But Theo said it will make it worse, I don't want to make it worse for him." I sigh.

Roman strokes my face. "I won't make it worse, I promise," he says, leaning in and kissing my neck. "Now, I believe I made a promise to show you exactly how much I love you," he growls, nipping my ear.

I laugh. "Hmm, I believe you did." I moan.

CHAPTER TWENTY-SEVEN

Roman

I offer to drop the kids at school personally today, there is some shit that needs sorting. I say goodbye to Theo and watch him as he walks in. He keeps his head down as the young lads walk in behind him. I notice the lads—that I'm guessing are the one that give Theo a hard time—walking behind him. It appears it's not just him they target. I watch as they walk in smoking and not one teacher even says anything to them. I pull out my phone and hit call.

"Sir," Simon answers.

"Ring Edward, tell him I want a meeting right now, if he's busy to cancel it, or I will be speaking to his wife," I threaten then disconnect.

Not two minutes later, Simon texts with the information to meet Edward. I smile to myself and drive to meet him.

I walk into the café and see Edward sat waiting for me. I take a seat and immediately he snaps, annoyed. "You need to stop threatening shit with me to get me to meet you," he spits.

"Well keep your dick in your pants then and I wont have to. Lori is a decent woman, she deserves better," I retort.

"What is it you want?" He sighs.

"You need a complete overall at Wentworth school," I state. He laughs and shakes his head.

"And where do you think I can find the money for that from? The budget for the year has already been allocated. I can't just magic money from my arse," he says smirking.

"Well, here's the thing, that school hasn't had any money spent on it for four years. There are dangerous electrics, and you've bypassed inspections for the last two years. I know for a fact that one teacher in that school is a previous felon. Now how would that look that you, head councillor of the district, has been filtering money out of a school, putting children in even more danger by hiring a convict? Let's see, who would eat this shit up? Maybe my friend at the tabloids would like the scoop?" I say, sipping my coffee.

"Are you threatening me?" he asks.

"Yes. But it's also a promise. The truth will always come out, I'm just giving you a little advance warning. Get that school sorted now, I don't care what it takes. Your time is up, and you know that. Maybe try to set things straight? It will look better in front of the judge when your case goes to court," I say, standing and chucking some money down on the table. I turn and leave.

I've know Edward my entire life, he is also a scheming low life. Always using people for what he could get. He bribed his way to being in the council, and now I know that his antics have caught up with him.

I make calls to the press and leave tip offs. I go back to the school and go straight to the headteacher's office. I don't knock, I walk straight in. What's more concerning is that no one has stopped me or questioned why a stranger has just walked in here.

When I walk into the office, the head teacher is asleep, snoring in his chair. I slam the door hard behind me, making him jump.

"What... Who are you?" he asks sleepy and confused.

"I'm your worst fucking nightmare. Now, in about ten minutes maybe, at least three of the national press will be down here, swarming the school, because it's been leaked about what goes on here. Now I suggest that you inform the poor staff that are half decent about what's going to happen and brace yourself, because you are about to be chewed the fuck up and spat back out for allowing what's been going on to happen here," I state. I don't wait for his response, I turn and leave and head back to the hotel.

It didn't take much digging to find out what had been going down. Ever since I met Cora and found out where she lived, I looked into the area and why it wasn't getting the financial injection like the rest of district. Money was being diverted to the already affluent areas, leaving the already poverty stricken areas in even more poverty. As soon as I found this out, I knew exactly who was doing it, and then finding out his cuts included the school. Now I've set the wheels in motion, Theo should start to enjoy school a little more in time, including getting those shitheads expelled.

I return back to the jewellery store to purchase Cora's engagement ring. I'm mad at myself for doubting my decision for listening to Camila. This time I spot the perfect ring, a yellow princess cut diamond, not too big and not too tiny either. The platinum band is woven and twisted around and up like vines to support the diamond. It's elegant, unusual, and perfect for Cora.

I pocket the ring and head back to the hotel, I have one thing to do and I know it's not going to be easy. I sit in the hotel restaurant and wait for them to arrive.

I sip my scotch, the only time I drink scotch is when I'm nervous or stressed.

"Coo-ee!" I look up and see Cora's mother, Margo, waving at me, her father, Felix, on the other hand, doesn't look so happy to be here.

I stand and greet them. "Thanks for coming and meeting with me today," I say, taking a seat. The waiter comes and takes our order and we sit and make small talk while we wait for our food.

"So, let's cut the crap, shall we? Why have you really got us here? You realised it's too much hard work taking on a woman and her two kids? Or have you realised that our type of people aren't really your thing?" Felix asks.

"Felix!" Margo chastises.

"It's fine, Margo," I assure her. I expected this reaction from Felix, he may be a hippy and seem like he doesn't know what he's talking about, but he does. He has an idea as to why I've asked him here today and he's testing me, calling my bluff. He has more of a problem about my wealth than anyone.

"Felix, you know none of that shit bothers me, you know I love your daughter and you know she loves me. Now, even though I think you have an idea as to why I have asked you here today, I am going to say it anyway. I would like your permission for your daughter's hand in marriage. She captured my attention from the moment I met her. I know it hasn't been that long, but I'm a believer of when you know, you know. And I know she is it for me. I know she is all I want and need, and that goes for the kids too. I want to marry your daughter, but I wanted to do things right and ask for your permission first," I state.

"Oh my God, Roman." Margo smiles happily, nodding her head.

"And what if I were to say no?" Felix says, crossing his arms across his chest. I could almost laugh at his attempt at being menacing, especially when he is sat there in a knitted rainbow jumper and his plaited beard dyed purple.

"I would say that it's a shame that I don't have your blessing, but I am going to ask your daughter to marry me regardless. I know what it would mean to her to have your support, I also know what it would do to her if she didn't have it," I point out.

Felix sits there for a moment, assessing me. Margo rolls her eyes and nudges his arm.

"For the love of Buddha, will you stop acting like you're not going to say yes? Of course we know you are. You love Cora and you know that Roman is the best thing apart from the kids that's ever happened to her. Now you're being exactly what you hate, what you protest against. You're being prejudice because of who he is. Remember you're a lover, not a hater, Felix, don't get your back up because this boy has some money in the bank," Margo snaps at him.

Felix sighs and rolls his eyes. "You see what you're getting yourself involved with? She has her mother's temper, she will stand her ground and be incredibly stubborn. You may be from the dark side, but I can tell you are a good'un under it all, just don't try and change my baby girl, keep her as loving and as caring as she always has been. Don't make her into one of these materialistic snobs, that goes for my grandkids too. I don't want her losing sight of where she came from."

I smile "Felix, as you said she's stubborn, I don't think she would let me change her or tell her what to do."

"Good point." Felix smiles.

"So do you have the ring?" Margo asks excitedly.

I nod and pull out the box and place it on the table. Margo practically snatches it.

"Oh, Roman, it's perfect, so beautiful. So unusual," she exclaims.

"Bet that cost you a pretty penny? You know, the miners get pittance for risking their lives mining for diamonds," Felix adds.

"For goodness sake, Felix, not now," Margo warns. "When are you going to ask her?"

"Christmas day. I have a gift I want to give her, so I need to take her off for about an hour and I am going to ask her there. I would appreciate it if you kept this to yourself until we return. Not even my parents know because my mother would not be able to keep it a secret," I say.

"Sure, your secret is safe with us," Felix states.

I release the breath I hadn't realised I had been holding. Less than two weeks today, I will be proposing. There goes those nerves again.

CHAPTER TWENTY-EIGHT

CORA

IT'S BEEN A CRAZY WEEK. FIRSTLY, THEO'S SCHOOL GOT SHUT down early for Christmas as so much leaked into the papers about what was actually going on with the school, including staff and even the local councillor. I asked Roman if he had anything to do with it, and his answer was simply, "All I did was make a couple of calls."

I'm doing some last minute shopping again, I had said to Roman that I had found and bought him his perfect present... It was a lie. I've even resorted to ringing his mother who said that he is the worst person to buy for. I know what music he likes, but he already has their back catalogue and has seen them in concert multiple times, and met them. I mean, I joked about the pound shop but I'm starting to think that will be my only option soon.

I'm wandering aimlessly, looking at shop windows, nothing jumping out at me. It then occurs to me, what's the one thing he doesn't have? A pet. I could buy him a dog. I decide to ring his mum and check, make sure he isn't allergic and that he actually likes dogs.

"Hello?" she answers.

"Hi, Audrey, it's Cora again. Sorry to pester you, but I have an idea on what to get Roman. I just need to make sure I'm making the right decision," I say, crossing my fingers.

"Fabulous, what is it you're thinking of?" she asks.

"I was wondering, what is Roman like about dogs?" I ask.

"Oh my, well, we used to have a family dog years ago, Juke, he was a boxer, absolutely lovely boy. He was Roman's best friend, followed him everywhere, sadly he died at ten from cancer. It broke Roman's heart, we always thought about getting another dog but as Roman was older, he was spending less and less time at home, and with George working away a lot, there was no way I could take care of a boxer all on my own . They are known for their energy and there was a time or two that Juke nearly had me over." Audrey laughs.

"Oh wow, okay, this is great. I think I have found him the perfect gift," I say excitedly.

"I can get in touch with the breeder for you, if you would like?" Audrey offers.

"No, no, that's fine, I'm going to go around the shelters, too many end up there, be nice to offer one of them a second chance," I state.

"You have a big heart," she states.

"Thank you. Right, I must go, I have a week to sort this out if I'm going to get him a dog," I reply, rushing to get to the shelter.

"Goodbye, dear, send me a picture when you find the dog, won't you? I will be sure to get some doggy provisions in for over Christmas. TTFN," she says before disconnecting.

I smile and head to the underground and to the local rescue centre.

When I arrive, the sound of barking and howling fills my ears. I smile as I approach the receptionist.

"Hi, how can I help you?" she asks.

"Hi, I would like to adopt a dog, please." I smile.

"Fantastic, if you could fill out this form with your details, and someone will be in contact to arrange a home visit." She smiles.

"Um, how long does that take?" I ask.

"Oh, you know, couple of weeks maybe." She smiles.

"I need a dog in time for Christmas, it's for my partner. I am happy to fill in a form, do a home check and whatever else you need to do but it's my gift to him," I state.

She bites her bottom lip and leans forward and whispers, "I'm not supposed to tell you this because, well, it goes against protocol, but my advice is don't say it's a gift, it goes against you, and also here is a list of dogs that we have had in the shelter for a long time, that will go in your favour too because we just want to see them settled. Fill that form out and I will get someone to come and show you around the dogs." She smiles.

"Thank you, that's great." I smile and sit down to fill out the forms. I keep hearing this howling and it breaks my heart. I wonder how Roman would feel if I adopted more than one dog?

Once I've filled out the form, I look at the list of long staying dogs. There is one that catches my eye. Good with children, one-year-old and he's a boxer cross Great Dane. His name is Mouse, which made me laugh because he's huge. A guy comes over to me and shakes my hand in greeting.

"Okay, so is there any dog in particular you would like to meet?" he asks.

"Yeah, I would love to meet Mouse." I smile.

He seems surprised by my answer. "Wow, okay. Before we meet him, I have to ask that you have a big enough house and garden for him, he's a big boy and I don't want to waste your time if you live in a flat or something," he states.

I point to the address on the form. His eyes go wide and he smiles, nodding his head. "This way," he gestures.

I follow him down a long corridor and all the dogs jump up at the bars and bark, wagging their tail in greeting. I can't help myself, I stop at each one to say hello because they are all too cute not to.

We finally stop outside a kennel, but I can't see any dog inside it.

"Um, where is he?" I ask.

The guy smiles and unlocks the door and steps in. He waits until I'm inside with him then he locks the gate. "Mouse," he calls and whistles. Then through a large doggy door comes Mouse, bounding through. I smile wide as he runs straight towards me and jumps up, knocking me on the floor. "Mouse, no," the guy says, panicking.

"It's okay." I laugh as he licks my face and tries to sit on my lap even though he's far too big to be a lap dog.

"Hey, baby, you are a beautiful boy." He's got the colouring of a boxer but is the size of a Great Dane. He is slobbering everywhere.

"I will take him." I smile and wheeze as he rests all of his body weight on me. "How much more growing has he got to go?" I ask.

"Oh, he will stop when he's about eighteen months to two years, probably about another twenty pounds or so." He shrugs. "Right, let's book you in for a home check." He smiles.

"Bye, baby, I will come for you soon, okay? I promise," I say, scratching his ear.

We leave him and I hear him howl which breaks my heart. I just want to take him now.

I manage to arrange a booking in four days' time, which is perfect. Now all I need to do is make sure Roman is out of the house.

CHAPTER TWENTY-NINE

Cora

It's Christmas eve and I am close to bursting with excitement. I'm about to go and pick up Mouse from the shelter. I've been secretly buying bits for Mouse, and luckily, Roman's house is so big, he will never find them.

Audrey and George are coming to pick me up, and the presents for Christmas day, pretending we are arranging and dropping them at theirs before meeting Roman and the kids at the homeless shelter.

I grab the black sack of wrapped presents and load them into Audrey and George's car. "I will see you in about two hours at the shelter, you okay picking Mum and Dad up?" I ask.

"Of course." He smiles and kisses me. "Love you, Kitten."

I smile against his lips. "Love you too," I reply before running down the steps to the car.

~

I bring Mouse out to the car and Audrey's eyes go wide. "My God, he is huge! I thought you said he was a boxer cross?" she says.

"He is crossed with a Great Dane." I wince at her reaction.

He pulls me to them, and Audrey and George greet him, his tail wagging happily. "You'll have to sit in the back with him, there is no way he will fit in the boot with the presents," George says.

"No worries," I say, sitting in the back with Mouse, his big droopy jowls hanging on the headrest of the passenger seat, drool running down it.

"I, err, will pay for the cleaning of your car," I offer, cringing at the trail of slobber sliding down the leather.

Audrey squeaks and moves forward, wiping her neck as a blob of drool lands.

"Sorry," I mumble.

It's a fair drive to their house and if I thought Roman's house was extravagant, I was wrong, this home is stately, the grounds are insane and I think there must be about fifteen bedrooms. We settle Mouse in the utility room. Audrey has paid for a trained, professional dog sitter to sit with him whilst we are out. "Be a good boy, Mouse, and we will be back later, okay?" I say, stroking and kissing his head.

We pull up at the homeless shelter. I was surprised that Roman's parents wanted to help too. What I didn't know is while I was seeing to Mouse, Audrey and George were loading up the boot with gifts and bags of clothes, blankets and toiletries.

Ren, the organiser, greets me as we enter. "Um, I see a lot has changed since last year." She smiles.

"Um, yeah." I shrug, smiling.

"Where do you want these?" Audrey asks.

"Um, what is it?" Ren asks.

"Presents, clothes and toiletries, etc." Audrey waves.

"Wow, thank you, um, just out back would be great, thank you." She smiles.

"Right, I guess I will get chopping." I smile and head to the kitchen where Theo and Betty are peeling potatoes... Well, Betty is peeling a single potato, it takes her a while. Roman comes up behind me and kisses me.

"Your parents are amazing," I tell him.

"Yeah, they are pretty good. What do you need me to do?" he asks.

"Can you help put up the decorations?" I ask.

"Sure thing," he says, kissing my neck.

People start arriving and I send the kids out of the kitchen to set the tables. We put the food into serving dishes. I see a couple of my old neighbours arrive. I always knew they struggled but I guess they have fallen on even harder times.

"Sarah? What happened? Are you okay?" I ask.

She looks embarrassed, tired and drawn out. "Aron lost his job and didn't tell me. He wasn't paying the bills. We've been evicted and are currently being housed at a local B & B by the council until accommodation becomes available, but because of the debt it's making it difficult. I feel Roman squeeze my neck, and I look up at him, sadness in my eyes.

"Um, Sarah, I'm so sorry," I say, hugging her. She smiles sadly and shrugs. Her kids hide behind her, looking dirty and pale.

"Go and get some food, and we have gifts this year, so the kids can get something too." I smile.

She smiles and brings her arms around her kids and ushers them forward. Her daughter is in Theo's year and I catch Theo looking at her with sadness in his eyes.

I turn to Roman. "I have to run to the shop for a second and grab some more gravy. Keep an eye on the kids, okay?" I say, grabbing my coat.

"I can go for you," he offers.

"No, no, it's okay," I say, grabbing my purse and running out the door. I run to the bank as they are just about to close and quickly run to the desk.

"Hi, can I take out all but one hundred pounds from my account, please?" I ask.

"Okay, so that means you would like to withdraw one thousand two hundred pounds. Is that correct?" she asks, and I nod.

I had been saving the wages from the last couple of pay packets, the only money I have spent is on Christmas presents.

I show her my ID and take the money. I run next door to the department store and grab toys for her youngest and a make-up set for her eldest. I run back to the shelter and run straight out the back and make quick work of wrapping them, doing the best I can.

I find Sarah and pull her to one side. I hand her the envelope, and she frowns then opens it. Her eyes bulge and her mouth drops.

"Cora, what is this?" she asks gobsmacked.

"It's just under one thousand two hundred pounds. I just bought the kids a little something to open tomorrow morning. I want you to have it, use it to help get yourself somewhere. Please. It's my Christmas gift to you." I smile.

Tears fill her eyes and her hands shake. "I can't... I can't take this from you, what are you going to do for money?" she asks.

"I have made sure we have enough for food until I get paid again. Honestly, it's fine, this is just money I was saving. I can save it up again." I smile.

She pulls me into a tight hug, sobbing. "It's okay, I will do everything I can to help you and the kids out, okay? You're not alone, Sarah," I say, trying to offer her some comfort.

"Sarah, tonight and over Christmas, you shall be staying at my hotel, free of charge, including no charge for all meals. After Christmas, we shall talk and see about work for you, and I know a few people, we can try and sort you somewhere to live in the new year," Roman says from beside us, making us both jump. I hadn't realised he had been listening the entire time, consumed in Sarah's sadness and in trying to help her.

Sarah wipes her eyes. "What? Are you serious?" she asks.

"Yes, of course, I'm not sure what more we can do about presents for the kids as all the shops are now shut, but at least I can offer you warmth, comfort and food over the festive period," Roman states, putting his arm around me. I don't think it's possible for me to love this man more than I do right now.

"Thank you, thank you so much," Sarah sobs.

"Our pleasure. Once you have finished here, I will drive you and your children back to the hotel and show you to your accommodation and let the staff know of your stay." He smiles.

"Go tell the kids, and merry Christmas, Sarah," I say, smiling.

"Merry Christmas and thank you again, really, I can't even begin to tell you what this means." She smiles.

We watch as she walks over to tell the kids. I cuddle into Roman and watch as their surprised faces light up. I sniffle back my tears. Roman takes my chin and lifts it, so I'm looking at him.

"Never in my life have I ever met someone so selfless, so caring and so giving. You have just given away nearly all of your hard-earned money because she needed it," he says.

"I don't need it." I shrug.

"You have no idea what your act of kindness has done for them, for her. I meant what I said, it is a true fucking honour to have your love, and to have your heart. An honour I gladly accept, an honour I don't ever plan on giving up," Roman whispers across my lips before kissing me.

"Excuse me, love birds! But it's time for presents!" Audrey yells.

I laugh as does Roman.

I help hand out the presents and I'm shocked and surprised at Audrey and George's generosity. New trainers and food vouchers for supermarkets, vouchers for takeaways, all things that are useful and vital to them. On top of all that, they bring out boxes of brand-new coats, blankets, and sleeping bags. Even single-sleeping pop-up tents.

"Your parents have bought so much," I say, shocked. Roman puts his arm around me.

"My parents will never do things by halves, it's all or nothing." He smiles.

"Well, I've got to hand it to you rich folk, you sure do know how to be charitable, I didn't know you had it in you," Dad adds.

"Dad," I say in a warning tone.

He holds his hands up. "Okay, I'm sorry, didn't mean it out of line, just saying it's good to see. It's nice to see people that can offer that kind of help doing it for a change." He smiles. I shake my head and roll my eyes.

"Right, I'm going to run Sarah and her kids back to the hotel, I will be back within the hour, okay?" Roman asks.

"Sure, we still need to clean up anyway," I say, kissing him.

I hug Sarah and the kids goodbye then get to work clearing up and making flasks of tea and coffee for them to take with them.

"Thanks again, sweetheart, you got a good one there. Don't let him go, will you?" Phillip, one of the homeless guys, says as he leaves.

"Oh, believe me, I won't be ever letting him go," I say honestly.

CHAPTER THIRTY

Cora

Once we all pile back to Audrey and George's house, we are shown to our rooms. Mum and Dad's jaws practically hit the floor at the place. Betty thinks we are in a castle and Theo is happy but obviously containing it and showing that excitement in the only way teenagers know how.

We all sit down to eat a delicious stew that Audrey had made and left cooking all day while we were out.

"Now, Felix, I know you're a very conscientious person when it comes to people rights and environment, so I thought you should know that none of our staff here work over Christmas, I do all the cooking and the cleaning. Also, all food here is sourced locally from farmers and local fruit and veg shop, so the only food you will be eating over this holiday period has been sourced from small and direct providers." Audrey smiles.

"Well, I appreciate that, and I thank you for supporting the smaller businesses, I know they need it." Dad smiles.

There's a loud bark and everyone freezes. "Do you have a dog?" Mum asks.

Audrey's eyes come to me. "Um, no," she answers.

"Mum?" Roman queries, giving her a look.

I stand and hold out my hand to Roman and he takes it but with a quizzical look on his face. "Come with me," I say as we walk.

I stop outside the door and turn to Roman. "So, you know I said I had gotten you the perfect gift?"

"Yes," he answers.

"Well, I lied. I had gotten you some gifts but they weren't perfect, so I tried to think of everything and, well, I had this one idea and I rang your mum who then told me the story about your dog, Juke. I decided it would be a great gift if I could give you that again, that bond that you only get from having a dog," I say nervously, fiddling with my hands.

"You got me a puppy?" he asks, his face expressionless.

"Um, well, he's a rescue dog, he is still a puppy but he's one year old. And his name is Mouse," I say as I open the door. Mouse barks and jumps full speed at Roman, knocking him to the ground and proceeds to start licking him all over his face.

"Shit. I'm sorry," I say, trying to pull Mouse off Roman.

Roman gets up and wipes his face and brushes himself down. He looks up at me and then the dog, and slowly a smile spread across his face." I can't believe you got me a dog." He laughs and starts to pat and stroke Mouse.

I sigh, relieved that he isn't disappointed at my gift. He stands and kisses me. I break away and scrunch up my face, laughing. "Eww, dog breath," I say, wiping my mouth.

"Yeah, Mouse got a little to up close and personal there." Roman laughs. "Thank you, I love him, even if he will be the size of a horse."

"Come on, let's introduce him to the kids." I beam, relieved that he is happy about Mouse.

It's safe to say that the kids love Mouse. Betty has already attempted to dress the poor dog up in a tutu, and Theo said he wanted to walk him to school so he would scare off all the bullies.

Audrey pulls out a folder and claps her hands. "Everyone, if you could please put on your coats, scarfs hats and then follow me." She claps.

We all put on our matching Christmas hats and scarfs that she provided, and we follow her outside, under strict instructions to leave Mouse inside.

As soon as we step outside, my jaw hits the floor. Fairy lights light up every single tree like a pathway.

"Wow!" Betty breathes.

"That is so cool," Theo adds.

"How much electricity is that using?" My dad grumbles.

"We have hired an environmentally friendly generator, Felix, and every bulb is an energy saving bulb," Audrey yells over her shoulder. "This way!"

We laugh and Mum clips Dad over the head as we follow Audrey.

Up ahead looks like a large barn. "Oh Christ," Roman mutters under his breath. Audrey stops and turns to us.

"Now, can I ask that you keep your voices low and be respectful to the animals. Betty, I am very lucky to be good friends with a certain someone who has dropped by quickly just to see us." Audrey winks. I look down at Betty whose eyes are wide with wonder.

Audrey opens the door and there inside is a small sleigh with two reindeers feeding off some hay, and there, sat in the sleigh, is Father Christmas.

"Oh my God," I whisper.

"Ho-ho-ho! Merry Christmas. Betty, come tell me what it is you want for Christmas just so I can make sure the elves have it just right," Father Christmas greets.

"Mummy! It's Father Christmas!" she whisper shouts.

"I know, baby, go speak to him, quickly, before he has to leave," I whisper in her ear.

She practically jumps from my arms and onto the sleigh. She leans forward and whispers in his ear what it is she wants.

I look to Theo, who obviously knows this is all fake, but the awe in his face is there, the happiness shining through. I wrap my arm around him and squeeze and kiss him on the cheek. "Eww, Mum," he mutters.

"Oh shush, it's Christmas, I'm allowed." I wink.

"Right, all together for a photo," Audrey organises.

We all stand where told and a professional photographer takes our picture. I'm not sure where she sprung him from but I'm starting to think it's possible that Audrey is Father Christmas with the amount of things she keeps whipping up.

Once we've said goodbye to Father Christmas, Audrey ushers us up to the top of the patio. She pulls out a small walkie talkie that I didn't even realise she had.

"Ho-ho-ho, stockings are in place. Over," she mutters into it.

With that, Betty squeals excitedly. "Look!" she says, pointing to the sky. We all look up and see what appears to be Father Christmas and his sleigh flying off from the Barn, followed by some fireworks. I don't know how she did it, but it even blew the adults away. "That was amazing, Audrey," I compliment.

She smiles. "It was nothing, now let's all go settle down with some hot cocoa in our pyjamas by the fire."

Dad goes to speak, but Audrey beats him to it. "It's fair trade cocoa, Felix, and naturally fallen logs for the fire. No trees were harmed," she says over her shoulder as we step inside.

Mum and I burst out laughing. "You've met your match there, darling," Mum says, patting his face.

Once we've all had cocoa—well, the adults got alcoholic cocoa—I put Betty to bed.

"Now, you need to get to sleep, okay? Because otherwise Father Christmas won't bring your presents," I say, kissing her head and tucking her in.

"I only wished for one present," She says, yawning.

"Oh? You did?" I say softly as her eyes start closing.

"Yeah, I asked him to make us a real family. So we can stay this happy forever," she says as she falls asleep.

My heart lurches and tears sting my eyes. I softly kiss her head again.

"Goodnight, my sweet baby girl," I whisper.

I smile to myself because if I had gotten to ask Father Christmas for one thing, it would have been the same.

To forever keep this happiness in their lives.

CHAPTER THIRTY-ONE

Cora

"Mummy! Mummy! It's Christmas!" Betty screams, running into our room.

Roman groans and buries his face in the back of my neck.

"Wake up! Wake up, he's been! Father Christmas has been!" Betty screams, bouncing on our bed. I laugh and nudge Roman, pulling Betty into my arms and kissing her.

"What time is it?" I yawn.

"It's seven-thirty," Roman says, stretching.

"Wow, you slept in this year, good girl," I say, smiling.

"Come on, Mummy, come on, Roman!" she begs.

"God, how can I ever say no to her?" Roman says getting up.

"You can't, she wont let you." I laugh.

I get up and put on a robe, Roman pulls me into his arms and kisses me. "Merry Christmas, Kitten," he says across my lips.

"Merry Christmas." I smile in return.

"Come on, stop kissing, we need to wake everyone up!" Betty

yells then runs off down the halls, knocking on everyone's doors and screaming "It's Christmas" at the top of her lungs.

Once everyone is downstairs, the adults all sit round with their coffees whilst Audrey hands out the presents from under the tree. Mouse is happily led in front of the fire, chewing on a giant bone I got him for Christmas. The kids are loving opening so many presents, they've never had a Christmas like it. I've never been so spoilt either, with perfume, clothes and pamper vouchers.

"Oh yes!" my dad says happily, holding up a jumper I got him made from recycled wool, even the paper it's wrapped in is all recycled. "This will be great to wear for the Workers Against Neglected Kids," he says, smiling.

"Jesus, Dad, W.A.N.K, really?" I say, laughing.

"Hold up a minute, were you at the nineteen-eighty-seven protest in Trafalgar Square?" George asks Dad.

"I've been to a lot of protests, you're going to have to be more specific than that," Dad answers.

"The protest for Pupils Education Artistic Diversity Organisation," George says.

Dad claps. "Yes! Were you there?!"

"Hold up," I say, hand up, pausing them. "You both attended a protest for pupils education for artistic diversity organisation, am I right?" I ask.

"Yes." They both nod.

"P.E.A.D.O," I spell out and they both pause for a moment.

"Ah," Dad says.

I shake my head. "You need to look at what the charities and organisations spell out before you start protesting for them."

"Always stand up against the big guy, always stand up for the little people," George says with his fist in the air.

"Don't be rude, the nicer way you're supposed to say it is, tall or larger than Everest and Dwarves." Betty tuts at them, rolling her eyes.

George looks to me. "She's been learning about feelings and political correctness at school," I inform him.

"Ah, I see, you mean larger than average." He smiles.

"That's what I said, larger than Everest." She shrugs.

I laugh and kiss her head.

We all get showered and dressed and then back to the tree for the remainder of the presents which were all bought by Audrey and George, they really have gone over the top with gifts.

I'm thankful Audrey hasn't brought us matching Christmas jumpers to wear. I feel Roman come up behind me and wrap his arms around my waist.

"Go get your coat and shoes on, I'm taking you somewhere," he whispers in my ear.

I look at him confused. "Go on," he orders, winking and smacking my behind.

I do as he's asked and go and put on my coat and shoes. He takes my hand and pulls me out of the door to his car. "What about the kids?" I ask.

"They will be fine," he says, starting the car up.

"Here, put this on." He hands me a black scarf. I frown and wrap it around my neck. "No, blindfold yourself." He laughs.

"I'm sorry, but you should have said." I laugh and tie it around the back of my head. "Is this some kind of new kink you're into? Because I have to say, it's a little out there, especially in public," I mock.

"Ha-ha, make sure you can't see anything, I don't want you spoiling your present," he orders.

"But you've already given me my present," I state, holding out my arm and the beautiful bracelet that is on my wrist.

"Just wait," he says. I huff and tap my fingers on my legs anxiously.

I feel the car stop. "Are we there?" I ask.

He doesn't say anything, he just gets out of the car and opens my door, helping me out. "I take that as a yes," I add.

"Watch your step." He directs me as I stumble and grip hold of him tightly. "Ah, bugger it," he says, chucking me over his shoulder in a fireman's lift. I scream and he smacks my arse, making me laugh.

"Shh, it's easier this way, I want to show you your gift before dark," he states.

I hear him unlock something and step inside, the smell of fresh paint and wood fills the air. He puts me down on my feet. "Merry Christmas, beautiful," he says before removing the blindfold. It takes a moment for my eyes to adjust to crisp white walls and bright spotlights.

I turn on the spot. "What is this place?" I ask. It's then that my eyes land on the stack of blank canvases, the shelves filled with every different type of brush. I walk to a unit and open the cupboard, it's filled with every different type of paint. Pencils, pastels, charcoal, you name it, it's there. My eyes start filling with tears. "Is this what I think it is?" I whisper.

"What do you think it is?" he replies back.

"You bought me my own art studio?" I question. I sniff and turn around to face him. He's stood there, smiling, his hands in his pockets.

"I didn't buy you your own art studio, I had them build you your own art studio," he says and nods his head towards the window.

I walk to the glass patio door and look out... there is the garden and Roman's house. "You said it was an office space," I mutter.

I turn back to face him, tears falling freely now, and when I see him, he is on one knee, holding out a small box with a ring inside it. I gasp.

"Cora, I've loved you from the moment I met you. Your fiery and smart mouth, your ability to care for anyone from any walk of life. Cora, you floor me with your kind and caring heart, your beauty, your body. There isn't anyone else I would choose to spend the rest of my life with. Marry me, Cora? Let me spend my life making you smile, laugh, and of course give you multiple orgasms." He winks.

I laugh and wipe my tears. "So romantic," I tease.

"Let me be the one to look after you, to care for you, to love you. Say you'll marry me?" he asks.

I bite my lip and nod. "Yes. Yes, I will marry you," I sob.

He slides the beautiful ring onto my finger then crashes his mouth down on mine. "I promise you will never have to worry about anything ever again," Roman says in-between kisses. "Fuck, I love you so much." He starts lifting up my dress and pulls down my tights and panties, chucking them across the room along with my boots. I make quick work of unbuttoning his jeans and sliding them down his thighs.

"Wrap your legs around me," he pants. I jump and wrap my legs around him, his hands go under my behind, he leans me against the glass patio doors and positions his cock at my entrance.

"Tell me you love me," he orders.

I smile, my fingers running through the hair at the back of his neck. "I love you, Roman, more than you'll ever know," I declare, the last word dying in my throat as Roman surges inside me.

"Dig those claws in, Kitten, and hold tight," he grits through his teeth. I grip his shoulders tight, my nails digging in. He thrusts up inside me, fucking me hard and fast pressed up against the cold glass. I moan, take his mouth and nip at his bottom lip, making him growl deep in his throat.

"Fuck," he groans. He continues to drive up into me, my thighs gripped tightly around him. His grip tightens on my behind as he relentlessly fucks me. I feel my walls clamp around him as my orgasm hits.

"Yes, fuck, Roman!" I cry out as my orgasm ripples through my body, he thrusts harder and his grip tightens as he buries himself deep inside me as he climaxes.

We are both panting, and Roman kisses along my neck and up to my lips.

"It's a good job your garden is so private right now." I smile.

He smiles across my lips. "I'm not done with you yet. We have over an hour left, and I plan on celebrating our engagement properly and christening every fuckable surface in this studio. You know, to give you inspiration when you come in here to paint." Roman winks and bites my lip playfully.

There is one thing I have learnt when it comes to Roman, what he says is his word, and boy am I happy about that.

CHAPTER THIRTY-TWO

Roman

I hold Cora's hand on the drive back to my parents, not wanting to let her go. As soon as we step foot into my parents' house, I know our little bubble of "just us" will be broken, and I'm trying to keep hold of that for as long as I can. I have no doubt that my mother will have a wedding planner on speed dial, Christmas or not, she will be setting things up, she just can't help herself.

I park up and switch off the engine. Cora goes to get out of the car, but I grip her hand tighter in mine. She turns to me. "What are you doing? Come on, my parents and the kids are all going to want to know." She smiles.

"I know, I just want to enjoy having just you for a moment longer, because as soon as we tell them, our mother's will be taking over and organising everything. Just give me this moment, peace and quiet, and your mouth," I state.

She rolls her eyes and leans in, kissing me. "Fuck, I love you," I whisper across her lips.

She smiles. "Well, Mr Pompous Arse is swearing, you must be

serious. I fucking love you too. Now, come on, I want to speak to the kids first before we tell the over excitable ladies." She winks and gets out of the car. I sigh and follow her.

I grab her hand in mine to hide the engagement ring. Those women are like vultures and would soon be circling us if they spotted it.

"Theo, Betty, come here a second, your mum and I need to talk to you," I call them over.

Betty looks up and stops herself putting her pink fluffy crown on Mouse. She sighs and pats his head and then comes running over. Theo groans and sighs, following her.

"What is it?" Theo asks.

Cora looks to me and smiles nervously. "So, Roman gave me a special Christmas gift. He built me my very own studio in his back garden," Cora states, pausing.

"That's pretty cool." Theo smiles.

"Wicked! I know loads of stuff I want to paint." Betty claps.

"There's more..." Cora bites her lip. "Roman proposed. He asked me to marry him, and I said yes," she says nervously.

The kids don't react, they just stand there and stare at Cora. "If you guys aren't okay with it then that's okay, just tell me and Roman and I will postpone it. Roman and I want you guys to be happy too," she says.

"Do we call him daddy now?" Betty asks.

"No, sweetie, you don't have to call him daddy," Cora assures. "Theo?" Cora asks.

Theo looks at her, then to me, and he smiles. "You make Mum happy, you're a good guy, so I'm happy." He shrugs.

"Oh, baby." Cora sniffles as she throws her arms around him.

"Betty?" Cora asks, wiping her tears.

"Well, I like Roman, and I like his house, and now I like his dog. And, Mummy, Theo is right, you smile a lot now. And you do that funny laugh where you make a pig noise. You didn't do that before. I don't like it," Betty says with a frown. Then she giggles. "I love it! It's a yes from me." She giggles. Cora wraps her arms around her, showering her with kisses.

"I think we need to limit the amount of time she watches Britain's Got Talent," I add.

"What's the matter? Why are you crying, dear?" my mum asks, concerned.

Hearing the word crying has Cora's parents and my dad walking over to see what the commotion is about. I look down at Cora who gives me a nod.

"Well, I took Cora to show her her Christmas present, which she loved. While we were there, I took the opportunity to get down on one knee and propose to her." I smile.

"I said yes!" Cora beams, showing her hand. My mum and her mum both let out a scream that I swear has set off the neighbourhoods dogs, even Mouse starts barking.

Dad walks over and pulls me in for a hug. "You did good, son. Proud of you, she is lovely," he says, slapping me on the back.

"Welcome to the family, son." Felix smiles and shakes my hand.

Margo showers my face with kisses and mum hugs me so tight I'm afraid I may pass out from lack of oxygen. "Alright, Mum, easy," I wheeze.

"I'm sorry." She sniffs. "It just, you're my baby boy and you're getting married to the most wonderful girl, and I'm so happy for you, and now I have grandchildren to spoil and it's just all so perfect," she blubbers.

"Oh Christ, alright, Mum, just calm down." I sigh.

"Calm down? Oh no, this calls for a celebration! George, go and fetch my planner, we are setting a date for the engagement party! I will call Phuc and he can organise and make it a spectacular event!" Mum claps excitedly.

"Sorry, who is Fuck?" I ask.

"It Ph-u-c, he's Japanese, and an absolute genius!" Mum beams.

"Oh Fuck." Cora sighs.

"Exactly! See? Even Cora knows him, he is world famous." Mum walks away almost skipping as she does.

"No I, erm, I didn't mean..." Cora tries to explain.

I pull her into my arms. "I wouldn't worry, whoever this guy is, if you don't like him or want to organise anything, just tell her, I will back you up. We can take her on, two against one." I wink. Cora laughs and I kiss her perfect mouth.

∽

AFTER I GOT MUM TO CALM DOWN AND NOT CALL THIS PARTY planner Phuc on Christmas day, she made a toast and got Dad to open a bottle of champagne she had been saving since I was born, for this very day. We all sit around the dinner table, ready to eat our food when Mum clinks her glass.

"I would like to make a toast to the happy couple. I think I speak for all when I say I couldn't have asked for a better Christmas present than getting new family members. To the future bride and groom, Cora and Roman," Mum toasts.

"Cora and Roman," our parents all toast.

"Right, everybody, let's tuck in, I don't want your food getting cold." Mum smiles happily.

"Wait!" Betty yells.

"What's the matter, sweetheart?" Cora asks.

"We haven't said grace," Betty chastises.

"But we are not religious," Cora points out.

"We need to do it. My teacher at school said it's good manners," she whines.

"Okay, okay. You want to say grace then carry on," Cora relents.

Betty puts her palms together and squeezes her eyes shut. "Lettuce pray..." she pauses.

We all choke down our laughter and let her continue.

"We thank you, Lord baby Jesus, for our presents, our food and Mouse. Thank you for making Mummy happy and giving us Roman. He's a nice guy, even though sometimes he makes Mummy cry. He's still a good guy. Amen," she says and starts eating her dinner.

I frown and look at Cora in question as to when I have ever made her cry.

She shrugs and shakes her head. "Betty, baby, Roman has never made me cry," Cora informs her.

"Yes he has, I heard you crying out and saying please, and oh God," she says, chomping on a carrot without a care in the world, not knowing that she's just shared with everyone at the table that's she's heard us having sex. Cora's face turns beet red and she avoids looking anyone in the eye. I cough on my food as the entire table has gone silent.

"I will just go and put some music on, shall I?" Mum says as she stands, putting on some Christmas music in the background.

After a while, conversation starts back up and the embarrassment wears off for Cora. "Don't worry, dear, you did the same to us when you were her age. Didn't she, Felix?" Margo chuckles.

"Yes, that went down well with your dad, the vicar." He snorts.

"Err, can we just drop that conversation? Thanks, it's bad enough hearing about my own mum, let alone my grandparents. I mean, eww, so gross." Theo gags.

We finish dinner and all sit around the large open fire. Mum eventually calmed down about engagement party planning when I gave her a look. And right now, looking around, Cora cuddled into me, the kids drinking hot chocolate and playing boards games on the rug with Mum, Dad, Felix and Margo, I know I'm complete. I know that what Betty said in her prayer was wrong earlier, it's me that should be thanking God for bringing Cora into my life. I don't know what I have done to deserve her, but I will fucking make sure that I cherish her every damn day.

CHAPTER THIRTY-THREE

Cora

"You're just going to have to tell him, babes, just rip that plaster off and tell him," Sylvia says, holding up the fourth dress she has picked up.

The kids are back at school after the Christmas holidays, and I promised to go shopping with Sylvia for what little would be left in the January sales.

"It's not that easy, I can't just say, 'Oh, Roman, by the way, I'm still technically married. Whoops, sorry, my bad.' I mean, come on, Sylvia!" I rant.

"Look, Roman is loaded, he can get you a top solicitor, and I bet because it's been so long since you've actually separated, there will be nothing to it. Hell, you're probably already divorced, just not by law, you need that little bit of paper to make it all legal and shit." She shrugs, taking her top off in the middle of the shop and trying the dress on. People look over to her, staring at this random woman, stood in her bra in the middle of the shop, trying dresses on. I'm just thankful she isn't taking her trousers off too.

"I don't know, I mean, I know we've been separated for over three years now, but I don't think that's grounds for automatic divorce, plus there's the small fact that I have no idea where Kyle is. I mean, he could be anywhere right now." I sigh.

"So tell Roman and hire a private eye or something. You know, go all Dog the Bounty Hunter on his arse." She pauses. "Oh, do you reckon he could hire Dog the Bounty Hunter? Because I have a thing for him, I think it's the mullet and the bad boy look. Mind you, his sons would totally get it too." Sylvia swoons.

"What the hell are you on? I'm talking about my mess of a life and you're there, getting off on—I'm pretty sure—an OAP with a mullet, and his kids. Focus, Sylvia, focus!" I clap in her face.

She sighs. "Fine, serious face on. Let me think for a minute." She pauses, tapping her finger on her chin. "Got it, give me your phone a minute," she states, holding out her hand.

I give it to her. "What's your idea?" I ask as she types away on my phone.

"Hang on... a... minute... there, all done," she says, handing me back my phone.

"What?" I ask, looking at my phone. It starts ringing and I see Roman's caller ID flash up. "What did you do?" I hiss.

"I told him, you're welcome." She smiles and walks off, looking through the rest of the shop.

I sigh and answer the phone. "So you text me that and then don't answer your phone?" he asks.

"I've answered it now." I sigh.

"It's not really something you just text, it's something we should talk about," he states.

"I know, I know, I'm sorry, I just didn't know how to tell you, it's not something you can just blurt out," I point out.

"This is true, it caught me off guard a little, and I think we need to be careful how we handle this, but if it's something you want then we can try," Roman says down the phone.

"Of course I want this, it's only you I want. I really didn't want to tell you like that." I sigh, sitting down.

"I will give you anything you want, you know that, and we can try tonight, if you like? I can get some lube after work," Roman says casually.

"What?" I ask.

"Lube, I can always pick some up," he answers back.

"Why would we need lube for filing for divorce?" I ask confused.

"You're still married to Kyle?" he asks in disbelief.

"Yeah, Sylvia grabbed my phone and text you. Hold up, what did she text you?" I ask, standing and looking around for her, ready to kill her.

"Well then, Sylvia text me pretending to be you saying, and I quote, 'I want your big dick in my tiny arsehole.' That is the message I got," he states.

"I'm going to kill her," I grit through my teeth, my eyes landing on her from across the shop. I signal I'm going to kill her.

"Cora," Roman calls my name, bringing my attention back to our conversation.

"Yeah," I respond.

"We need to talk. When you're done, come by the hotel," he says sounding pissed and disconnects.

"Shit!" I shout loudly causing everyone to look at me. Sylvia comes over to me, looking sheepish.

"What happened?" she asks, biting her lip.

"He said to stop by the hotel so we can talk. Why did you do that? He's pissed off and it's just made it all one big mess." I sigh.

"Sorry, babes... Look, as my way of apologising, let me take you for a couple of cocktails, give you that Dutch courage you need to face the music," she offers, and linking her arm with mine, she leads the way to the bar.

∼

"So, who wants another mojito?!" Sylvia sings, swaying on her stool.

"Overrr here!" I giggle, holding my glass up in the air.

"So, remember to stand up for yourself, you have nothing to be scared of, it's normal for most people to not be divorced yet. Totally acceptable," Sylvia states, pouring me another mojito from the jug she bought.

"Why am I slur-uring and you... are... not," I say, stumbling over my words.

"Because I am a hardcore drinker and you, my dear, are a lightweight!" she says, smiling. "Give me your phone, I will ring Roman and tell him to come pick you up," she says, holding out her hand.

"Nuh-uh," I say, shaking my head. "I gave you my phone last time and yooou got me in this mess!" I slur.

"Just give me your damn phone, I want to ring my mother," she says.

"O-kay, here you go." I smile, handing her my phone.

"Jesus, no more drinks for you. You are not safe when inebriated," she says whilst putting the phone to her ear.

A little while later, and after my fourth mojito, I am happily swaying in my chair, singing along to Elton John playing over the bar speakers.

"Rocket man!" I sing.

"Shit, how many drinks did you give her?" I hear a deep voice ask.

I lean back over my chair, hanging upside down. "Hey! Roman! Baby! I is having a little drinkie with her!" I laugh, pointing. My chair wobbles from me leaning back and I fall, landing on the floor with a thud.

"Ouch!" I yell.

"Christ, come on, let's get you home and to bed, before the kids come home from school and see you like this. Give you a chance to sober up." He sighs, helping me up from the floor. I wrap my arm over his shoulder and smile at him.

"I really love you, like more than pizza." I giggle.

Roman smiles and shakes his head. "Come on pisshead, let's get you home," he says, leading me to the car.

I fall asleep in the car and stir when Roman lifts me out of the car and lays me in bed. I groan and curl into my pillow, snuggling in. I feel Roman kiss my temple before I completely black out again.

CHAPTER THIRTY-FOUR

Cora

I STIR AND MOAN AS MY HEAD FEELS LIKE I HAVE A HERD OF elephants dancing on it.

"There's water and pain killers on the side for you," I hear Roman say.

I sit up and drink the water and take the pain killers. Roman is sat in the chair across the room, his shirt sleeves rolled up and his top few buttons undone. He looks pissed off, sat there with his drink of scotch, the room is in darkness apart from the soft glow of the lamp by Roman.

"The kids," I panic.

"Mum and Dad have them for the night. I told them you're unwell," he states firmly.

I fiddle with the stitching on the bed, biting my bottom lip. " You're mad at me," I state.

"No, I'm disappointed," he answers.

"Oh, man, that's so much worse." I sigh.

"Why couldn't you tell me? Why did it take a text from Sylvia to get you to tell me? We've been engaged over a week. The fact that your still legally fucking married is something that generally comes out when you accept a proposal," he snaps.

I feel my chin wobble and I bite my lip harder to stop myself from crying. He's right of course, I know he is. "You're right, I'm sorry. I didn't even think about it at the time and then I didn't want to ruin the moment. I never had the money for divorce and neither did Kyle, it never mattered before because I didn't honestly think I would ever meet someone. I will book an appointment first thing Monday and arrange to get the divorce put through," I apologise.

Roman doesn't say anything, he downs the last of his whiskey and places the glass on the table. He stands, his jaw tenses, and his eyes burn into mine. He walks across to the foot of the bed, his hands in his pockets, just stood there, not saying a word. I crawl across the bed to him and kneel up in front of him. My hands glide slowly up his stomach, chest and up around to the back of his neck.

"I'm sorry I didn't tell you sooner. I want you. I want to marry you. I promise I won't keep anything from you again," I say softly. I stroke my thumb across his bottom lip.

"I'm not mad at you still being married, I'm pissed that you felt that you couldn't tell me. You never have to worry about telling me anything, ever," he assures.

I lean up and kiss him. His tongue sweeps against mine and I moan. "How's your head?" he asks between kisses.

"Totally fine," I breathe. Roman smiles and steps back. I go to protest, but I stop myself when he starts unbuttoning his trousers.

I watch as he undresses himself in front of me until he's stood there completely naked, my eyes automatically landing on his thick, hard cock. He wraps his fist around it and strokes himself. "Take your clothes off," he orders, his voice deep and raspy.

I don't waste time, I remove all my clothes with lightening speed. Roman smirks at me. "Get on all fours, facing me," he orders. I do as he asks, feeling my arousal grow as I watch him. He walks towards me and stops just in front of me, his cock just an inch from my face. I lick my lips, wanting to taste him.

"Do you want my cock in your mouth?" he asks, continuing to stroke it.

I nod.

"Say it," he orders. "Tell me what you want."

"I want your cock in my mouth, I want to lick and suck it until you come. Then I will swallow every last drop you give me," I breathe.

His eyes darken and he lets out a low growl. He grabs the back of my head and practically thrusts his cock into my mouth. I moan and take everything he gives me. I suck, my tongue swirling around the tip. His grip tightens on my hair as I take him deeper, his hips thrusting, fucking my mouth.

"Fuck, I'm going to come, baby," he groans.

I moan and suck harder. "Shit." He growls as he comes, and I swallow every drop.

I kneel up and he runs his thumb across my bottom lip and places it in my mouth. I suck, my eyes fixated on him. He withdraws his thumb and grazes his fingertips slowly down my body, between my breasts, and continues down between my thighs. I gasp as he ever-so-softly runs his finger along my centre.

"I feel how wet you are, how turned on you are from having my cock in your mouth. Tell me, do you want this?" he says as his plunges two fingers inside me, curling them around and hitting my G-spot. I moan and grip onto his shoulders.

"Or do you want this?" he whispers in my ear as his thumb circles my clit. My nails dig into his shoulders. "Or maybe, you want both those things?" he says, biting my neck, moving both his fingers inside me and his thumb on my clit. It's too much, my orgasm is building quickly. I cry out and my nails dig in harder, so hard I'm surprised I don't draw blood.

With his other hand, he cups my breast, pinching and rolling my nipple between his fingers. That's it, my climax hits, it hits me so hard my body jolts and I arch my back as the pleasure takes hold of me.

"Fuck, Roman," I cry out, but he doesn't ease up, he continues moving his fingers over and over.

"You're going to come for me again, I can feel you building already," he whispers in my ear. I whimper as I feel my walls begin to tighten again.

"Yes, oh God," I moan. With quick movement, Roman removes his hand and flips me on my back and slams himself inside of me. I scream out, the feeling too much to handle.

"Fuck, I feel it, baby. You're about to come, but hold it back, you wait. Wait for me, wait I until I tell you," he growls, unmoving inside me.

I nod.

"Answer me," he orders.

"I will wait for you," I pant.

"Hands to the side and grip the sheets tight, baby, you're going to need something to hold on to." He smirks.

He wasn't wrong, no sooner have the words left his mouth, he starts thrusting forward, relentlessly slamming himself inside me. My entire body moves with each thrust. I feel myself start to tighten, and I tense my entire body to hold it back. Both our bodies are covered in a sheen of sweat.

"Hold it, wait for me." He growls and pants as his relentless pace doesn't ease. "Yes, fuck, now, come for me now," he growls. I arch my back and scream his name as my orgasm tears through me.

"Fuck!" He roars his release.

He falls forward, his body caging me as we both come down, trying to control our breathing. "If this is what happens when I keep things from you, I might do it more often." I pant, smiling. His head comes up and he gives me a glare, making me laugh.

"Kitten, I will fuck you like that anytime I want; I don't need a reason or an excuse," he says before kissing me. "Now, let's get cleaned up and order in some food. I've built up an appetite." He smiles, pulling me up to my feet.

CHAPTER THIRTY-FIVE

Roman

I lay there, Cora sprawled across my body, fast asleep. The sun is slowly rising through the windows. All I can think about is last night, the shit I gave her over not being able to tell me, when I haven't told her about Kyle being in rehab. He's been there a while now, and from the reports from the doctor there, he's doing well. I hope she sees why I kept it from her and doesn't throw this in my face, although I have a feeling she will. I didn't give her the nickname Kitten for nothing.

She stirs and moans, her eyes fluttering open. She smiles up at me, her chin resting on my chest. Looking at her right now, I wonder how in the fuck did I get so bloody lucky.

"Morning." She smiles, placing a kiss on my chest.

"Morning, beautiful," I reply, tucking her hair behind her ear.

"So, what's the plan today?" she asks.

"Well, I will ring my solicitor, get him on your divorce. Then Mother is bringing the kids back and apparently we are venue shopping for the engagement party," I inform her.

"What? Are you serious?" she moans.

"Oh yeah, very. Can't we just have it at your parents' place, like with a marquee or something? Just keep it simple?" she asks.

"Sure, tell her that's what you want, don't let her railroad you into something you're not comfortable with," I say as I sit up. I kiss her before getting up and getting into the shower.

I head to my office and ring my solicitor. "Why are you ringing me on a Saturday?" he answers, annoyed.

"Sorry, Daniel, but I promise I will see you right for it. I have an urgent and important task. My fiancé needs a divorce done quickly, been separated for over three years, the ex is currently in rehab. How quick can you work your magic?" I ask.

"Shit, you're getting married? I'm guessing this is the cleaner girl that has everyone talking down at the club?" he asks.

"Yeah, that's the one," I answer.

"You want me to make up a prenup? With your wealth and all, I'm sure you want to protect your investments," he says.

"I don't want a fucking prenup, she isn't with me for my money and I don't ever plan on fucking letting her go," I snap.

"Okay, easy, as your solicitor I'm just doing my job, offering you your rights and options. Give me the name and I will draw up the divorce. Assets, kids or pets?" he asks.

"Two kids, both live with her. He has no fixed address," I answer.

"Okay, got it, send me across full names and personal details of your future wife and I will draw up the divorce papers in the week," he offers.

"Thanks, Daniel, will do," I say before disconnecting.

Now I need to figure out a way of breaking the news to Kyle while he's in rehab and hope it doesn't tip him over the edge to start using again.

∽

"Oh yes! Fabulous idea, the theme can be winter wonderland as it's January. Oh yes! This will shit all over Beatrice's ball, a winter masquerade ball. And I have Phuc to organise it." Mum claps excitedly. Cora looks at me and mouths 'who is Beatrice?' I shake my head, warning her not to go there. Mum's always had a rivalry with Beatrice ever since I was at school, it was battle for the head of the PTA committee. Nothing like a bit of mother competition to bring out the evil side of a school fundraiser.

"Now, give me a date to go on?" Mum asks, looking at the both of us.

"Make it the end of the month, give people something to look forward to. You think you can organise an entire ball in three weeks?" I ask her.

"Oh, my boy, I could do it sleep walking," she boasts, patting my face.

"Cora, make sure you give me a guest list of people you want there," she says, kissing our cheeks. "I'm off, your father wants a special night tonight." She winks.

"Christ," I groan and Cora laughs.

"Well, the force that is my mother is throwing a not very low key engagement party, are you sure you're okay with this?" I ask her.

"It's fine, honestly, it will just be a marquee in the garden, no big deal." She shrugs.

I laugh and shake my head. "Have you forgotten Christmas already? She had reindeer and a barn built in the garden for the kids to enjoy for all of thirty minutes. Don't underestimate her, she will pull out all the stops," I warn her.

We spent the weekend just relaxing, walking Mouse in the woods and enjoying a bit of down time. The weekend goes far too quickly and soon Monday is here.

I was surprised by Monday afternoon to have Daniel call me. "What's the problem?" I ask.

"No problem, I'm having the papers delivered to you now," he says.

"Wow, that was quick," I state.

"Simple case, they had nothing of any value, the kids are with their mum and the husband is a drug addict. He has nothing to fight with, even if he wanted to take this to court, no solicitor would touch him. All that is required from him is his signature on the bottom of the papers, then you are both free to marry," he informs me.

"That's great, thanks. Send me your bill and I will get Simon to pay it," I state.

"Already sent." He laughs.

"Of course it fucking is," I retort. "Catch you later," I say before disconnecting.

Not thirty minutes later, Simon knocks at my door. "This just arrived for you." He hands me the envelope.

"Thanks. Um, can you do me a favour and clear my schedule for the afternoon? There's something I need to take care of," I state.

"Sure thing." He nods.

I grab my coat and keys and head out of my office. I spot Cora in the foyer, training up a new employee. She sees me and blows me a kiss. I give her a wink in return, making her smile brightly.

I drive for over an hour to the rehabilitation centre. I park up and walk into reception. "I'd like to see Kyle Whitman, please," I ask the receptionist.

"Do you have a visitors appointment?" she asks.

"No, this is a quick visit, an urgent matter," I state.

"I'm sorry, all visits are pre-booked and have to be approved by the councillors and doctors," she states.

"Call Dr Greeves, tell him I'm here," I demand.

"Okay, sir, please wait." She calls him through and I stand, feeling too agitated to sit down.

"Roman, what are you doing here?" Dr Greeves asks.

"I'm here to see how Kyle is doing considering I'm paying for his treatment. Wondered if I could see him?" I ask.

He looks at me sceptically. "That's not how we normally do things here, Roman, I won't risk the patients being set back," he states.

"Come on, why would I want to set him back when I'm paying for this? Just ten minutes, that's all I need with him," I state.

"Fine, ten minutes in the communal gardens. I will go tell him you're here," he says, walking off.

I stand in the communal gardens under the patio heater, pulling my coat closed from the bite of the cold winter air. I look up and see Kyle walking towards me, his hands in his pockets, his eyes assessing me. He looks better, he's gained some weight and looks a lot healthier.

"Roman," he says in greeting. He pulls out a cigarette and lights it.

"Kyle. You look good," I state.

"Yeah, well, these past few weeks I've stopped throwing up and the cramps and pain is manageable. What do you want, Roman?" he asks.

I hold out the divorce papers. "I asked Cora to marry me, she said yes. Need you to sign the divorce papers," I state.

I watch as his jaw sets tight. "Why would I sign those?" he snaps.

"Because you owe her a decent life, because you failed as a husband and a father, and you ruined her life. She's happy now, she doesn't have any worries. That goes for the kids too," I point out.

"I know I've made mistakes, I know I messed up our marriage, but this is my chance to make up for that. This is my chance to prove to her and the kids that I can be that good husband and father," he bites back.

I laugh and shake my head. "You're delusional. It's been three fucking years. You're done, she is mine. She loves me, and I love her. Now I paid for you to be here for the kids, so you could be a decent father to them. Do not dredge all this up for your own selfish reasons. This is fuck all to do with her, this is to ease your own guilt because of what you've done to them. Don't make this harder on her and the kids, sign the damn forms and do the right thing," I growl angrily.

He stands there and takes a drag on his cigarette. "I will take my chances, we were high school sweethearts, you can't just wipe that kind of bond, that kind of love. You might have the money, but it's never been about the money with Cora. I will always have her, she and I are meant to be."

"Jesus, you sure you're off the crack? Because to me, it sounds like you're still fucking smoking it. Don't fight me on this, and if you cause them any pain, any tears, I will finish you, do you understand?" I threaten, getting in his face.

"What you going to do, cut me off? I'm clean and plan on staying that way. I get out of here in two weeks' time, then I start stage two of recovery. This place provides me with accommodation for three months to help keep me clean. Which you've already paid for, so thank you for that. Thank you for giving me a chance to get my wife and my kids back," he states before walking away, leaving me standing there, wishing I had left him on the streets. He would probably be dead by now and I wouldn't have this shit to deal with.

CHAPTER THIRTY-SIX

Cora

Roman was out of office for hours. When I asked Simon where he was, all he could say was that he was attending some business. I go to his office and sit at his desk, waiting for him. I lean on his desk and rest my head. Can't go anywhere, he's my ride home, so I may as well rest my eyes whilst I wait.

"Wake up, beautiful," I hear Roman whisper in my ear.

I groan and sit up, rubbing my face. "What time is it?" I yawn.

"Three o'clock, I've sent Simon to pick up the kids," he says.

"Okay, where were you?" I ask.

He looks at me, and it isn't a good look. Something's wrong, I can tell. "What is it?" I ask, worried.

He sighs and perches on his desk next to me. He hands me a large envelope. "What's this?" I ask, opening it.

"Your divorce papers," he states unhappily.

"Well, that's great news, isn't it?" I ask, confused by his reaction.

"Yeah, great. Except Kyle wont sign them," he states.

"Is that where you've been? You found Kyle?" I ask.

"I've known where he was all along, Cora. I paid for him to go into rehab around three months ago," he informs me.

"Why didn't you say anything? You made this big deal about being honest with each other, yet you've been keeping this a secret from me? Why?" I ask, annoyed.

"I know, I should have told you sooner. He came to me after we saw him. I didn't tell you because I didn't want you getting your hopes up, or the kids. I didn't want him coming back into their lives unless he was clean and sober," he defends.

He has a point; I know what he was trying to do, and I appreciate him paying for Kyle to be in rehab. But he should have told me.

"I'm guessing Kyle refused the divorce?" I sigh, knowing what Kyle is like.

"Yeah, said he was coming back for you, for the kids. He used me for the rehab. He's coming for you, according to him. You and he are meant to be, and you will always love him and choose him over me," Roman says, looking pissed.

"Oh Christ. Well, he's wrong, I don't love him. I did once, but not anymore. I mean, what is he playing at? He thinks after being separated for three years and he spent all our money on gambling and drugs that I'm going to forgive him?! Seriously? He is insane, are you sure he's still not on drugs?!" I rant now, pacing Roman's office. He reaches out and grabs me, pulling me in his arms.

I look at him and he's smiling. "I don't know why you're smiling, this is shit. He's just being a selfish prick, like he's always been, only ever thinking about himself," I snap.

"I know, and I was pissed too, but hearing you say you don't love him and that it's me you love, seeing you get riled up and passionate about it, makes me happy," he says, smiling.

I smack his chest. "Well, you're a moron too, because you should know that it's you I love, that it's only you. And now I'm getting annoyed at you for not knowing it." I huff.

Roman throws his head back and laughs.

"Don't laugh at me," I growl. This only makes Roman laugh more. Damn it, why does he have to be so incredibly handsome?

Especially when he laughs like that, it makes it hard to stay mad at him.

"Come on, let's get home, I told Simon to take them straight home and that we will meet them there," he says.

"Okay." I sigh.

"Kiss me," he orders. I smile and lean forward, kissing him. I bite his lip, making him hiss.

"Yeah, I'm still annoyed, and yes, this kitten still has her claws out, so, Mr Nash, see this as your warning." I wink.

∼

"No, guess again!" Betty yells. We are playing a game of charades before bed.

She dances around the lounge, making funny noises.

"Um... Hippo?"

"Um... BFG?"

"Monsters?"

"Jack and the Beanstalk?"

We all yell out our guesses.

She puts her hands on her hips and stomps her foot angrily. She looks up and sighs. "Cheese and rice! I was a ballerina!" she yells.

"Cheese and rice?" Roman whispers to me in question.

"She means Jesus Christ." I giggle.

Roman laughs. "It's not funny, Roman!" Betty chastises.

"You're right, I'm sorry, how about we stop playing this game and have some ice cream instead?" Roman offers.

Gone is her angry face and in it's place is now an angelic smile. "Yay!" She claps, jumping up and down.

"Thank God, that game was painful," Theo complains, getting up and following them into the kitchen.

After ice cream and getting Betty to bed, I decide to go into my art studio. I sit there, staring at a blank canvas for a while, contemplating what to paint. Roman walks in and hands me a glass of wine.

"Thanks," I say, sipping the wine.

He hands me a little remote and I frown. "Press play." He smiles. I press play and the room fills with Natty's, "She Loves Me." I smile and look to him.

"It's set up to play any song you request, either type it into the controls or press that mic button and speak into it with your request. Now, paint me a masterpiece," he says, kissing the top of my head and leaving me alone.

I sigh and close my eyes. I start painting, feeling myself relax and allowing myself to get lost in the music and my art.

I hear the patio doors open and turn and see Roman stood there, smiling at me. "You camping out here all night or are you going to come inside to bed?" he asks.

"Why? What time is it?" I ask.

"It's one a.m.," he answers.

"Oh shit, really? I've been out here for like four hours! I had no idea, I got so swept away with it all, I didn't realise," I state, standing and rinsing my brushes in the sink.

I turn and see Roman staring at my picture. "It's Kyle," he states.

I bite my lip and nod. "Don't read too much into it, it was because he was on my mind," I defend.

"I know, it's incredible," he says, pulling me into his arms.

"It's nowhere near finished yet," I point out.

"Well then, it just goes to show, it will be a masterpiece," he says before kissing me.

"Come, let's get to bed, we are both going to be shattered in the morning," he says, taking my hand. He locks the door and leads me to bed.

∼

Sunlight streams through the gap in curtains. I squint and stretch to look at the time and see it's after nine in the morning.

"Shit!" I yell and jump out of bed and run out of the room to wake the kids. Only when I get there, their beds are empty. I frown and run downstairs and into the kitchen, and I come to a skidding halt, seeing Roman stood there, drinking his coffee.

"Kids, school," I pant.

He laughs. "Yeah, they are in school. I let you sleep in. Take the day off, I told Sylvia you won't be in today," he states, walking towards me.

"Oh." I puff, blowing my hair from my face. Roman tucks my hair from my face behind my ear.

"Coffee?" he asks, smiling.

"Yeah," I mumble. "I shouldn't just take a day off like this, it doesn't look good to other members of staff," I point out.

"I don't give a shit what other staff members think, I'm the boss and you're my fiancé. Take the day off and spend it in the studio. You haven't had a chance to get out there since Christmas," Roman says, handing me a cup of coffee.

"But—"

"No buts, this is a direct order from your boss. Go paint, I will pick the kids up and will be home later," he says, kissing me and walking out of the house before I can even protest. I look around the empty kitchen and listen to the silence. I sigh and smile to myself, boss' orders, yes sir, I can definitely do that.

CHAPTER THIRTY-SEVEN

Cora

It's the day of the engagement party, me and Roman have been kept away from their house and from seeing any arrangements. It is a complete surprise, even down to all of our outfits. I've had a woman show up to do my hair and make-up, even though I will be wearing a mask covering half of my face.

Betty comes running into my room whilst I'm getting my make-up done.

"Mummy! Look at my dress!" she screeches excitedly.

She spins on the spot. Audrey got her a beautiful white dress with snowflake crystal details on it, and of course, a silver sparkly tutu to match and tights. And a little silver lace mask with a handle for her to hold it to her face.

"You look beautiful. You will be the most beautiful person there." I beam at her.

"I know!" She twirls again. I laugh as she runs off.

"What's your dress like?" the woman asks.

"I don't know, it's in that zip bag, I'm under strict instructions to not open it until I put it on," I say nervously.

"Wow, I would have ripped that thing open by now and peeked at it," she states.

"Believe me, I was tempted. But then with Audrey, I wouldn't be surprised if she hasn't rigged an alarm to it to go off if I opened it before I was supposed to."

She laughs and continues to do my make-up. My eyes are fixed on the dress the entire time, praying to the dress Gods that it isn't some pouffy ballgown.

She leaves, wishing me luck. Roman is already at his mother's—as ordered by his mother—to greet all the guests, and something to do with important business connections there.

I stand in front of the bag and unzip it. I remove the bag and gasp at the beautiful dress in front of me. A light silver dress with detailed lace overlay of delicate leaves over the bodice, and it continues to flow down to the floor. There is a white fake-fur shawl to wear with it and diamanté silver heels. Christ, let's hope there's some spanks in here to suck it all in with because this dress will reveal everything.

I get myself into my dress and heels. I stand in front of the full length mirror and almost don't believe it's me staring back. My hair is in loose curls, pinned to one side, and the dress hugs my curves. There's a knock at the door which makes me jump.

"Yeah?" I answer.

I'm surprised to see Audrey and Mum poke their heads through the door.

"Oh my goodness, would you look at how stunning your daughter is, Margo." Audrey gasps. "I knew this would be perfect for you."

"Oh, I wish I had my camera," Mum sobs.

"Don't worry, I have that covered." Audrey winks.

"Why are you both here? I thought you would be at the party?" I state.

"Oh, sweet girl, we came to get you, the kids are already on their way there with your father. And we had to give you this too," Audrey says, handing me a box.

I frown and open it, and inside is my masquerade mask. It's a crystal eye mask and the detailing is stunning.

"Here, let us help you put it on, don't want to ruin that pretty make-up and hair," Audrey says.

After I have it on, not forgetting the stiletto heeled silver pumps, I actually feel like a goddess. "Oh my, you look incredible." Mum sighs.

I grin at her. "I actually feel it too," I say, turning to Audrey. "Thank you for this, I can't even imagine the cost. I mean, maybe after tonight we could auction it off for charity?" I suggest.

"Oh for goodness sake, woman, for one night, just think about yourself," she says, rolling her eyes. "Right..." She claps. "Let's get going, I can't leave the men too long to greet the guests, if I'm not there overseeing it all, it will all go to pot!" she flaps, leading the way down the stairs.

Outside is a limo. "Of course," I mutter as we climb inside. I'm excited to see Roman, to see his reaction to this dress.

The drive there felt longer than usual as Mum and Audrey chatted away about possible wedding venues and themes. I would love nothing more than a quick wedding. Maybe we could just run away together and avoid the massive wedding day? Although, I'm sure Audrey and Mum wouldn't ever forgive us for it.

We pull up and my jaw drops. Every tree that lines the property and driveway is lit up with white fairy lights. There's even a fake snow machine in front of the property, dusting the bushes and ground with snow. A young guy opens the door and hold out his hand to help me out of the car.

"Err, um, thank you," I say awkwardly.

We round the red carpeted path, around to the side of the house and into the back garden. "Oh my God," I say, stunned. A huge marquee is all lit up with fairy lights. It really is a winter wonderland.

"See? Phuc is a genius!" Audrey beams.

My eyes scan for Roman but I don't see him. "Come on, let's go find Roman, I know he's just going to die when he sees you," Mum says, linking her arm with mine.

As we enter the Marquee, we are handed a glass of champagne

by men in white suits with masks on. "I am starting to feel like I'm in that movie with Tom Cruise and Nicole Kidman," Mum whispers in my ear. "What's it called? Nine and half weeks? Nope, that's Mickey Rourke. Oh, Eyes Wide Shut, that's the one, where all the posh rich people meet in a big fancy house with these very same masks on and they all bonk each other," she states.

"Mum!" I hiss.

"What? It's what happens. I mean, I don't particularly find Tom Cruise attractive, but I bet he's a bit of a goer. He is quite enthusiastic, I would imagine. He puts in one hundred and ten percent every time. Probably has a little dick though," Mum says, downing the champagne. I take her glass.

"No more champagne for you," I state.

Mum rolls her eyes. "Oh, there's Roman, who is that woman?" she asks.

My eyes scan the dance floor, and I spot Camila dancing with Roman, whispering in his ear, her hands on his chest and moving up around his neck intimately.

"More champagne, madam?" a server offers. I take two and knock them back.

"Oh, Cora, there you are. Can I introduce you to Alec? He's a long-time friend of the family and recently sold his hotel to Roman," Audrey says from behind me. I reluctantly turn and plaster a fake smile on my face.

"Hi, Alec, lovely to meet you," I greet.

"Well, I see the boy has mighty fine taste. My lassie, it is a pleasure to meet your acquaintance." He smiles, taking my hand and kissing the back of it.

I immediately warm to Alec, he seems like a larger than life character. He has friendly soft eyes.

His eyes look over my shoulder and I know they land on Roman and Camila. "Jesus, that damn woman is like a damn leech," he mutters. I turn and look, seeing her running her nails through his hair at back of his head. Roman looks uncomfortable.

"I'm sorry, Alec, please excuse me," I apologise.

"Of course. I like her Audrey, got fire in the gut," he states.

"Yes, and now world war three is about to kick off." I hear Audrey's heels click along the wooden floor as she runs after me.

Roman's eyes land on mine and he smiles, but they soon fall when he sees how pissed I am. I don't think, I just act. I grab Camila by her hair and yank her back, except it's extensions and they come off in my hand. I scrunch up my nose in disgust and chuck it to the floor.

"What the hell?!" Camila screeches.

"Get your claws off my fiancé! You vile gold digging whore!" I yell.

The entire marquee goes silent and all eyes are on us. I'm past the point of caring, I'm sick of this bitch trying to hit on Roman.

"You are unbelievable! You've just proven who you are. You can take the girl out of the council estate, but apparently, you can't take the council estate out of the girl. You have just shown everyone here that you are not for this world, you are not right for Roman. You have no idea how to behave, you're low life scum with a junkie husband and you'll never be anything else," Camila sneers. She takes a tray of hors d'oeuvres and tips them all over the floor and stamps on them with her heel. "Now, do your job and clean up this mess." She smiles.

Tears sting my eyes and I look around the room at people muttering, watching. I feel humiliated. I swing my hand back and slap her hard across the face before storming off.

"She just slapped me!" I hear Camila cry.

"Get out, and don't ever come near me and my family again!" Audrey yells at her.

I don't look around to see the commotion. I kick off my heels and run, needing to get away from these people.

I find a quiet spot out of the way, hidden by some bushes. I sit down on the stone bench and sniff back my tears. Maybe she is right? Maybe I don't belong here? This is supposed to be our engagement party, but not one person stopped her, not one person defended me.

Why would they, I'm not one of them?

CHAPTER THIRTY-EIGHT

Roman

I stand there, my blood boiling from what Camila did, the way she humiliated her like that. "Go and find my daughter, right now. She's going to need you," Felix says, gripping my arm.

"Roman, are you going to let your mother speak to me like that?" I hear Camila whine behind me.

I turn and storm towards her. "What did she ever do to you, Camila? All she has ever been is kind and caring. She has more class than you ever will. Get off of my parents' property, and I never want to see your face again," I growl.

"But, Ro-ro," she whines.

"Fuck off and get out!" I roar. She flinches and people escort her out.

"Calm it, son, go and find her. I know what she's going to be thinking right now, don't let her be alone in her thoughts," Margo orders.

I nod and go in search of her. It's now that I wish my parents didn't have acres of land to search. I notice her heels left on the ground. I bend down and pick them up and carry on my path to find her. I run between the bushes and pause. I hear her sobs.

"Cora," I call. I see her sat on the stone bench, her shoulders slumped forward. I walk to her and crouch down in front of her. "Cora," I whisper. Her tear-filled eyes come to me and my heart shatters.

"She is gone, I'm sorry, we were just dancing. She got a bit handsy, I told her to stop. She wouldn't take no for an answer. I didn't want to cause a scene," I apologise.

She smiles and shakes her head. "She's right. I mean, I'm not meant for your world. I don't know how to speak to these people or how to behave. I'm always going to say the wrong thing, I'm always going to be different from them and I'm never going to change." She sniffs.

I reach up and take her mask off, wiping away her tears and cupping her face. "Exactly, that is one of the reasons I love you, that is why I want you. You are different to them, but not in a bad way. In a fucking good way. You make me laugh, you care and you're not afraid to say what's on your mind. I love you, not them. I want to marry you, not them. I couldn't give a shit what they think. We are not worlds apart and we don't have separate worlds from each other," I state, stroking her cheek. "We have our world, you, me, the kids and Mouse. That's our world, it's us, just us. Only us," I say before kissing her.

She rests her forehead against mine. "I love you, Roman, so much." She sighs.

I smile. "Kitten, right back at you, and don't ever forget it."

"Come on, let's get back to the party and in the warmth because it's bloody freezing," I state. There's a snap of a twig and we both turn and see Kyle stood there. I stand, immediately feeling my blood boil. "You've got to be kidding me, how in the fuck did you get in?" I say, standing in front of Cora.

His eyes flick from mine to Cora. "Kyle, what are you doing here?" she asks, standing behind me, her hand connecting with mine, holding it tight. Kyle's eyes drop to our hands and his jaw tenses.

He sighs and looks down. "Honestly, I came to tell you how I feel, to show you that I can be clean, to beg you for a second chance."

"A second chance?" Cora questions, raising her eyebrow.

"Fair enough, okay, maybe like my fifth chance." He smiles sheepishly.

Cora grunts. "Well, whether it's giving you your second or your fifth chance, it's not happening. I love Roman and I'm marrying him. If that means having to fight you in the courts for a divorce, I will, because it's him that I want."

Kyle smiles. "Yeah, I heard. Even after that shit that snobby bitch threw at you. I knew her plan wouldn't work," he mutters.

"What plan?" I snap.

"That Camila invited me tonight, said I was to declare my love for Cora while she seduced you," he informs us.

"That conniving bitch!" I growl.

"It's cool though, man, I saw the scene play out, I saw everything, and I heard you guys just now." He smiles sadly.

"What do you want, Kyle?" Cora asks.

He looks at her, his eyes soft. "I want you, Cora, but I know I'm too late. I know too much has happened. I've fucked up too many times, you're happy now, you're in love. I may not be able to make up for everything I've done to you, all the pain I've caused you over the years, but maybe I can give you a little something to say I'm sorry... I'll sign the divorce papers," he says, shocking us both.

Cora lets go of my hand and walks to him. She wraps her arms around him and hugs him, he hugs her back. "Thank you," she whispers.

She kisses his cheek and steps back. "You look good, Kyle, promise me you won't return to that life," she says, smiling.

"No way in hell, thanks to your man here." He nods. He reaches forward, holding out his hand. I reach forward and shake it. "Thanks, man, and look after her." He smiles.

"I will," I answer.

He doesn't say anything else, he smiles and leaves. Cora turns to me, her eyes wide, her face stunned. "Okay, what in the hell just happened?" she asks, stunned.

"I have no fucking idea, but I do know it means I can marry you now," I state.

Cora smiles and kisses me. She sits down on the bench and bends down to put her heels back on. I crouch down and take hold of her other heel. I gently hold her ankle, smiling at her.

"Why, thank you, sir," she teases.

I slide her heel onto her foot. "A perfect fit." I wink.

She laughs. "A real fairy tale ending, so I guess that makes you my prince?"

"Of course, I came and rescued you, my damsel in distress. I fought the evil jealous witch and her henchman. And now I get to make you my queen. This fairy tale may be ending, but there's a whole new story waiting for us," I say, kissing her.

"A sequel?" she asks.

"No, Kitten, more like the R-rated version."

EPILOGUE

Cora

"I'm so nervous, I've been to the toilet like twenty times already," I mutter.

"Well, I would normally calm you down but after the drama that unfolded at your engagement party, I think it's proven that anything can happen. I have my little bag of popcorn at the ready should drama unfold," Sylvia says, patting her handbag.

I give her a look, and she holds up her hands in self-defence. "Our wedding day went by smoothly," I defend.

"That's because you guys eloped to Scotland, only taking the kids and your parents," she argues back.

Roman's arm snakes around my waist. "It will be fantastic. I promise you." I grin nervously and nod, biting my lip, hoping he is right.

"Oh, I'm so proud of you, sweetie!" Mum cheers, walking up to us with Dad.

They both hug and kiss me, Dad's eyes are looking around. "Dad, it's all energy saving, as much organic materials used as they possibly could, and all local tradesmen were used," I say, rolling my eyes at him.

"That's my girl." He smiles.

"Darlings!" Audrey yells, making her way through the crowd with George trailing behind her.

She kisses each of us. "This is just fabulous! Beatrice is over there looking like she's chewing on a wasp. Ha!" She turns and yells to Beatrice. "Beatrice, darling! This is my talented daughter-in-law! Isn't this spectacular?" She says bitchily.

"Audrey," George warns.

"Oh shush, let me have this. For years she's been lording it over me, rubbing it in my face that her son was an MP, and where is he now? In prison, probably getting probed by a large man called Tank." Audrey laughs.

"Dad, no more booze for Mum," Roman states.

"Gotcha, son." He nods.

"Oh, you're no fun!" Audrey whines.

"Ladies and Gentlemen! Can I have your attention?" Phuc yells. It turns out that he is an organising genius, I had to hire him.

"Oh, shit, here we go," I say nervously.

"I would like to officially announce the grand opening of Cora Nash galleries. Please browse, sip champagne and spend your money!" Phuc winks. The crowd chuckles, while I'm close to hyperventilating.

"Now for the artistic genius herself, Cora Nash," he introduces. Everyone claps and cheers, and I feel like I'm going throw up. I hate speaking in front of large groups and there are at least one hundred people here. My hands shake and I can feel the sweat trickling down my back.

"Hi, I will make this quick as I hate public speaking..." I pause and people laugh. "I cannot thank you enough for being here for the grand opening of my very own gallery, it still seems surreal to me. I wouldn't be here now if it weren't for the amazing support of my family and my husband, Roman." I pause and blow a kiss to Roman who is watching me intently. "So, every piece in here is for sale, and every penny goes to the Nash Fresh Start For Families charity. So please, spend big!" I laugh. "I declare Cora Nash Galleries open," I say as I cut the ribbon in front of the doors.

I walk to Roman who pulls me into his arms and crashes his mouth down on mine, kissing me like there's no one but us.

"I'm so fucking proud of you," he whispers across my lips.

"Why, thank you, sir," I say, fluttering my eye lashes. Roman growls at me, making me laugh.

"Come on, let's mingle, and when this party is over, we are locking up and I am fucking you on every surface," he growls low in my ear.

I look to him and lean up on my toes to whisper in his ear. "Is that an order, sir?" I tease.

"It's a threat, Kitten," he promises.

"Good, because I'm not very good at following orders," I state before sashaying away to mingle, leaving Roman stood there. I can feel his hungry gaze on me the entire time.

As the evening continues, I take a moment and stand back, taking stock of everything in front of me. Theo stood with his arm around his girlfriend from college. Betty stood in front of her painting, telling every person that stops in front of it to buy it. My parents happily talking and laughing with Audrey and George. The entire warehouse filled with my artwork.

If five years ago you had asked me where I would see myself, it wouldn't be here. I would see myself still in our little council flat, still struggling day to day to get by, still alone, just me and the kids. But by chance, I got knocked off my feet—literally—by a handsome, generous and fantastic in bed man.

We came from different sides of the tracks, two completely different worlds colliding together, creating our own world just for us, just for our family.

Fairy tales don't exist, but once in a lifetime when you least expect it, someone will come crashing into your life, knocking you right out of your once comfortable but tired shoes, bringing you new sparkly ones. Step into those new shiny glass slippers and embrace your new life, your new love, and an entirely new world.

THE END

ACKNOWLEDGMENTS

I cannot thank enough my lovely talented friend Lindsey Powell for saving my behind and working her magic editing, proof reading and formatting this book for me, finding the time to fit me in amongst writing your own amazing books. Love you my fellow West Country gal.

Not forgetting my amazing husband for making me yet another beautiful cover. I love you always.

Also a little special mention to Robyn my super PA, without you I'd be drowning in a sea of disorganised chaos.

Readers to you always I am beyond thankful for your continued support.

ABOUT THE AUTHOR

L.G. Campbell lives in South West, England with her husband and children and writes in her spare time. She loves to write romance that will have your heart pounding but will also make you laugh out loud.

You can follow me on social media for latest news and exclusive teasers.

instagram.com/author_lgcampbell
facebook.com/Authorlgcampbell

ALSO BY L.G. CAMPBELL

Thank you for reading Worlds Apart.

If you would like to read more of my books they are all available on amazon and kindle unlimited.

Rocke Series

Rise Above

Wallflower

Fortress

The War Within

Standalone

Tiers of Joy

Satan's Outlaws series:

Hidden Truths

Printed in Great Britain
by Amazon